Bitter SWEET

BITTERROOT MONTANA VETERANS

BOOK 3

ANNE M. SCOTT

Developmental Editing Lia Huni

Proofreading Paula Lester, Polaris Editing

Anne M. Scott
Visit my website at www.amscottwrites.com/romance

First Printing: September 2023

Lightwave Publishing LLC

Dedication

In memory of my cousin, Coleen, who left us too young.
May perpetual light shine upon you and your family.

Contents

Chapter 1

DEB BOULANGER SMILED AT her phone's camera. "And that's our specials for tomorrow! We'll be open at seven, and I'll have prepacked boxes ready to fly out the door." She wiggled her fingers. "See you then!" She clicked the video off, reviewed it, added captions, hashtags and music, then posted it to the Deb's Bakery website and social media profiles, plus community pages. Her last chore done, she turned off the sign in the front window of her bakery, and then rose on her tiptoes and reached for the sky, her back popping and cracking. At a mere five foot two, she didn't have a prayer of reaching the ceiling, let alone the sky.

Crossing the small dining area in front of the counter, she checked for stray crumbs or napkins, but Jeff, her clean up person, was meticulous. Behind the bakery counter, she pulled mostly-empty trays out of the glass front display cases. If only she could find more people with Jeff's dedication. Her employees were nice enough, but had no real love for baking; they were there for the paycheck only. Which would be fine, if she could afford to pay them more hours. But she was stuck in what her small business advisor called the muddy middle. She had more business than she could handle, but not enough to afford full time workers with benefits and insurance, no matter how much she wanted to.

After wrapping the few leftovers in plastic, she placed them in the day-old sales basket. Those left from yesterday had already gone to the food pantry, along with loaves of fresh bread. She'd like to send more to them and the family shelter, too, but she couldn't.

Marcus Bank's President, Sharlene Murphy, had strongly suggested Deb accept investors. She'd sent eager candidates ready to shovel capital into Deb's Bakery. An influx of cash would allow her to hire full time employees, but at the cost of losing control. The men she'd interviewed at Mrs. Murphy's request—and they were all older men—took a look at her balance sheet and told her to buy cheaper ingredients, get rid of Jeff, and contract a commercial bakery to make her most popular cupcakes with preservatives, then distribute to grocery stores.

Deb didn't want to do any of that. She wanted to bake, design new creations, and make her customers happy. Cheaper ingredients and preservatives—required if she wanted to distribute her goods more than a couple of hours away—changed the taste and texture too much. Besides, there were more than enough cheap cupcakes in stores already. High quality local goods kept her customers coming back. Plus, going commercial meant shutting down her dining area, and she liked talking to customers.

Even if some of those customers were a pain, like Charles "Chaz" Cust and his horrible, but wealthy and influential mother. But she'd take the Custs any day over the most recent so-called investors Sharlene Murphy sent her way.

Rough men in boxy suits, with wary glances on entering the bakery, they reeked of cologne and gunpowder. Once Ryan, Erin's fiancé, pointed out the signs, she could spot the bulge of concealed pistols under their arms or at their waists. These men were demanding and rude, too, pushing in front of customers and practically shouting that Marcus Bank sent them to invest, and not taking no for an answer. She'd had to threaten to call the cops twice. The last three investors had heavy accents as well; Nadia, one of her regulars, told her they spoke like Bratva—the Russian mob—and she couldn't come into the bakery anymore. She bought cupcakes at the Saturday Farmer's Market when Deb opened, then scurried away.

After the last uninvited mobster made a fuss on a busy morning, Deb had Sam Kerr, her attorney and other best friend, send a cease-and-desist letter to the bank, stating formally that she was not interested in investors or franchising. Ms. Murphy had stormed in the next day, her normally calm, pale white face flushed and glaring, accusing Deb of backstabbing, underhanded behavior and trying to get her fired. Deb had replied calmly, reminding Sharlene that she'd called, emailed, and sent personal letters, and yet, more so-called investors kept showing up and attempting to intimidate her and her customers.

Deb had another reason for taking the nuclear option; the idiot "investors" attempting to intimidate her didn't understand the people of Marcus, Montana. At least half of her customers legally carried firearms. The last thing she needed was a wild west shootout in her shop. Filing that insurance claim would probably get her dropped as too big a risk, and insuring a bakery was difficult enough already.

"Hey, Deb, are you here?" Erin's voice rang over the hum of cooling fans.

"Up front!" She stacked the display trays and carried them to the sinks. Her night worker, a student at the local community college, would clean them, and the next day's goods were ready for tomorrow's sales on covered trays in the back.

Erin's bright red hair appeared between the racks of cupcakes, cookies, and bread, then she leaned against the sink next to Deb. "It smells amazing in here."

Deb chuckled. "You always say that."

"And I always mean it. You are the superhero of baked goods." Erin pointed her elbow at Deb, a gesture left over from her days in the Air Force, where pointing with a finger wasn't polite for some odd reason.

Deb put her hands on her hips. "That's me, Cupcake Woman!"

Erin laughed. "Funny every time." She sobered. "How are you doing after my mother went 'Terror of the Town' on you? Any fallout?"

She grimaced. "I got an official letter back through Sam, stating my wishes would be followed, but that my loan was under review." Other than her first year, she'd made every payment on time, and paid extra on the original amount during good months.

"I don't know what's gotten into her lately." Erin sighed. "First, she tries really hard to set me up with slimy Chaz Cust, then she alienates me and Ryan publicly, and she sucks up to her wealthy customers in all kinds of weird ways. Now she's sending mobsters to your door. I'm afraid she's gotten into something really, really bad, and can't find a way out." She shook her head, her expression sad. "I hate to say it, but I'm glad we took Wiz's warnings seriously and opened accounts at other banks. I can't trust my own mother anymore."

"I've opened new accounts, too, but I really don't want to go through the hassle of getting a new business loan." That would take time and effort, and she was short on both already.

"Me either, but my loan and a tiny business account are all I have left at Marcus Bank. Another good year, and we'll be paid off." Erin grinned. "And speaking of business, with Ryan downrange, I need to get back to mine. My boxes are in their usual places?"

Deb grinned. "Sure are. And I put a special present in there for you and your snuggle stud."

Erin's expression turned dreamy. "He's coming home late tonight, and I can hardly wait."

"I bet." Deb waggled her brows and grinned, but couldn't help the jealousy spearing her heart. If only she could find a guy like Ryan. Her first marriage had been a total disaster; they'd both been too young, and she'd been blindly stupid, too. After her sister Kim met and married Nic Acer, Deb had hoped she'd have a chance with Nic's brother, Michael. Kim even suggested the two of them date, but Michael had scoffed, claiming the idea was ridiculous. His words had stabbed her in the heart, but stiffened her resolve. No man would ever make her feel less than enough ever again; she'd had enough of that with her first marriage.

Deb still used Acer Home Repair when she needed help with her bakery, but she called Nic directly. Both Nic and Kim told her that Michael still struggled to accept his medical release from the Army and deal with his continuing health issues despite creating an extremely successful business.

"Speaking of studs, did you know Michael Acer was in Louisiana helping with the hurricane cleanup at the same time as Ryan?" Erin raised her brows.

"No, really?" Michael had seemed totally focused on his business and he was just plain grumpy. Volunteering halfway across the country seemed out of character. But she didn't know him that well—he'd made sure of that.

Erin showed her a photo on her phone. "Yep. Ryan had no idea Michael was a Team Rubicon member until he was assigned to Michael's team to muck out a flood victim's house. Since he's a contractor, they made Michael a team leader immediately. Ryan said he did a great job." The photo showed a grinning Ryan and a grimacing Michael, the two of them in mud-covered white plastic suits, carrying a battered white bathtub. Despite having a mechanical gripper instead of a left hand, Ryan didn't seem to have any trouble with his end of the load. Michael looked more pained. "They're on the same flight back late tonight, though, so I'm giving Michael a ride home."

"I'm sure Kim and Nic appreciate that." Deb pretended to pout. "But now I won't get to watch her kids." Isabella and Sophia, her nieces from Kim's equally disastrous first marriage, were the joy of Deb's life. But she had a ton of cupcakes to decorate for the Farmer's Market, and the two girls made that difficult. If she was smart, she would close the shop on Saturdays, and concentrate on the market, but her regulars would whine.

Erin chuckled. "The girls are cute, but I'm sure you'll have more opportunities."

"Guaranteed." The back door buzzer made her jump. "Wonder who that is?"

Erin followed her to the door, picking up her boxes on the way. "You don't have afternoon deliveries?"

"Rarely. Almost everything comes in the morning." Deb opened the back door, revealing a harried-looking FedEx worker. "Can I help you?"

He thrust a flat white cardboard envelope with his black handheld on top at her. "If you're Deborah Boulanger, I have a letter for you, and it requires a signature." He pointed at the screen on the handheld.

Suspecting she'd rather pick up a rattlesnake, Deb put her hands behind her back. "Who's it from?"

The guy turned the handheld around. "George Franks."

"Nope. Send it back." She'd rather pick up a double batch of bread dough without yeast—and that stuff was heavy, bulky and awkward. She pulled her phone from her pocket and snapped a picture of the envelope and handheld.

"You sure?" The man's eyebrows crinkled.

Deb pointed at his handheld above the screen. "Yes. Look at the sender's address."

"Deer Lodge, Prisoner num...oh. Got it." He pulled out the stylus and tapped. "Refused. Have a nice day."

"You too." They watched the big truck drive away.

Erin walked to her silver hotrod, Smoky, and opened the trunk. "Does that happen often?"

Deb grimaced. "Often enough, although this is the first time he's sent something by a commercial carrier. He's always trying to get money out of me. He almost ruined my life the first time around. His second and third tries weren't any better, and now I'm done." After the first year, she'd written "Return to Sender" on every single letter. As much as she wanted children, she was thankful they hadn't had any, because then she'd be tied to the idiot for life.

Erin nodded firmly. "Good for you. Does Sam know this is going on?"

Deb shrugged. "Yeah. There's not much either of us can do until he comes up for parole. With any luck at all, his record of harassment will keep him in prison."

"Here's hoping." Erin frowned at the dust left by the speeding truck.

Even if Franks got out, he wouldn't be Deb's problem, and there was no sense in worrying about it. Besides, Erin had better things to do. "Have fun tonight!"

Erin laughed, blushing. "Thanks. But let me know if there's something I can help you with, whether that's Franks or my mother."

Deb appreciated the offer, even if Erin couldn't do anything. "Thanks, Erin." They hugged and her muscle car rumbled away.

Deb returned to her bakery and the hundreds of cupcakes waiting. Erin was so lucky to find true love, twice. A bitter person would believe it wasn't fair, but Deb knew better. Love grew slowly between two people, with mutual care and trust, not instant attraction, desperation or pretty words. The right person would come along someday, and he'd be worth the wait.

Despite her pep talk, the image of a mud-spattered, grimacing, dark haired man lingered.

Chapter 2

Michael

Michael Acer hauled his heavy bag into his house, waving at the retreating lights of Erin's hotrod. It was a beautiful car, but loud—conversation between the three of them had been impossible. Which was just as well. Being the third wheel was bad enough, but Ryan and Erin acted like teenagers. At the airport, he'd pulled out his phone to find another ride before the two of them finally broke apart.

But if he had a woman like Erin, he'd probably do the same. Unfortunately, the odds against that were astronomical. His constant back pain, hearing problems, and debilitating, unpredictable migraines made him unreliable and short with customers; a relationship would never survive, no matter how much a certain cheerful, gorgeous, curvy blonde baker made him wish otherwise.

He dropped his duffle bag in the laundry room and carried his smaller backpack to the bathroom. Yanking his toiletry kit out, he pulled and replaced the ridiculous number of pill bottles he required to remain a functioning human being. Flying with meds was such a hassle. If he'd been able to drive, he'd have packed everything in daily dosage containers. But flying required carrying the original prescriptions, especially since one of them was an opioid. He'd taken all his meds with him every day, locking them in a vehicle while they were working, and never letting them out of sight otherwise. He'd also been very discrete when taking them. He needed the stronger drugs occasionally to function and he didn't want to tempt a recovering addict. Or a thief—disaster zones attracted the best and worst human beings.

Michael loaded his day-of-the-week pill holder, took the doses he needed, brushed his teeth, and plopped into bed. The work in Louisiana, clearing muddy, water-logged furniture, appliances, wallboard and everything else from flooded houses was physically hard and mentally challenging. The exertion was good for him; he'd usually fallen asleep quickly and woken from only a few nightmares. But the faces of the homeowners were hard to forget. They were all grateful for the help, but many couldn't accept that they'd lost everything, while others shut down, unable to face the devastation.

He stared up in the darkened room. If a flood swept through his apartment, he'd lose little he cared about. Their few family heirlooms were safe in Nic and Kim's house and most of his remaining possessions were the simple things needed to live, like clothing, food, and furnishings. The only things he'd be sad to let go would be the shadow box he'd built to remember the Army brothers and sisters he'd lost in Afghanistan.

He raised his right arm, bringing it close to his face. With the blackout curtains, it was too dark to see the memorials inked on his skin. Even if he lost the shadow box, the tattoos would remain.

Remembering those terrible events wouldn't help him sleep. He could take a sleep med, but didn't want to be groggy on his first day back. Instead, he concentrated on his breathing, attempting the meditation the Veteran's Administration shrink taught him. But rather than blanking his mind, a woman with long blonde hair in a high ponytail, bright blue eyes, and a short, curvy figure appeared.

Forgetting Deb Boulanger was impossible at the best of times; trying to fall asleep after a long day on the road was far from his finest hour. But dating her was impossible. She was too young, too positive, and simply too good for him. Plus, her sister was married to his brother, which made the whole thing just too weird. Any relationship between them was doomed to fail and she deserved a whole lot more, especially after her first marriage. George Franks had been a high school football hero, but a druggie even then. Michael had never understood why anyone fell for his so-called charm. But Deb had been a soft-spoken sophomore; with less than stellar parents, she didn't stand a chance of resisting fifth-year senior Franks when all the jocks and cheerleaders were "shipping" the two of them.

Busy learning his new job in the Army's Striker units eight hours away at Fort Lewis, Washington, Michael heard about the marriage after the fact. A year ahead of Frank's original class, he'd known Kim and Deb only by sight in their tiny school, but if he'd known ahead of time he might have warned her off. Someone certainly should have.

Woulda, coulda, shoulda. So many things in his life fell into those categories and thinking like that only brought guilt, which wasn't helpful. Michael concentrated on the air going in and out of his lungs and the rise and fall of his chest until he finally fell asleep.

The next morning, Michael opened his eyes and immediately slammed them shut, the sliver of light shining through the shades piercing his brain like a laser. The left side of his head throbbed, his stomach churned, and he reached for the medication he kept beside his bed. But it wasn't there—he'd probably left it with all the others in the bathroom.

Stupid. He'd known travel might trigger a migraine; he'd been lucky on the way to Louisiana, but the potential was just as great going home. Maybe more so, because he'd changed his sleep schedule, gained altitude and eaten unusual food all week.

Despite his pounding head and the tossing waves in his stomach, Michael slid his legs to the edge of the bed and stood, leaning on the nightstand, then the wall. Ignoring the flashing lights partially obscuring his vision, he shuffled into the bathroom, forced down a glass of water, and then found his medication, popping the pill under his tongue. Patting the countertop, he grabbed and squeezed his emergency ice pack and shambled back to bed, sliding under the covers and putting the cold pack under his neck.

With no actions left to distract him from the pain, he concentrated on his breathing. All he could do was endure until the meds kicked in, and then call Nic. Fortunately, Kim had set up a voice trigger on his phone. "Phone, migraine alert." Other people had clever names for their phones; he only wanted it to work when he needed it.

"Notifying Nic you have a migraine." The phone's voice was a soothing, low female tone that didn't make his head hurt worse.

Michael endured until the throbbing lessened and the ice pack warmed. He pulled it away, letting it fall to the floor, and slept.

He woke, pain free but groggy and tired, and checked his phone. A little before noon; not his worst episode. Nic had sent a "got it, sleep" text he hadn't noticed while suffering through the waves of pain. Fortunately, Michael hadn't scheduled any estimates or committed to finishing a project; experience had proven his health was too shaky after travel.

Getting out of bed, he showered, shaved and dressed, then drove to Nic's worksite.

Nic was putting tools away in the work truck. "How're you feeling, bro?"

"Better." Michael shrugged. "Are you done here?"

Nic nodded and slammed the tailgate. "Sure am. Time for a coffee. Join me?"

"Sure, why not?" He could get a decaf. With all the extra sleep, he'd have a hard enough time falling asleep at his normal time, and regularity was critical to preventing another episode.

Nic's lips pursed. "Actually, I need some food too. Let's stop by Deb's."

Michael grimaced. "I'll head back home and work on the books."

"Kim's got the books." Nic huffed. "Come on, don't be a chicken. Deb's cupcakes are the best and you know it."

Michael glared at his brother. "Don't be trying to set us up. The sisters and brothers thing is too weird." And she deserved better than some broken down guy who couldn't even get out of bed at least one day a week.

Nic guffawed. "Yeah, only if you make it weird. It's not like we're related to them by blood or marriage other than me and Kim. But no, I'm not messing with your love life." He smirked. "But Kim might not be so restrained, and I'm not telling her no."

"You're so whipped." He didn't really mean the words, and Nic knew it.

Nic grinned. "Happily. I'm getting a cupcake, whether you are or not."

"Fine." He'd admit Deb was the best baker in town, probably the best in the state, and her treats were almost worth the certain awkwardness. He got in his truck and followed Nic. With any luck, Deb would be so happy to see Nic that she'd ignore him. They parked in the small lot behind the bakery and he followed Nic in the back door.

The heat hit him like a hammer, reminding him of summers in Afghanistan, but the smell was much better. Browning sugar and bread, cinnamon, yeast, vanilla, and a dozen others swept over him. They wove through the machinery and cooling racks to the front of the store. Just before the bakery display case, Deb sat at a table, rotating a cake on a stand with one hand while spreading white frosting with the other.

Cold air blasted down his neck, fighting the heat of the commercial ovens, and Michael stepped to the side. Deb—and her cake—needed the air conditioning more than he did. Besides, extreme temperature shifts could bring on another migraine.

"Nic!" Deb grinned.

Nic put an arm around her shoulders and squeezed. "Hey, how's my favorite sister-in-law?"

"I'm your only sister-in-law." She chuckled, then her eyes met his and the smile fell from her face. "Michael."

"Hey." He lifted his chin like an idiot kid.

She turned back to Nic. "So let me guess. Cupcakes?"

"For your nieces, of course." Nic nodded like a bob-blehead doll.

Deb chuckled. "Right, just for them."

"Well, if you insist, I'm sure Kim would like one, too. And I wouldn't mind either." Nic grinned. "I'm sure Michael appreciates your expertise as well."

"Yep." She smoothed the frosting into a thin layer, then spun the cake. "Good enough for the base lay-er." Hopping off the stool, she sashayed to the bak-ery counter. "Luckily for you, I made a test batch." She bent and pulled a small tray out from under the back counter.

Michael quickly averted his gaze from her backside, but couldn't help staring again once she stood and turned to them. Deb was short, curvy, and smoking hot.

She placed four cupcakes in a box, then held the tray out to Nic. "Take one." Nic did and the tray swung to Michael. "Go ahead."

He grabbed one of the elaborately frosted treats, almost squishing the cake out of the wrapper before he gentled his grip. "Thanks."

She nodded and placed the tray on the counter. "Let me know what you think. It's a new recipe for this fall. It's only a few months away."

Michael peeled back the paper and bit, trying to get some cake with the enormous pile of creamy frosting. Sweet cinnamon and vanilla, with a little bite of heat, and a delicate cake that almost fell apart in his mouth. Wanting every bit, he licked the remaining frosting from his lips. "It's delicious no matter what season it is." Deb's eyes were on his mouth. He raised the treat to take another bite when pounding from the bakery's front door made him jump.

Deb scowled and marched around the counter to the front door, putting her hand on the knob, but not opening it. "Sorry, we're closed. We open at seven tomorrow."

"I've got a message for you." A raspy man's voice, the tone carried an edge of menace.

Michael exchanged glances with Nic. They put down their treats and moved closer to Deb, but hidden behind the door. She raised her brows at them, then cracked the door open. "Can I help you?" She kept her hand on the knob.

Michael leaned over to peer through the window. A tall, hulking man, with a bit of a gut and a five-day shadow glared down at Deb, hands clenched at his sides. "Are you Deb?"

"Yes." She raised her chin.

"Deb Franks?" He emphasized the last name.

Her neutral expression turned into a glare. "No."

He put a hand on the door, and she shoved her toes against the other side. "You used to be Deb Franks, though, right?"

"Yes. For my sins. What do you want?" She scowled.

If looks could kill, the guy would be flat on the ground. But the pretty blonde wasn't a superhero. Good thing he and Nic were there, or the confrontation could go badly for her.

"George has a message for you." The man pushed the door harder and threat coated his words.

Michael raised his brows at Nic, and slid closer to Deb. Nic shadowed him.

"Well, I don't want to hear it, or anything else from him ever again." She stabbed the air in front of the man's face with her pointer finger. "He should have gotten that message loud and clear when I divorced his slimy self and returned his letters."

"If you know what's good for you, you'll take this message." He drew back his arm and slammed his palm against the door.

Deb stumbled back into Michael. He grasped her around the waist and held her until she was steady. She pulled her phone from a pocket on her apron. "Back off, buster! Leave now, or I'm calling the cops. Nobody threatens me, especially in my own shop."

He knocked the phone from her hand. "You're gonna listen and listen good!"

Fury swept through Michael, but he locked it down. He stepped in front of Deb and shoved the man back. "No, she isn't. Leave now, or you'll be leaving on a stretcher."

"Gonna take more than you to take me down, short stuff." The man poked his finger into Michael's chest. "And this is none of your business, so butt out!"

Michael grabbed the man's finger and bent it back. "Don't think it'll take even me, but guess what? I got lots of help."

The man yelped. Then Nic pulled the door wide, grabbed the man's pants and spun him around, yanking his finger from Michael's grasp. Nic grabbed the man's right arm and pulled it up toward his neck. "This is my sister's business. Get out, and don't come back. We see you here again, you're done for."

Together, Michael and Nic crowded him out the door. Nic let go of his pants and Michael shoved him hard, sending him sprawling. Nic pulled out his phone and clicked a picture of his face. "Don't come back. And tell George to back off, or he'll be staying even longer."

The man scrambled to his feet and walked down the sidewalk backwards. "You'll regret this!" He shook his fist in the air, then jogged away.

He and Nic watched until the man crossed the street and walked out of sight. Then they returned inside and Michael locked the door. He shook his arms out, trying to shake his anger away, too.

"Deb, are you okay?" Nic held out his arms.

Deb nodded, but her lips trembled and she threw herself into Nic's hug. "Yeah, I'm fine. Thanks for the help. Are you guys okay?"

If only he'd thought to offer a hug first. But that would be stupid. She deserved a better guy; someone healthy and happy.

Nic let her go, chuckling. "Sure, that was easy."

Michael couldn't laugh, not with rage and fear still coursing through his body. "Deb, has this happened before?"

"No." She wrapped her arms around her waist. "George has been sending letters, but I return them unopened. Don't want anything to do with the sleaze ball." She shivered.

Nic's mouth twisted. "Can't blame you there. He must want something pretty bad to send someone to threaten you in person. Maybe you'd better report this?"

Deb sighed. "Yeah, probably. I'm really tired of dealing with this."

Michael raised his brows. "Exactly what is this?"

Deb's lips pressed together for a moment. "Want another cupcake? It's a bit of a story." She walked away from them and put the cake she'd been frosting into a nearby commercial fridge. She pulled out the remaining cupcakes and carried them to a table. "Water or coffee?"

"Water would be great, thanks." Michael knew he needed to rehydrate after his migraine, and more sugar wasn't going to help. But he couldn't resist her sweets. He followed her behind the counter, taking the glasses she filled, and then returned to the table, sitting after she did.

Nic took a bite. "You should be on one of those cupcake shows on TV. No way anyone could compete with these."

Deb smirked. "No thanks. Those shows have deadlines and pressure I don't need. And I'm not exactly TV material." She rolled her eyes and waved a hand from her head to her waist. "I eat too much of my own product."

Michael couldn't help himself. "You look perfect to me."

Nic elbowed him, hard. "Dude, bad timing." He kept his volume low, but Deb's face reflected amusement and disbelief.

"What else is new?" He was generally bad with women but everything came out wrong around Deb. "Sorry, never mind. I know the basics of what happened with Franks, but I don't think Nic does, so if you could tell us the whole story, maybe we can help." He had to stay calm and project reassurance. Displaying anger might make Deb more anxious, and it wouldn't help him either.

Deb took a deep breath. "I got married in high school to George Franks. He was a jock, and the picture-perfect boyfriend for an insecure fat girl who'd been teased her whole life. George's dad was pretty well off, so George was more than a little spoiled, and it turns out, a whole lot lazy. We got married right after he graduated high school when I was a junior. I found out later his mom pressured him hard to marry the 'right kind of girl' thinking that would keep him on the straight and narrow when he went to college." She rolled her eyes. "It did for a while. Then he started partying harder, and he lost his football scholarship, and he really wasn't good enough that they were willing to overlook his academics, so he dropped out." Deb looked down at the table. "I'm pretty sure he cheated on me the whole time he was there. He lived in a big house with his teammates, and there were girls there all the time. When I confronted him, he blamed me for trapping him into marriage and gaslighted me hard." She shrugged, still staring at the table top.

Good thing George was in prison, because if he was here, Michael would be rearranging his face. George had always been sleazy but emotionally abusing a woman made him into true scum. "Did he physically abuse you, too?" Michael hardly recognized his own voice, his words coming out in a growl.

Deb shook her head. "No. He knew I wouldn't stand for that. Anyway, after he dropped out, he went from job to job, while I supported us by working in a bakery in Missoula. His dad cut him off, telling him to grow up and get a real job, but he got fired time after time. Then he got into drugs, and before long, he was dealing, not that I knew that." She shuddered and glared at the wall in front of her. "When I found needles, I kicked him out, packed my stuff and got the cops to search the place. There wasn't anything there but paraphernalia, but it wasn't long before he got caught the first time with drugs, and I started divorce proceedings. Then he got caught dealing at the high school, which sent him up to the state prison at Deer Lodge for a very long time." Her mouth twisted and she glanced between the two of them. "Sam drew up the divorce paperwork for me, even though she doesn't usually do domestics, and George actually signed it, so it wasn't even contested. But he kept sending me letters, mostly asking for money, and while I sent him some early on, I quit after the third request. Then I sent the letters back unread. But something else must be going on now, because this is the first time I've been threatened." She shook her head. "I'd better call Sam."

"I think you should spend the night with us." Nic pointed at the front door. "Too much glass, not enough security here."

"Here?" Michael wasn't sure what Nic meant.

Deb pointed at the ceiling above her head. "I live in an apartment above the bakery. No commute for me."

"Nice. Normally. But Nic is right." Michael glanced around the front of the business, trying to remember what the back door looked like.

"I'm not going to let some thug scare me out of my home. Or my business." Deb glared at him, but it was like a kitten glaring.

Michael smirked. "Guess I'll be spending the night." She was family, and he never abandoned family. Remembering that would keep him on the straight and narrow.

She raised her eyebrows. "I don't think so. I don't even know you."

He chuckled. "We can fix that. One night with me, and you'll know me real good." He'd already veered way off the straight and into a race track full of curves.

Nic punched his arm. "What is wrong with you?"

Michael held up his hands, palm out. "Just kidding, trying to lighten the mood." *Badly.*

"Kim is going to kill you, and I'll cheer her on." Nic scowled.

"Thanks, but no thanks." Deb rolled her eyes. "I'll call Sam, we'll talk to the Sheriff, they'll keep an eye on my place, and everything will be fine."

Michael snorted. She was being completely unrealistic. He'd seen the same tactics in the Taliban-controlled towns. The cowards always targeted women, and they were successful, more often than not. "What are you, five? Do you live in a cartoon? Gonna start wailing some feel-good song so you can hope and pray your way out of this?" With every word, Deb glared harder. But evil looks didn't scare off drug dealers; it took force or leverage.

Nic smacked him harder. "He may be a rude jerk, but he's right. What kind of protection do you have here? Surveillance? Security? A weapon?"

Deb sighed. "I have a security system with monitoring, because bakery equipment is expensive and flammable. No cameras; never needed them. No guns. I have a taser upstairs."

It was a miracle she hadn't been robbed or attacked before. Even the little town of Marcus had criminals. "You have to get too close to use a taser. You're too tiny to take that chance. Unless you know some sort of martial arts?" It was highly unlikely. Deb was softly rounded, pretty in a cute cheerleader-girl-next-door way, and about as menacing as a stuffed bunny. Although she probably had strong arms and hands from baking, so he could teach her a few techniques easily.

"No, do I look like a karate expert? I bake." She spread her arms wide, raising her hands in the air, and looked down at her pink apron decorated with her logo and yellow sunflowers.

She looked as delicious as her cupcakes, but he wasn't dumb enough to say that. "I don't think you're safe here by yourself. You should stay with Nic and Kim, or I can help." He'd resisted temptation before, and he'd do so again.

Deb rolled her eyes. "I'm not abandoning my business, and I'm staying here, by myself. I have 911 on speed dial, the cops love me because I bring them goodies, plus I have my security system and my taser. I'll be fine. I'll call Sam, and we'll warn the police, and file a complaint with the prison." She glanced at her phone. "Nic, wasn't Kim expecting you home early for the girl's dance recital?"

Nic winced and tapped his phone. "Yep, got to go." He stood. "Michael, you got this?"

He nodded. "Yeah. I'll get a few things from home and come back." Good thing he hadn't unpacked his duffel bag; his sleeping bag, pillow, and some clean clothes were still inside. He'd add a few of his business T-shirts, repack all his meds, grab his weapon and he'd be good for guard duty.

Deb shoved her chair back with a screech. "Stay home. I don't need your help."

Michael stood, and moved to deliberately loom over her. "Too bad, cupcake queen. You're getting it. I can sleep in my truck, but I'm not leaving you here alone tonight."

Deb's lip curled. "Hope you have warm blankets, because you'll need them."

"Don't you worry, I'll be fine, and I'll make sure you're safe." Staying in his truck was a better idea, anyway. Deb was too tempting, too distracting. Outside, he'd stay alert and aware, and he'd remember she was too good for him.

Michael followed Nic out of the bakery's sugar, spice and everything nice, back to his truck, coated in the dust, muck, and dirt of his life. A little reminder that sweet Deb was too young and too clean for him. A cupcake queen deserved a king, not a guy who couldn't get out of bed because his head ached. He drove faster than usual; fear for Deb simmering in his gut. She brought so much joy to so many; she deserved a safe, happy life.

Chapter 3

DEB READIED THE CASH drawer for the morning, placed it in the safe, checked the front and back door locks, engaged the security system, and threw her apron into the laundry hamper. Despite her brave words, she was grateful for the commercial steel doors leading to her apartment. She checked the deadbolts on the door separating her stairway from the bakery and the exterior door, then trod up the narrow stairs. She should do a sale video highlighting the next day's specials, but she couldn't, not after that.

Opening and locking the final door at the top of the stairs, she entered her sanctuary and took a deep breath of relief. Most would find the tiny studio apartment claustrophobic; her queen size bed took up most of the space, with just enough room for a reading chair and an ottoman. The bathroom squeezed into the space behind the kitchenette; both were small, but so was she.

A narrow island with tall stools separated the kitchen from the bed and gave her a little storage.

The sunny yellow walls with dark brown furnishings were a bold design choice, but the splashes of bright white and pale blue lightened the intense shades. Since she woke very early, and the winter nights were long in Montana, strategically placed full-spectrum lights started her day on a bright note. In the evenings, she used dimmer lighting, the relaxing hues signaling her work day was done.

Michael Acer in her space would be anything but re-laxing. The man, with those broad shoulders, constant scowl and blunt words simply didn't fit, physically or emotionally. At least he wasn't unfairly tall, although he could still hover over her physically, but everyone could. She was used to it, but she wouldn't let anyone intimidate her in her own home. Or attempt to intimi-date her in her business. She wasn't the shy, needy, in-secure girl George had groomed, and she wasn't giving into his demands or anyone else's. Including Michael's or Nic's, no matter how well-meant.

Slipping off her shoes and putting on slippers, she drew the shades on the tall, narrow windows. She hated to shut out the view, but having glass in the three walls surrounding her sleeping space seemed too accessible, too vulnerable. She shook the sensation away; she was on the second story above a high-ceilinged business. It would take a lot of effort for anyone to climb up. But contacting her security company to install additional sensors upstairs seemed prudent. Maybe some cam-eras, too, depending on how affordable they were. She could get doorbell cameras at the very least.

She wanted to plop down in her chair and mindlessly eat chips, but instead, she put on an apron and fixed a heathy meal with chicken and veggies. Owning a bakery meant eating too much sugar and butter; a healthy meal every night was the only way she could keep her weight in check. At least baking meant plenty of steps and weight lifting without deliberate exercise, something she'd always hated.

Deb ate her meal at the island, cleaned and then took a shower, drying her hair and readying her clothes and makeup for the morning. Tightening a silky robe around her waist, she could no longer resist. She peered out the tiny bathroom window, the only one that looked down on the small parking area behind her business. A white truck, with a large work box on the back was parked directly in front of her back door. She couldn't see the words, but she knew the stark black and white logo on the door: Acer Home Improvement.

Michael really was going to camp out in his truck. That couldn't be comfortable. And while the worst of the winter was over, the nights were still chilly. She couldn't leave the man down there to shiver, no matter how misguided he was.

Part of her said she should; she hadn't asked for his help. In fact, she'd objected, strongly. She was perfectly capable of calling 911 and she had a taser on her nightstand. Although, she wasn't sure it was charged; she'd carried it every day when she worked in Missoula, but Marcus seemed so safe, and she didn't even have to go outside to reach her apartment.

But maybe Marcus wasn't safe anymore. Wiz had warned all of them that Erin's mother, Sharlene Murphy, had made some bad decisions regarding investors into Marcus Bank. Erin still had trouble with Chaz Cust, and he'd harassed both her and Sam, too. Then there were the men who attacked Wiz last fall, trying to assault her and burn down her house. None of those seemed related to George Franks, but the so-called investors Marcus Bank sent her way might be. Organized crime was into drugs, and George had dealt them. Maybe there was a connection.

And in that case, Michael might not be safe, alone in his truck. She couldn't do much to help a soldier, but she could provide a secure, warm place for him to stay. Her alarm system would alert both of them, where he might be surprised in his truck, especially if he slept. She put her hand on the deadbolt to the stairs. Offer or not?

She was kidding herself. She wouldn't be able to sleep knowing he was down there, cold and uncomfortable. Especially with lingering medical problems related to his military service. Sleeping in a truck wouldn't be healthy. She tied her robe securely, grabbed her keys, opened the door, and padded down the stairs. At the outside door, she hesitated again, putting her eye to the peephole. The white truck with the shadowy figure in the passenger's seat mocked her cowardice. She shut off the alarm and left the building, making sure her keys were in her pocket, and marched to Michael's truck.

As she neared, he scowled. Regret made her grimace, but she wasn't turning around.

He rolled down the window. "Yes?"

She clenched her fists. She had to be polite, even if she didn't mean it. "It's going to get cold, and you won't know if my alarms go off until it's too late. Would you like to come upstairs or at least inside?"

His scowl deepened. "I'm fine. I'm not sleeping, and if I was, this seat is more comfortable than a Striker."

She had no idea what a Striker was, but it didn't matter. "That might be, but you don't have people sharing your watch. And you have jobs to do tomorrow, right?"

He grimaced. "It won't be the first time I've worked without sleep."

"But if you slipped because you're tired and injured yourself, I'd feel terrible." Which was true, even if she hadn't asked for his help. "If you're insisting on guarding my business, which for the record, I don't think is necessary and I didn't ask, you can at least stay warm and comfortable, and maybe get some sleep." She clenched her fists and gritted the words out. "Please?"

He glared, then nodded. "Step back." She did, and he opened the door. From the back seat, he pulled a large dark green bag, closed the doors and locked his truck with a beep. A big, black holster secured an equally big, black pistol to his muscular thigh. "Lead the way."

Grimacing once her back was turned, Deb opened the door, letting him in. She locked it behind him and entered her alarm code. The tiny landing at the bottom of her apartment stairs was much too crowded with Michael's wide shoulders. No matter how she tried to squeeze closer to the keypad, her backside brushed against him. The alarm system flashed and beeped—she'd entered the wrong code. Carefully pushing each button, she entered the right number and jumped when it flashed "Alarm On." She sucked in her gut, and turned to face him, regretting it instantly.

Michael glowered down at her. "Can I open the door to the bakery now?"

"No, I have to unlock it." Deb winced at the anticipated awkwardness and shuffled to her left. He slid to the right, trying to keep his giant bag from knocking her over.

Despite their care, every inch of her brushed against him, trying to send shivers down her spine. But she was in control and she wouldn't let his body affect her. She opened the inner door to the bakery, her tension fading with the comforting scent of flour, sugar, butter and vanilla. Skittering away, she waited until Michael stepped inside, then closed and locked the door. She swallowed, wishing for a glass of water. "Do you want to stay down here, or upstairs?" She didn't want him in her apartment, not one little bit.

"I wouldn't be effective up there." He turned a full circle, then glared down at her again. "Can I get the alarm codes and a set of keys in case I need to go outside?" He walked toward the dining area, pulling cooling racks out of their neat rows, making her move around them. After she grabbed one and stopped him from blocking her, he growled. "I'm trying to create obstacles for anyone coming in the back."

She put her hands on her hips. "Well, tell me where you're headed, and I'll get in front of you."

He snorted, stepped back, and bowed, sweeping an arm out to the side. "Yes, milady."

It was her turn to glare. "Look, I didn't ask for this. I don't want you here. But I'm not going to leave you outside either, so can the sarcasm." She marched in front of him, stopping at her decorating table, which stood at the end of the divider between the sales area and the bakery. Customers liked watching her decorate; sales had increased when she moved her table to that location. Plus, it was right under an air conditioning vent, so it was a double win.

Michael stopped right behind her, blocking her between his body and the table. She stepped to the side and turned.

He surveyed the space and turned back to her. "I'll stay here, between the two areas, where I can hear and see everything. Give me keys and codes, and you can go."

"Oh, thanks for dismissing me from my own business." Deb marched to her safe, opened it and pulled an extra set of keys, throwing them at him and glaring harder when he caught them easily. "I'll send the codes to you on a text. I hope your phone is properly secured. I'll be back here at four." She walked away, wanting to get back upstairs.

"Four in the morning? That's when your day starts?" His voice sounded incredulous.

Like so many, he probably thought baking was easy, but she worked really hard for her success. "Yes." She spoke over her shoulder, not wanting to spend even one more second with him.

"Right. See you then."

She marched to the stairway, not looking back, and after locking and alarming every door, she retreated to her apartment, trying to calm her nerves. Men came in, took command, never listened, and blamed the female when things went wrong, no matter how many times they were warned. She paced the small floor space between the kitchenette and island and texted him the alarm codes. At least he was down there, not up here making everything worse. He'd undoubtedly make fun of her décor and lack of space, and complain about her lack of a television.

Her rugs would be softer than the sealed concrete floor of her shop. But no, he didn't belong in her sanctuary.

Deb untied her robe, draped it over the footboard of her bed, turned off the lights and climbed into bed. No matter how angry Michael made her, she still had to work very early tomorrow morning, and if she didn't want to waste hundreds of dollars in ingredients, she had to sleep.

After a restless night of tossing and turning, and wondering far too much about Michael, Deb rose. She dabbed on extra concealer; dark circles stood out against her pale skin, and that didn't match her bright and bubbly image. Happiness sold more cupcakes.

Precisely at four, she turned the alarm off and unlocked the deadbolt on the shop's back door. Her morning employees had keys to the doorknob, but they wouldn't show up for another hour. Inside, she put on her apron and slid her cell phone in the pocket, checking for all her other necessary items. She pulled the rack of already decorated cupcakes, cookies, and other breakfast items from the big walk-in cooler, and rolled it to the front, pushing the Michael-created obstacle course of cooling racks aside.

Standing next to her decorating table, Michael stuffed a dull green sleeping bag into a smaller bag. A thin, red mattress with more holes than cushion was on the floor next to his feet, a bright green pillow on top of it. Maybe she'd worried for nothing. Erin had said something about Ryan taking his backpacking gear with him last week, because plain cots weren't very comfortable for a full week of hard work. But that mattress looked too thin for concrete, though.

Well, no matter how lousy her night had been, she could be polite. "Good morning." She rolled the rack past him, flipped the coffee maker on, and loaded trays into the bakery case. "Help yourself to anything in the back, and coffee will be ready shortly."

"Thanks, but I'm going home to get a little more sleep, and I can't eat this sugary stuff anyway." He rolled and stuffed the rest of his things into his duffle bag, then walked away without another word.

Deb finished loading her trays, careful not to slam them into the case. The last thing she needed was broken glass. She placed bread into baskets, letting the loaves fall with a little more force than necessary. How dare he dismiss her products as "sugary stuff" when she had so much more. She made a great selection of gluten free products and low sugar products, too. The guy was determined to be nasty; at this point, mustering gratitude was far beyond her capabilities.

Good thing she had bread loaves to shape; trying to bake cupcakes with all this anger would end in dense blobs of overworked batter. She could punch the bread dough and pretend it was Michael's glowering face.

After a full day of happy customers, Deb was exhausted but restless. She'd tried to take her normal twenty minute nap after closing the front door, but memories of the brute George sent wouldn't let her rest. She rose and worked with Jeff to clean the shop, started savory and sweet batches of bread dough, then decorated the cupcakes her decorator Joan couldn't finish. After Jeff left, she checked her special orders, confirming she had nothing left tonight; the next evening, she'd be baking big layer cakes for a weekend wedding.

Deb stretched her fingers and jumped at the pounding from her back door. She had a buzzer; no one should knock. She yanked her cell phone from her apron pocket and trotted through the bakery, peering through the peephole. The same brutish man who'd confronted her the day before stood there, one hand thrust under his jacket at his waist. He might have a gun. He raised his other arm and pounded on her door again.

Deb took a deep breath and yelled. "Go away. I have nothing for you!"

"You owe us money. Open up, or I'm coming in!"

She moved away from the peephole, pressed the emergency button on her security panel and dialed 911.

"Marcus Dispatch, what's the nature of your emergency?" At the same time, a man's voice came from the speaker in her panel. "Do you need police response?"

"Help! There's a man with a gun at the back door of my bakery and he's threatening to break in. Please send the police, fast." Her back door shook and thunderous bang sounded, followed by a ringing thwack. "I think he's trying to shoot my door!"

"An officer is responding to your location. Please take shelter behind a locked door if possible and confirm your address for me." The 911 operator's voice was calm.

Deb entered the stairwell to her apartment, gave the 911 operator the address, and her name. The alarm company confirmed they'd requested response too, then hung up. She jumped again when a second double-bang sounded. She peered around the stairwell door into the bakery; bits of glass glinted, spread across her floor with a mangled bit of brass in the middle. "He shot the peephole!"

A siren wailed in the distance. The man outside yelled nasty names at her, then a car door slammed, and an engine rumbled then roared, fading as it sped away. A few seconds later, flashing red and blue lit the front of her bakery for a few moments, then the normal evening light returned as the officer's car squealed around the corner to the back. A car door slammed.

"Deputy Miles has arrived at your location. Please remain indoors and away from windows while he searches the area. Other officers are responding. An officer will call this number when it's safe to open the door. Do you understand?"

"Yes, thanks for your help. I appreciate it."

"You're welcome. Hang tight, they'll be with you momentarily. Take care." The call disconnected and Deb slid down the wall to sit on the floor. Turning in George had been bad enough and she'd done that at the station with Sam at her side. Talking with police after a shooting would take forever. Not wanting to tie up her phone, she texted Sam. "Man threatened me, then shot my door. Cops are here. What do I tell them?"

Sam texted back immediately. "Nothing. Not one word. I'll be there in ten minutes or less."

Deb climbed to her feet, entered the bakery again and grabbed a broom to sweep up the shattered peephole. The debris sprayed at least ten feet inside the door all the way to one of her work tables; fortunately, she hadn't been mixing batter or she'd have to throw away entire batches of dough. She'd have a lot of cleaning to do, though, because a piece of broken glass or plastic in a cupcake would be a death sentence for her shop. She sighed and grabbed a bucket of bleach water and a rag.

If she'd been looking through that peephole... At least cleaning would keep her from thinking about how close she'd been to getting shot.

Chapter 4

MICHAEL ANSWERED HIS CELL phone. "Hey Nic, what's up?" After a good night's sleep in his bed, he'd started a new job, rebuilding a decrepit deck. Yanking old planks and pulling nails had been a great workout and the perfect way to expend excess emotional energy. He would have stayed at Deb's bakery last night—with an inflatable mattress rather than a hiking pad—but she hadn't called him, Kim, or her friends about more problems. The bad guy must have gotten smart and left.

"You weren't at Deb's last night, right?"

His shoulders rose at the tension in Nic's voice. "No. What happened?"

"Same guy who threatened her came back. Tried to shoot the lock—" they both snorted at the stupidity "—and then shot the peephole out."

"Is she okay?" Shooting out a modern lock with a pistol wasn't possible, but if she'd been looking through the tiny window, she could have lost an eye or even her life. She wasn't stupid; she'd have run if someone pointed a gun at her, even through a metal-clad door.

"Yeah, she retreated to her stairwell after the first gunshot and called the cops. Kim says Deb's furious. Guess the peephole shattered and she had to deep clean everything within twenty feet of the door."

Michael's fists clenched, the edges of his phone biting into his palm. "I should have been there."

Nic snorted. "Why? We all figured the guy learned his lesson and left. I thought you staying that first night was overkill. Those kinds usually give up when they run into hard targets—they go for the weak or defenseless. We made it clear Deb wasn't either."

The muscles between his shoulders tightened, like a sniper was watching from a hideout. "Yeah, that's what worries me. The guy must be more than some local drug dealer's thug. I'm going to go talk to her later."

"Kim says all Deb's friends are upset, too. A bunch of them are ex-military and one of them is a security specialist, so I guess they're insisting Deb make some changes and accept some help. There's a meeting at the bakery at six. Can you make it? I've got a school thing for the kids."

"Yeah, I got it. Tell Kim not to worry. I'm not leaving Deb alone again, but I need an inflatable mattress or a cot if I'm going to sleep in the bakery." His broken body couldn't handle another night on barely cush-ioned concrete.

"We've got an inflatable. I'll drop it off this afternoon. Let me know how else I can help, and don't say I don't know what I'm doing. Being an Air Force RED HORSE member means going to some pretty lousy places and defending our equipment while we build the base, remember?"

"Hey, I wasn't going to say it." He wasn't; as a member of the Rapid Engineer Deployable Heavy Operational Repair Squadron, big brother was the real deal, not some fighter pilot raining death from thousands of feet above. Of course, Michael never complained about air power when it was saving his guys. But Nic had two daughters who needed him; he couldn't be risking his life.

"Sure you weren't. See you later." Nic ended the call.

Michael took out his anger at Deb's situation on the decking, and exposed the joists in half the time he'd estimated. Still breathing hard, he pulled the remaining nails and screws while inspecting the structure carefully. No sign of rot or insects; the homeowner should be happy. He spent the rest of the day staining the joists, and cutting the new decking. After cleaning up, he spoke with his customer, who was very pleased, then went home.

He showered, packed all his things including Nic's inflatable mattress, strapped on his pistol and drove to Deb's bakery, noting the lights on inside. He parked at the back, so his truck wouldn't be obvious later, and tried the back door. Locked; excellent. He rounded the building, noting that Deb's apartment above the shop had large windows on three sides, and an emergency escape ladder that hung too low for comfort. Anyone could reach it from the bed of a pickup truck.

At the front, he checked the knob—locked. He peered inside; a larger group than he'd anticipated. He knocked; heads twisted toward him.

Ryan opened the door. "Come in. We've got pizza & beer from the brewery, and Deb's got lots of treats." Ryan joined his wife, Erin, seated next to Deb at the head of the table. "I'll introduce you to everyone. Erin and Deb you know; that's Sam Kerr. She's Deb's lawyer and ours." Ryan pointed to a gorgeous woman on Deb's left, with long, auburn hair, fancy clothes, and per-fect makeup. She looked more like a model than a lawyer—and high maintenance.

Sam scanned him from head to toe and back again. "Lovely to meet you, Michael. Come join us." He didn't move. He didn't want to sit next to Sam; she had trouble written all over.

Ryan waved his mechanical grasper toward the next people sitting at the table. "This is Wiz, her fiancé Tom Borde, and Tom's dad, Pete Borde. They own the Rock-ing B Ranch." Ryan grinned. "Pete's a Vietnam sniper, Wiz is ex-Air Force, a kick-ass martial artist and com-puter security expert, and Tom's a financial expert and cowboy, but still a good shot."

The tiny, dark-haired, elfin Wiz looked fragile be-tween her towering fiancé and father-in-law, but Michael believed Ryan's assessment. Wiz was clearly assessing him and he wasn't sure if he made the cut. Pete held out his hand, and they shook. Pete gripped firmly, but without any silly contest.

Michael sat next to Ryan, wishing he was closer to Deb, but happy he wasn't at the same time. He twisted his chair to watch both doors.

"I've got your back." Wiz lifted her chin.

"Thanks." Michael watched Deb and Sam discuss points on the paper between them while surveying the rest of table; an interesting group of people. Wiz cast glances around the room constantly. Her chair was pushed back from the table, probably so she could easily get up. Tom leaned his arm against her shoulder, but kept his hands off. Pete seemed less wary, but also scanned the bakery carefully. Then Michael remembered; they'd been involved in a huge mess with Wiz's ex-husband committing arson, and a self-defense shooting in her house. Some of the press had tried to paint Wiz as a criminal, because she'd killed her attacker, which was ridiculous. More importantly, she was cool under pressure and a crack shot—and Deb might need both.

A smack of metal on wood drew his attention back to the end of the table. Sam picked up a stamp from the paper; most likely, she was notarizing Deb's signature. She retrieved a slim leather portfolio from the floor and slid the papers inside. "Okay. I'll file this with the court tomorrow. Thanks, Wiz, for figuring out who the guy is. Having a name makes it much easier to file a restraining order." Sam turned to Deb. "But, finding this guy to serve him will be hard, and as you all know, orders only work with basically honest people. This serves more as a way to increase a sentence if the police catch him. We need evidence. You need cameras, Deb."

"Deb." Wiz's voice was quiet, but urgent. "I've done a quick assessment of your shop and I can help you with a security system like Erin's, except we'll use both wifi and cables since you're in town where there's more electronic interference. I've already emailed you a parts list; you can buy it locally or order online. You can add the visual monitoring to your existing security service, although they won't like using my system rather than theirs, but mine's much more secure. I'll walk you through the steps to keep a backup on a cloud service as well as on your computer and a physical backup."

Wiz tapped her phone. The picture of the man who threatened Deb appeared. "This particular guy isn't an issue. I'm fairly certain he's a low-level contractor paid by the job. But the next person they send might be real trouble. This man is connected with the Russian Mob, the Bratva. Plus, Marcus Bank has connections there too." She took in a breath. "I've got some contacts with the Federal Bureau of Investigations, but they're not local, and not organized crime." Wiz turned to Sam. "You have the right contact."

Sam scowled. "Of course you found out. Fine. I doubt it will help, but I'll reach out." Her lip curled.

Deb put her hand on Sam's clenched fist. "Don't do that. It's not worth the heartache."

Sam turned to Deb. "What heartache? It was over a long time ago and you're my best friend. These guys are dangerous, and next to your life, a simple email and follow-up phone call is nothing." She shrugged. "I'll keep it professional. No problem."

Erin snorted. "Sure. How'd that work out for you last time?"

Sam flipped her hair back. "That was years ago. I'm over it. Why waste my time? I've got better men in my life now."

"Of course you do." Deb put an arm around Sam's shoulder. "But let me know if you don't want to. I'll reach out to him myself." She frowned. "He deserves a piece of my mind anyway."

Sam flicked an imaginary fly. "It's water under the bridge. I've got this."

Michael lowered his voice and leaned closer to Ryan. "Sam's ex is FBI?" That might be helpful, but definitely not something to rely on. In his limited experience, the feds were more trouble than they were worth.

Ryan turned toward him and shrugged. "Guess so. Before my time."

"I'm concerned my issues with local law enforcement may cause you problems, too." Wiz scowled, the first real emotion she'd displayed.

Deb laughed. "Not a chance. Do you know how many cupcakes I take them? Plus, I donate to their fundraisers, along with the fire department and the hospital too. Pay it forward is my motto." She rose. "Be right back." She walked into the back of the bakery.

"You." Wiz pointed at Michael. "You be careful. I don't have a lot of friends, and Deb is one of them."

Michael raised both hands in surrender. "I have no bad intentions. Just trying to keep my sister-in-law safe." Attraction could and would be ignored. "And speaking of that, I'm grabbing my gear. I'll guard the bakery every night until this is resolved." He followed Deb into the warmth of the bakery. He still had the keys and alarm codes, and he'd only have to open the door for a few moments.

But when he arrived at the door, it was wide open. "Deb?"

Silence greeted him. He pulled his sidearm, slid to the side of the doorway, crouched, and peered around the doorframe quickly, ducking backing inside. Nothing moved in the small parking lot. He checked the other direction. Nothing and no one.

Deb wouldn't have gone upstairs and left the door open. She might be a ray of sunshine, but she wasn't stupid or ignorant. Michael closed the door gently, then sprinted for the front, twinging pain lancing up his spine with every step. Pizza boxes were opened and beer fizzed. "Where'd Deb go? I found the back-door open, and no sign of her."

Wiz sprang to her feet, pulled a pistol and sprinted for the back, Tom, Pete and Ryan following. Staying at the table, Erin and Sam went for their phones, thumbs flying. Erin looked up. "Nothing."

Michael raced to the back. Wiz stood just inside the open back door, pistol drawn and pointed at the ground, while Ryan, Tom and Pete searched the back lot. They returned quickly. Ryan shook his head. "Nothing. Her car is here, and your truck. No sign of any other vehicle, but one could have rolled in and out without us noticing if the car was quiet."

Erin and Sam joined them. Erin pointed at the ceiling. "Has anyone checked her apartment?"

They all shook their heads. Erin crossed to the apartment's stairway door and checked it. "Locked."

Tom leaned out of sight, then returned. "Exterior door is locked too."

Michael pushed through the crowd. "There's a fire ladder outside. You can reach it from a pickup bed."

"Wait," Wiz hissed, holding her big black .45 low. "Don't start your truck. Tom can lift me to the ladder." She slid her pistol into a thigh holster, and took Tom's hand, pulling him around to the side of the building. "Just like boosting me on to a horse, but a little higher and harder."

They all followed, weapons out except Sam, who carried her phone. Wiz peered up at the ladder, and pulled Tom into place below it. When she turned away, he caught her shoulder. "You sure about this?" Wiz nodded.

"Okay." He kissed her quickly, then stood, bending over, his feet spread wide. He laced his fingers together, forming a cup. Ryan moved behind Tom, and Pete to the other side, probably to catch her if the throw was short.

Wiz backed away and sprinted to Tom, jumping so one foot landed in Tom's hands. He exploded upward, tossing her into the air like a circus performer. She caught the ladder's second rung and pulled herself up, then climbed the remaining rungs. Clinging to the top of the ladder, she lifted herself to the side of the window and peered inside. She ducked down, looped an arm through the top rung, and pulled out her phone, texting with both thumbs.

Tom and Ryan both pulled out their phones, the rest of them gathering around to read.

"Deb tied to a stool next to the sink, behind a counter, gagged. At least two men, they're searching, tearing things apart. Both near the bed at the front of the room. One team should go up the stair. I'll try to lower the ladder quietly, so we can get a couple more up here. Shorter people, because getting through a window isn't easy. Text when you're at the top of the stairs. I'll send a go message. Count three seconds after it arrives, then go. Whoever comes in first, go for Deb, knock her over behind the counter. Michael, you cut her free and make sure she gets out. One verbal warning, fire only when fired upon. Clear?"

Michael scanned the group. "I'm the shortest, I'll go up the ladder if Wiz can get it down quietly. Erin is behind me. Ryan, Tom and Pete go for the stairway." He'd take Ryan, but with only one hand, a ladder and a weapon was iffy.

Erin put an arm on Ryan's shoulder. "Check her apron pockets for her keys. What about the window? Is Wiz going to break it? And if we have to break down the door, that will be noisy. They're steel. It will take a while."

"Great points." Michael had brought his work truck. "I've got breaker bars in my truck. Tell Wiz we're getting tools, but if she has to go in to protect Deb, we'll be right behind her. Ask her how she's getting in." He sprinted for the back, grabbing the workbox on the truck and unlocking it. He opened the lid, and gently moved the tools off his bars, handing them to the others gathered around him, to reach the buried bars faster. "Just put them on the ground. We'll pick them up later."

He stuck a short claw bar in his back pocket for the window, handed his two-foot wrecking bar to Tom, and grabbed the three-foot crow bar for himself. "Tom, if you have to, pry right at the lock. Deadbolt first; since the door is steel, try to break the frame instead. If they're both steel, you might have to go through the wall to the side instead, if there is one. Take the reciprocating saw and cut through the wallboard between the studs. Or just smash through with the bar. It will be noisy either way."

Tom hefted the bar. "Got it. Too bad we don't have a door ram."

Erin's phone lit up. "Wiz says the windows are shut. She'll break it with her gun if she has to."

"Pry bar might be faster and quieter." Michael ran back to the ladder. The fire ladder was fully deployed, the bottom rung three feet off the ground. It was metal, so he'd have to climb carefully to keep the crow bar from clanging against the ladder. Wiz stood to the right side of the window, pistols in both hands, legs braced on the steep roof. Her right hand was turned ninety degrees so the butt of the gun faced the window; she was ready to break it and shoot at the same time, which was impressive. He'd never try it; he wasn't a good enough off-hand shooter.

Michael climbed quietly to the top, then slid off the ladder to the left. Taking the small bar, he placed it right at the window latch, then glanced inside. As Wiz said, Deb was tied to a high stool, a kitchen towel tied around her head as a gag. She was jerking against the restraints, but carefully, probably because she didn't want to tip over. Hopefully, she'd let herself fall if bullets flew.

At the front of the room, white fluff filled the air—the men had cut the cushions on her chair, and sliced the mattress open. Which was ridiculous; if Deb had money, it would be in her safe or invested in her business. So that meant these guys weren't bright, or they were trying to intimidate her. Either way, they'd be likely to shoot first, ask questions later. At least their weapons were holstered.

Erin climbed up but remained crouched on the ladder. "I'll use the small bar on the next window, you use the big one here." She pulled the small bar loose and stepped around him carefully. "Sam got Deb's extra keys out of her safe. The guys are at the top of the stairs, ready to go."

Wiz holstered her left-hand pistol and put her left foot on the window sill, grabbing the window frame above his head with her left hand. "Erin, send the go."

Erin whispered, "Sent. Three, two, go!"

Michael jammed the crow bar into the window frame and yanked down, hard enough that he almost fell off the roof. The window latch gave way with a screech and the window flew up, hitting the top with a bang. Wiz jumped inside at the same time the door slammed open, her voice matching Tom's. "Hands up!"

He pulled his weapon, his fingers wrapped around the grip and off the trigger, then jumped through head first, letting his arms collapse, rolling on to his shoulder and across the floor to the island. Ryan crouched next to Deb, who was flat on the floor, and he was cutting her gag loose. Michael holstered his gun, pulled his pocket knife and sliced through the restraints on her feet. A gunshot rang, followed by a second. He and Ryan ducked but kept working on Deb's bonds.

Men yelled as Michael helped Deb to a sitting position on the floor. "Come on, we're getting out of here." He put his arm around her waist; her feet might be numb. "Hang on, stay low. We're going for the door, then down. Ready?" He glanced at Ryan; he nodded and drew his weapon, raising it to rest on the countertop above them.

Deb wrapped an arm around his shoulders. "Ready." Her voice trembled.

He tightened his arm. "Three, two, go." He tightened his core muscles and thrust upward, like a jump squat, carrying Deb with him, and bounded to the door. He turned sideways, half-dragging her down the steep, narrow stairs, and then to the corner of her bakery near the walk-in refrigerator. He pointed at the floor, and she crouched. "If anyone shoots, go in the fridge, understand?"

Her big blue eyes blinked up at him. "Okay."

Michael rose, standing over her, holding his gun, while sirens grew louder. "Sam, we're back here!"

Sam sprinted toward them, her phone to her ear. "Deb is free. There were two gunshots. I don't know the status upstairs." She raised her brows, obviously asking him.

Michael shook his head. "I was getting Deb out."

Thudding sounded from the stairs. Michael shoved Sam behind him. "Down."

A man appeared in the door to the apartment, hands behind his back, Tom behind him, followed by another man, with Ryan behind him. "Down on the ground. Face down, flat." Both men dropped to their knees, then Tom and Ryan lowered them to the concrete. Michael would have pushed them, hoping their noses broke. Bright red stained one man's arm.

"Attackers are secured in the bakery. One wounded, so we need an ambulance." Sam rose and pushed past Michael.

He turned to Deb, offering her a hand up. Scowling, she refused and used the refrigerator door handle to pull herself up. She stomped to Sam, who held an arm out to prevent Deb from getting too close. Probably wise, because Deb's clenched fists implied she was furious.

Michael followed Deb. The original thug who threatened her, plus another guy who looked enough like him to be a brother. He was moaning. Ryan rolled him to his side, cutting away his shirt to expose the wound on his upper arm.

Sam leaned over and said something quietly to Deb. She scowled, but turned on a toe. "I'll get it."

Michael followed her to the front, where she pulled out a big red bag with a white cross. "Big first aid kit." He put out his hand to take it from her.

She ignored him, carrying it to the back. Red and blue flashed inside the bakery, and people crowded the area. Marcus Sheriff's deputies, Marcus City police, and a State police officer stood near the bad guys, most listening to Sam, one deputy handcuffing the men on the floor. With the trouble Wiz had encountered with the cops, Michael was happy to leave the talking to an attorney.

Wiz and Pete entered the room, sliding behind the crowd, and an ambulance crew pushed a gurney inside. A crime scene technician headed up the stairs with one of the deputies.

Pete joined them. "Deb, can I get some big garbage bags?" He put an arm around her shoulder. "They trashed your place. I'm so sorry." Deb turned into Pete's chest, and he hugged her. "Don't worry, when the cops release the scene, we'll take care of it. Wiz got pictures for your insurance, and she said you're welcome to her guest house as long as you need it."

Michael would rather be holding Deb, but if cleanup was all he could do to help, then he would. Deb's cleaning supplies were neatly stacked below the handwashing sink. He grabbed the box of black garbage bags, and other supplies. When the deputy released the upstairs, he slid behind the remaining cops, and trod up the stairs.

Dropping the box near the door, he pulled a bag and shoved armfuls of stuffing into the black bags, along with the chair cushions when he reached the window. Erin, Wiz, and Ryan joined him shortly, all of them working together to pick up the tatters of Deb's once-lovely home. They had most of the mess cleaned up in minutes, but the ripped mattress would be a challenge to get down the stairs.

Wiz looked out the still-open window. "I can pull Pete's truck below the window, then we can dump all the bags out there and take them to the dump tomorrow. How do we get the mattress out?"

"We'll have to cut it in half." Michael shrugged. "Then out the window." He joined Wiz and inspected the remains of the latch and the window frame. "These are terrible latches. I'll replace all of them with better ones, and install some additional security measures. I wonder if she'd go for bars?"

"No, she wouldn't go for bars." Deb stomped across the room. "I'm not living in a prison because of some thugs."

Michael scowled at her. "I'm not proposing a jail, just a little additional security."

"The answer is no. And I'll decide what goes on my windows, when, and who." Her brows almost met above the bridge of her nose, her cheeks were flushed, and her fists clenched.

Evidently, he'd infuriated her again, but she was too cute to be intimidating. "Okay." He raised both hands. "It's your house." Once she'd calmed down, she'd agree. She probably just needed to feel in control after being captured.

"Yes, it is." Erin put an arm around Deb and spoke quietly to her.

Michael kept cleaning. But whether she agreed or not, he was still upgrading her latches, if only for his peace of mind. It had been too easy to break in; he wouldn't sleep knowing she was so poorly protected. Despite capturing the two thugs downstairs, he was certain the threat wasn't over—they had to be ready for the next battle or they'd lose the war.

Chapter 5

Deb sat upright on the springy bed, heart pounding, mouth dry, shaking like the middle of an undercooked cake and feeling just as raw. For the fifth night in a row, she'd relived the terror of a hand covering her mouth, the hard, frigid barrel of a gun to her temple, and a man's voice warning her to shut up and tell them where the money was, or she'd die, and so would all her friends. Not wanting to put her friend's lives at risk, she'd told them all her money was upstairs.

In hindsight, she'd been stupid. All her friends except Sam had been armed, and they were all smart enough not to shoot wildly. She should have stomped on the top of the man's foot, then let her legs collapse, jerking her head out of the man's grip, and then yelled while rolling away. But she'd frozen. Unlike her friends, she wasn't military, or a martial arts expert, or a fierce negotiator. She designed cute aprons, baked and decorated. She didn't ninja her way out of life and death situations; she created heart attacks and weight gain. Mostly her own.

Her alarm went off and she climbed out of Wiz and Tom's incredibly comfortable guest bed. Commuting in the dark wasn't fun, but the safety of Wiz's super-se-cure-to-the-point-of-paranoia compound let her fall asleep at night. Even with the security upgrades Wiz and Michael were implementing at the bakery, she wasn't sure she'd be able to sleep in her apartment. But she had to try. They'd completed their work and given her a tour after she closed the day before. On the sur-face, little had changed, but it no longer felt like home.

She dressed, gathered her remaining things from the guest house and packed them in her suitcase, rolling it out to her car and putting it in the trunk. Security lights flashed on with her movements, and the gates opened in front of her car. It was a little spooky, but she was sure that no matter how hard she tried to be un-obtrusive, Wiz woke whenever she left the guest house. She wasn't the kind to sleep through anything, let alone movement near her home.

Deb drove down the dirt road and turned on to the highway, watching for deer, elk and other critters. Since spring was coming, they were gaining seven min-utes of daylight every passing day, but it was never light at four o'clock in the morning. Another reason to return to her apartment—commuting was dangerous. She couldn't afford a new car on top of the security equipment.

She'd insisted on paying for the work, but neither Michael or Wiz would give her a bill for their time, just the materials. She'd objected, but knew it was useless.

Someday she'd be able to pay them back; until then, they'd get all the baked goods they ever wanted for free.

She couldn't afford to turn down their generosity, not with Marcus Bank reevaluating her loan and all the other things she had to replace. Michael was sort-of family, at least, but Wiz was just a friend. But after Tom had explained that Wiz wouldn't be able to sleep well leaving a friend unprotected, and she'd be doing him a favor to accept Wiz's help, Deb had given in gracefully. Kim had keys to Deb's apartment, and told her bluntly to accept Nic and Michael's help, because real family helped each other. Even if their parents hadn't.

Deb and Kim had always relied on each other, but Michael's presence in her apartment bothered her. He avoided her whenever he could, and when he had to ask a question or give an explanation, he used as few words as possible, via text if possible. Clearly, he couldn't stand her.

His dislike bothered her. As a recovering people-pleaser, that was her problem, not his, but it still wasn't easy to overcome. Especially when she found him so physically attractive. Not overly tall but muscular, a striking face but not conventionally gorgeous, Michael's ingredient list was the perfect mix of raw materials. But his grumpy attitude and clear aversion baked into a lumpy, tough mess. She didn't need more of those in her life, so she swept her daydreams of romance into the trash.

She pulled into the lot behind her bakery, the new motion-detector lights flaring, leaving nowhere to hide except the dumpster, which was on the far side of the parking lot and backed up against the building; only the short side was hidden. And that was watched by a camera, like the rest of the parking lot, the interior of the bakery, and her stairwell.

As instructed by Wiz, she backed into her parking slot next to the apartment's exterior door, and pulled up the security system, checking for alerts—none—and the cameras. Nothing moved and there was nothing unusual inside, either, except Michael's sleeping form on his inflatable mattress near her decorating table.

Since the security system was fully operational, there was no need for him to guard the bakery. But as usual, he wouldn't listen to her, and neither did Kim or Nic, so Michael had a set of keys and full access to the alarm system. At least he didn't invade her apartment for any-thing but work.

Deb put her keys between her fingers, disarmed the back door with her phone, locked her car and let herself inside, then re-locked and alarmed everything behind her. Despite her unease with the new system and the lingering effects of the attack, the scent of dark choco-late, sugar and spice comforted her enough to keep moving. Hanging up her coat, she put on an apron, transferred her keys and phone to her pockets, and turned on the lights along the back wall. No matter how much she didn't want Michael camping out in her bakery, she tried not to wake him.

But despite her care, he was rolling off the bed. She winced at his slow, jerky rise; Nic had shared that Michael had chronic back pain along with frequent migraines after surviving multiple roadside explosions in Afghanistan. She offered a quiet "Good Morning," knowing anything cheerful would only get a scowl. He was grumpiest in the morning, and she didn't need to see his sleep-creased face, making her think of more pleasant things to do than work. She turned on ovens and readied the bakery for the day.

Opening the big walk-in refrigerator, she pulled the display case rack, avoiding Michael as she passed. She flipped the coffee machine on, and got ready to open, ignoring the hiss of escaping air from Michael's mattress and the close of the restroom door. When she was done with the sales setup, she returned to the back and rolled a huge mixing bowl of bread dough out of the refrigerator. Kneading her frustrations away was the best way to deal with both the aftermath of her nightmares and her ridiculous, one-sided attraction to the grumpy handyman.

She locked the heavy bowl into place and turned the bread hook on low, the whine of the motor loud. After the dough was knocked down, she'd portion, knead and shape it. A few minutes later, Michael towed his things past her. She turned the machine off. "Have a good morning and sleep in your own bed tonight, please." He grunted, raised his chin, and kept walking.

Typical. Unless she could convince Wiz to lock him out, he'd be back at the end of the day. And she'd be upstairs, trying and failing to ignore his presence below. She weighed out the perfect portion and shaped the loaf. Twenty more of these might relieve her tension and tire her enough to sleep through the night. Even if that hadn't helped yet.

Late that afternoon, Deb splayed her aching hands against her waist and bent into a backwards stretch. She was almost done with customers, and the day couldn't end soon enough. For the third time in a row, one of her employees hadn't shown up. When the woman finally answered her phone, she admitted she wasn't coming back. The attack on Deb had scared her too much.

Deb had told her employees about the incident in great detail, and they each assured her they were fine with the addition of the security system. She'd brought in a couple of cans of bear spray, too, putting them near the front register. But she couldn't blame the girl for being frightened.

The bell on the front door chimed, making Deb sigh. She'd hoped she was done, but there was always someone rushing in at the last second.

The man was average height, probably in his fifties from the gray hair in his temples, his face slightly pockmarked, and he had smoker's brackets around his nose and mouth. He wore a tailored, expensive gray suit. He strode to the counter. "You are the owner, Deb?"

"Yes, I am." Interesting. Many older men thought she was an employee, and didn't expect much in the way of brains simply because she was blonde and short.

"Your cupcakes are delicious. Have you considered expanding? I don't usually invest in small businesses, especially bakeries, but for these?" He tapped the front of the bakery case. "These could go national."

Deb forced a smile. "Well, thank you very much, sir. I appreciate your compliment, but I don't have any desire to expand nationwide. I couldn't ensure the same quality, and I'd have to use preservatives, and worry about packaging, and marketing, and all the other business things that I don't want to deal with. Or deal with franchise owners. I like baking and I don't want to be a business manager. But thanks anyway."

"I can understand that, but that's where I come in. With my help, you wouldn't need to manage the business, I would. You'd be free to invent new flavors and designs instead." He handed her a thick business card. "Take a look at my company's track record. I think you might be pleasantly surprised." He tapped a black Amex card on the top of the counter. "And give me a dozen assorted cupcakes, please."

Deb grabbed a box and loaded cupcakes. The order would add a nice cushion to her bottom line for the day. "Certainly. But I enjoy being a small town baker." She smiled at the man as she handed him the box, ran his card, and gave him the receipt.

The man nodded. "You could keep your shop open, too." His eyes narrowed into a fierce stare. "But more importantly for you, my help would keep criminals from targeting you and your shop. Everyone knows to avoid challenging my organization." He raised both brows. "Everyone." He turned and walked out the door. In the parking lot, a man opened the back door of a big black Mercedes, and closed the door behind the man, then drove away. Deb locked and alarmed the front door behind him, then returned to the cake she was decorating. But she didn't pick up the pastry bag, because her hands trembled.

That pleasant, slightly grandfatherly man had essentially threatened her. She picked up her phone and texted Wiz, concentrating hard to combat the shaking. "Can you run a facial recognition for me?"

Her phone rang—it was Wiz. "Someone in your shop?"

Deb swallowed to wet her dry mouth. "He just left. Nice suit, chauffeured car, subtle sort of threats."

The taping of keys sounded. "Got him. I'll run it and let you know. Looks like everything's secure, but stay on the phone with me and walk around the back of the shop. Make sure there's no surprises back there. Don't go outside."

She did, carrying one of the bear spray canisters even though she felt slightly ridiculous with the big can in her hand. She returned to the front. "Nothing out of place, Wiz. Thanks for staying with me. That guy was kind of creepy at the end."

"I've run the video and I'm glad you called me. He knows more than a stranger should, and that was definitely a hint about his possible capabilities or threat level. Looking at the driver, I'm thinking this guy is organized crime, but I'll find out. Or Sam will if she ever follows through with her contact."

"Thanks Wiz. I appreciate your help." Deb wasn't touching that comment about Sam; she knew why Sam was so reluctant, and didn't blame her.

"That's what friends are for. Let me know if anything else happens or anyone else visits." The call dropped. Deb smiled. Wiz was a little short on words, but a good friend. Very few people would offer her a super-secure guest house for as long as she wanted while teaching her some self-defense moves, too. Erin had offered a room, as well, but living with the newlyweds wasn't ideal, and no one wanted her staying above Erin and Ryan's coffee shop; it was too far out of town, not close enough to their house, and undefendable. Sam's house wasn't very big, it was in the middle of town, and it didn't have any alarms. She definitely wasn't staying with Kim and Nic; she'd never endanger her nieces. Regardless of the situation, she was lucky and she had to remember that, even when things were hard.

Deb closed, then washed the dishes and filled the mop bucket. Her regular cleaner, Jeff, was at Camp Eagle Mount, a camp for developmentally challenged adults, and his mother at a nearby spa. The physical labor helped Deb sleep better, but despite going to bed early, she was exhausted from the stress.

Her phone chimed with an alert from her alarm system, so she checked the back cameras. Michael's truck pulled into the parking lot. Either he was early, or it was later than she thought. She glanced at the time; it was late. She needed more help, but finding anyone who wanted to work was so difficult and time consuming. And with the ongoing problems, potentially dangerous for the employee.

She mopped. The faster she got done, the faster she could get upstairs and avoid the grumpy handyman. As Michael entered, her alarm system chimed again. She couldn't hear his footsteps over the sound of the mop and the cooling fans, but she knew he was there.

"Why are you still here?" His tone was snarly and aggressive.

She turned to face him, but kept mopping. "I have work to do. Don't worry, I'll stay out of your way."

Michael left his bag on the floor and marched toward her, scowling. He reached for the mop. "Give me that. Go upstairs and get some rest. You look tired."

Deb didn't let go. "Gee, thanks. It's my business and my responsibility. And I know you've been working hard all day too. If you're insisting on staying, go set up your bed. I'll finish mopping and leave you alone."

He yanked the mop from her hands. "Go. I'll finish. Don't worry; I did a lot of mopping in the Army." Turning away, he swept the mop back and forth, overlapping the strokes perfectly.

Deb threw her arms up, then stomped away. Objecting or trying to fight over the mop would be humiliating and useless. He was much stronger than she was, and she was too tired to fight about it. She spun on her toe and marched to the back. The man was so exasperating. She unlocked the stairway to her apartment, and grimaced when an alert on her phone reminded her to turn off the alarm before the cops showed up.

The constant stream of law enforcement stopping by was comforting, but eventually they'd quit. Already, the Marcus County sheriff's deputies drove by, but rarely came inside; the Sheriff hated Wiz. Then Wiz had shot Deb's attacker, protecting her before the police had a chance to arrive, and the Sheriff considered that an additional insult. Wiz had deliberately wounded the man rather than killing him, wanting to know who he was working for. Unfortunately, the police had shown up before they could question him, and the investigators weren't sharing any information. Sam said the men had gotten out on bail already, too, no matter how stridently she'd objected.

All in all, Deb's life was filled with uncomfortable drama and more threats than she could handle. She unlocked the door at the top of the stairs, stepped inside, and hung up her coat and purse. Her pretty curtains were closed, concealing the new metal security shutters. The scent of fresh paint overwhelmed the smell of the bread cooling below; between the damage from the attack and the security installs, Michael and Nic had to cut and patch a lot of drywall. They'd painted it the same sunflower yellow, but the reason for the fresh coating made it seem dull and dreary rather than cheery. She plugged in the inflatable mattress, her niece Sophia's twin for backyard "camping" and breathed a sigh of relief when it began filling.

Her cell phone rang; a restricted number. She was tempted to let it go to voice mail, but some of her most lucrative orders came from celebrities and politicians vacationing in the area, and they often had restricted numbers. "Hello, Deb's Bakery, how can I help you?"

"This is Warden Provost of the Montana State Prison. Is this the former Deborah Franks, now Boulanger?"

Dread sank her stomach to her toes. "Yes. Can I help you?" She plopped down on the edge of her folding chair.

"I regret to inform you that George Franks was attacked and fatally injured today. His attacker has been apprehended and charged, but Mr. Franks did not survive. I know you were divorced, but he kept you on his medical power of attorney and notification list. I'm sorry to notify you over the phone and for your loss."

Deb bit back her initial reaction that her drug-dealer ex wasn't much of a loss. "Thank you. I appreciate you telling me. Do you know the motive?"

"No, although the attacker has multiple murder convictions, including others in the prison. We're trying to move him to the federal Supermax prison. I'm sorry we couldn't do it sooner. I know you've returned all of Mr. Frank's letters unopened. Do we have permission to open them to assist our investigation? We'll send you copies, if you'd like."

"You can open them and anything else he's got. Please send the copies to my attorney, Samantha Kerr, and let her know of anything you find. You should have her name on file."

"Ah, yes, I see it. Thank you. Again, I'm sorry for your loss. We'll keep your attorney informed. Goodbye, Ms. Boulanger."

"Goodbye." She'd lost all love and respect for George, but despite her initial reaction to his betrayal, had never wished him harm. She'd hoped he'd take advantage of his incarceration and find a new calling, a way to succeed once he was released, but someone had made sure that would never happen. She was relieved she'd never get another letter or have to worry about him showing up on her doorstep, but she regretted his death. He'd never have a chance to redeem himself.

The hits just kept coming, one after the other. Her phone chimed; her bakery's back door had opened with the correct security codes. She brought up the camera; Michael hauled his big bag in her back door, securing it behind him.

She violently swept the view away. He was the last man on Earth she wanted around when all she could think about was collapsing into a comforting embrace, because he'd be anything but consoling. Despite that, she couldn't help wishing for strong arms to hold her,

like George had during the early days of their relationship.

She fell flat on the bouncy bed and cried. Some for
the man she'd sworn to never shed another tear for,
but mostly for herself. After she stopped, she completed
her nightly routine, and counted cupcakes until she fell
asleep, but it took forever.

Chapter 6

THE NEXT MORNING, DEB rose and went to work, but every day seemed harder than the next. Even a girl's night—held at Erin's house rather than the Brewery—didn't help, much. The threatening man hadn't come to her bakery again, but he mailed her a contract with a very lucrative offer. She didn't bother reading it before sending it to Sam. In three days, another letter came, and another three days after that. She sent all of them to Sam unopened.

On Friday, Sam entered right before closing, her smile turning upside down when she spotted Deb. "Oh, sweetie, I'm sorry you're going through all this." She held open her arms.

Deb gratefully accepted her hug. "It sucks."

Sam squeezed her tight, then let go. "It does. And I'm not going to make it better." She reached into her luxurious leather portfolio case and pulled out a sheaf of papers, placing it on one of Deb's tables. "Can you talk?"

Deb locked the front door, turned the open sign off, poured Sam a glass of iced tea, and plopped into a chair across from Sam. "Yeah. Obviously, I need to."

Sam nodded. "Yes. On the surface, this is a great contract. The compensation is extremely high, and you are in complete control of all the recipes." One brow rose. "However, compensation is a percentage of the income, not the gross, and we both know that it's easy to lower profits to zero with equipment purchases and marketing and all the expenses of a business. Also, the company, TriWestCo Holdings, would be in control of the baking and they could use whatever ingredients they want. There's nothing in here that says they have to use *your* recipes at all. But they get complete ownership of the bakery and individual product names, and all associated intellectual property. Your name becomes theirs."

She tapped on the contract. "Not only that, but there's a non-compete clause. You can't open a new bakery for ten years. There's also a brutal non-disclosure contract. You can't tell anyone who else is involved, that they're not using your recipe or anything else about these so-called investors. Nothing about them personally or even the company name. You have to claim they're using your recipes and you can't say anything that's uncomplimentary."

Sam scowled. "I talked with Wiz. TriWestCo is a shell company with dozens of layers above and below. The guy who visited you goes by John Scott, and he's a known organized crime associate, both in the US and overseas. He arranges money laundering. Wiz is digging into his background, because she's pretty sure there's even more to this guy than it seems. But for now, Tri-WestCo will contract with some huge commercial bakery and bake mass market crap with substandard ingredients, but they claim it's your special recipe and you have to back them up. You'll probably make some money, but they'll be making a whole lot more and hiding the profits from trafficking people, guns, and drugs. Don't sign it." She sipped her tea.

"No kidding." Deb shuddered. She didn't want anything to do with that man, his contract or his dirty business.

"Wiz believes his offer of protection is a scam, too. He's the one threatening you, forcing you to accept his assistance; reason number five hundred and fifty-five not to accept the contract. She thinks he's hitting a lot of the small businesses in town with similar offers. We should call a meeting of the Marcus Business Association."

Deb looked at the ceiling, then back at Sam. "Except, remember who's in charge?"

Sam's shoulders drooped. "Yeah, Erin's mom and she's involved up to the top of her shiny bright red hair."

"Yeah." Deb shuddered, imagining Sharlene's reaction.

Sam frowned. "Well, I know the majority of the business owners, and I know all the local attorneys. I'll send a letter to all of them with a 'look out for this scam' that keeps the threat generic, so I can't be accused of libel, but makes it clear I'm talking about what this particular guy is doing." She sighed. "Wiz said that occasionally,

a town gets together and makes it clear they'll protect their own. Then this guy will move on. But more
often, he succeeds with enough businesses that before long, he owns the whole town."

"That's terrifying." She wrapped her arms around
her waist.

Sam shivered. "It gets worse. Because once he
owns the majority of the businesses, he starts pro-
viding workers. He brings in people from around the
world, and makes them work long hours for next to
nothing. They are given drugs, and become addicts,
and if they get injured, because they're high or sick
while they're working, they simply disappear." She
grimaced, closing her eyes for a moment, then met
Deb's gaze again. "I contacted Trevor."

Deb put her hand over Sam's and squeezed. "You
know I'd never ask you to do that." Sam had loved
Trevor Mills with every bit of her heart through high
school and the first two years of college, even though
they'd gone to different schools. She'd dressed in
baggy clothes, didn't wear makeup, turned down
every advance, and avoided parties and social events,
all so Trevor would know she'd stayed true. Accord-
ing to rumor, he hadn't done the same, partying hard
with his team mates in the athlete's dorm. And then,
after their second-year finals, Trevor texted, telling
Sam he'd joined the Navy, was shipping out the next
day, and she was free to date other people, because
he wasn't coming back. She'd been devastated and
cried for a week. Deb had nursed her through it,
bringing compassion, electrolytes, moisturizer, junk
food, and tissues.

But after the initial shock, Sam had decided that living outrageously was the best revenge. She worked out, dressed in sexy clothes, dated extensively, refused to go exclusive with anyone, went to every party, and had a blast all summer. She slowed the partying during school, but kept refining her look and attitude, becoming a flirty, unobtainable beauty. Sam's façade was almost perfect, but Deb knew that even a decade later, the wounds of Trevor's betrayal remained. "We'll have a sleep over soon and make voodoo dolls, right?"

Sam snorted. "Not necessary. It was a kid's crush. I'm better off without him. But Wiz was right. It turns out, Trevor is a big deal in the FBI's organized crime unit. I had to work my way through several layers of admin assistants before I could talk to him. When I told him what was going on, he confirmed our suspicions. He seemed excited that we were seeing the very start of the process and they'd be able to catch the organization in the act, get real evidence and make the charges stick. He called me the next day, asking lots of questions, and more the next. Then he stopped communicating. He ghosted me." She glared at the tabletop. "When I called the next week to ask some questions in return, his *assistant* told me that the Bureau was grateful for my help, but they didn't need anything else, and to never contact him again. The FBI would handle the case and they didn't need the assistance of a small-town attorney." She rolled her eyes. "Typical."

Trevor was a monumental jerk. If he dared to show his face in Marcus, Deb would kick in his kneecaps. Hurting a lovely person like Sam was the act of a selfish ass. She squeezed Sam's hand again. "I'm sorry. Some people only change for the worse."

"Yeah." She shrugged. "Like I said, I'm better off without him. But more importantly, that reaction tells me he's not going to do anything, he's just too much of a coward to tell me. We're on our own. I don't think we can trust the Sheriff's department, or the city. Maybe not the state either. I'm sure Wiz will help us as much as she can. But even with her help, banding together against Marcus Bank will be hard. They own so many loans in town; businesses, mortgages, and personal. I quit advising the bank because they were making really risky loans and bad business decisions. With the information Wiz has dug up, I'd bet my Louboutin stilettos that Sharlene planned the whole thing with this TriWestCo Holdings guy." She scowled. "I wouldn't put it past that greedy woman. She's terrible."

"She is. Poor Erin." Deb's parents were neglectful and lazy, but not actively evil.

Sam shrugged. "Erin's got Ryan, now, and Wiz, and the Bordes, and us. Better than her mother any day."

"True, but it doesn't make dealing with your mother becoming a criminal easier." Deb's parents had moved away years ago and rarely contacted either of their daughters, but they hadn't been reliable from the start. Sharlene hadn't gone bad until Erin's dad died, and even then, she hadn't become a threat until recently. Erin struggled with her conflicted feelings, but Ryan's steadfast love made dealing with her emotions easier.

Sam stood. "I've got to get to my next appointment. Hang in there, Deb. We'll get through this."

Deb rose, and hugged Sam tight, then let her go. "Be careful out there, Sam. I don't like any of this."

At the doorway, Sam looked back with a sad smile. "I don't either. I'm carrying mace, and asking Wiz about an alarm system for my house and my office. This could get a whole lot worse before it gets better." She left the bakery, getting into her shiny red hybrid SUV and driving north.

Deb locked up, finished closing, and cleaned up, scooting upstairs before Michael arrived. She couldn't take anymore drama today. She made a semi-healthy dinner, had a glass of wine, and unable to stay awake another minute, went to bed an hour early.

Tomorrow had to be better.

In the dead of night, Deb woke, shivering, her hip and shoulder aching. She reached for her phone, but her entire arm hit the floor rather than only her fingertips. The dim light of her phone's screen saver lightened the gloom. No wonder she was cold—she was on the floor. Her inflatable mattress was flatter than a fallen souffle.

She rolled to her hands and knees, found a fleece jacket and knitted hat, then put water in the microwave for tea. While the water heated, she paced, swinging her arms. Even if she had a patch kit, finding the hole seemed impossible when she was so exhausted. It seemed that everything was going wrong and only getting worse.

At the knock on her door, she spun, her heart pounding.

"Deb, are you okay?" Michael's bellow was muffled only slightly by the steel door.

Hand over her chest, she unlocked the deadbolt and opened the door. Michael scowled with a key in one hand, his gun in the other. She glared. "I'm fine. Just cold. Go back to bed."

"Why are you cold? Did the heater quit?" He slid the gun into his holster, pushed past her and checked the thermostat, mounted on the short wall leading to the bathroom behind the kitchen. "It's working." He turned back, scanning the room. "Your bed is flat. Why haven't you bought a real mattress yet? I told you I could work around one a week ago." He glowered.

The microwave dinged, and she turned away, pulling her cup, dunking an herbal tea bag and cupping her frigid hands around the mug. "I haven't had time. Workers aren't showing up, so I'm not going to get the time, either." She held up a hand to stop his objections. "And I can't afford to close. I need the income."

"Can you afford to get injured? Because zombies make mistakes. I've watched you; baking can be hazardous."

Deb spun, scowling. "I'll be fine. I've got it all down to a routine." A shiver ran from her head to her toes, and she turned her back to him. Strong arms closed around her, warmth pressed against her back, and she stiffened.

"Relax. I'm just trying to warm you up, nothing else." His voice rumbled in her ear and down her spine. She wanted to remain stiff, but between his warmth and the comfort, she relaxed. "Drink your tea. Let's speed this up."

Deb blew and sipped; the tea too hot to gulp. Of course he wanted to hurry. He couldn't be truly attracted to her; merely forced into proximity by a family connection. After she drank half the tea, she stopped shivering.

Michael let go and stepped away. He bundled her sheets and blanket on to her folding chair, picked up her mattress and examined it. "There's no obvious hole, and it's too late to be searching. I'll bring my mattress upstairs." He stomped out of the apartment and returned before she could object, spreading her blankets across the floppy full size mattress and plugging it in to fully reinflate. The motor buzzed.

She put her mug in the sink. "You're going home to sleep, right?"

He shook his head. "No. I've got a backpacking mattress in the truck. I think."

Deb grimaced. Nic had loaned him the larger in-flatable—Isabella's mattress—because of Michael's bad back. "Then you can give me that one, and take the bigger one back. I'm smaller and will fit better."

"No. I'm not doing that." He crossed his arms.

"Well, I'm not taking your bed." She mimicked his stance.

"So neither of us get any sleep? That's stupid."

Deb pointed at the door, shaking with fury. "Get out. I don't let anyone call me stupid. Not anymore."

"Your ex called you stupid? What an idiot." Michael grimaced. "I wasn't calling *you* stupid. I was saying not sleeping was stupid, because you need sleep. I'm used to going without."

Deb glared. "You *used* to be able to go without. Now you get migraines. Go home."

"I'm not leaving you or the bakery unprotected. I'll get my backpacking mattress and be fine." He stomped away, again, and thudded down the stairs.

Deb watched him search his truck through the surveillance camera. After opening every door and box, he finally carried a roll of dirty foam inside. She met him at the exterior door, blocking it. "Go home. You can't sleep on that."

He pushed past her again. "I've slept on worse."

"Recently? Go home." Men were so stubborn, and Michael was at the extreme of the spectrum.

He turned. "Lock the door, alarm it and go upstairs. Sleep."

"Go home."

"No."

Deb locked the door and followed him to the front. Neither of them would get any sleep if the standoff continued. "Look, you're not going to sleep well on that, and I'm not going to sleep if you're on that. So grab your sleeping bag and we'll share the mattress." He looked up, eyebrows raised. She frowned at him. "We're adults, right? I'm not going to attack you while you're sleeping."

He glared. "I'm not worried about you."

She grabbed his sleeping bag and turned away. Of course, he wasn't worried about her; she wasn't anything to him. "Then come on. We'll both have a semi-comfortable mattress and get some sleep."

He said something too soft for her to hear, then material swished. "Fine."

She climbed the stairs, aware of his presence behind her, and headed straight to the bed. She rearranged her sheet and blanket, folding it in half and creating a makeshift bag with the crease in the middle. That way, even if she reached out in her sleep, she wouldn't touch him.

He laid his bag on the other side of the mattress and pulled his phone. "I'm alarming everything. If you're ready, get in. I'll get the lights."

"Sure." Deb wasn't too sure she was ready, but she'd made the offer. She plugged in her phone, pulled off her fleece jacket and knit cap, then slid under the blankets, shivering slightly when the cool sheets pressed against her skin. She curled into a ball with her back to him.

The other side of the mattress dipped, and she rolled to her back. She grabbed the edge of the mattress, pulling herself back on to her side and held on until Michael got himself settled. All that muscle probably weighed a lot, because his side of the bed was lower than hers, and her body wanted to roll. Eventually, she gave up, lying on her back so she wouldn't move, and tried to ignore his breathing and warmth. She counted cupcakes and faded into sleep.

Chapter 7

MICHAEL

A TINKLING MELODY PENETRATED Michael's sleep. His left arm was numb and his chin nestled in a mass of soft hair smelling of strawberries, comfort and home. His right arm cradled a blanket-draped, soft, warm woman. He pulled her closer.

She rolled away, smacked her phone and then snuggled back into his embrace, so he closed his eyes. Then they snapped open so hard his eyelids ached. Deb—he was holding Deb. She'd wake up any second and scream. He desperately wanted to keep her close, but once she realized what he'd done, she'd be up and yelling. He had move before her alarm went off again. He rolled to his back, letting his upper arm fall off her waist, then stealthily slid his right arm out from under her head, pushing her pillow into place, and then rolled onto his left side. Pins and needles jabbed his arm, and his back protested, but the greater pain came from the loss of Deb's supple heat.

As she'd said, they were both adults. Unfortunately for Deb, his body wasn't so mature, reaching out for comfort, warmth, and more. Not wanting to wake her, he held back an exasperated snort at his excuses. He couldn't blame his body or subconscious for his behavior. No, that was all him, wanting what he couldn't have. She deserved better. He waited for her alarm to sound, then rolled off the mattress, moving slowly so she didn't bounce or sway.

Deb slapped at the cell, sighed and returned to sleep, full pink lips pursing in a purring snore. Michael would give almost anything to get back into bed with her, but it couldn't happen. He'd already taken liberties he wasn't allowed and couldn't justify. He gathered the few things he'd brought upstairs, slid his weapon into his holster, then stepped silently to the door, checking the surveillance on his cell before unlocking and turning off the stairwell alarms.

Downstairs, he washed his face, brushed his teeth, put on a fresh set of work clothes, and took all his morning meds, grateful his interrupted sleep didn't spark a migraine. Knowing Deb would be down shortly, he flipped the coffee pot on, and turned on the ovens to save her a little time. Then he packed his gear and got out of the bakery before he scarfed down a half a dozen cupcakes. Tomorrow was Friday; he'd allow himself one then, and maybe one during the Farmer's Market. Deb didn't know it, but he'd be watching, along with many of her friends.

Hauling his gear to the back door, he opened it and almost crashed into a stranger. He dropped his gear and grabbed the man's arm. "Who are you? What are you doing?"

The man wrenched his arm out of Michael's grip. "I'm going to work. Who are you?"

Michael's head jolted back, trying to avoid the man's horrific breath. "Deb's brother-in-law. I've never seen you before." He couldn't imagine Deb hiring a guy who let something die in his mouth.

The man swore and ran. Michael ran after him, but stopped after a few paces. More important to find out what the guy had done to Deb's business, if anything. He pulled up the video surveillance and rolled the cameras back to the stranger's first appearance. The man, about his height, a black knit cap covering greasy brown hair, a scraggly beard trying to hide the sores of a meth addict, wearing blue jeans and a dirty black jacket, sauntered up to the back door and tried the handle. When it didn't budge, he inspected the seams of the double-wide doors, then moved on to inspect the rest of the back of the building. He returned to the doors, crouched and jammed something long, thin and white into the gap between the door and frame. He jumped to his feet, and on the video, Michael walked out the door and grabbed the man's arm.

Michael moved to the edge of the door, dropped to one knee and peered at the gap. Something that looked like putty had been forced into the gap. He sniffed, snapped a picture with his cell, stood and backed away, calling Deb. Even with the bakery's delicious scents, up close, the smell of C-4 was obvious.

"Yes? I know, I'm late."

"Deb, you need to evacuate, now. Go out the front. Wait, check the cameras first. I'm calling 911 next, because I think someone was trying to use plastic explosives to blow open your back door. Get your keys, coat, cell, ID and get out, now!" He didn't mean to yell, but couldn't help it. The stairway was way too close to the back door.

"Explosives? Seriously?"

"Deb, move, now!"

"I'm going. There's no one out front I can see in the cameras."

There could be a car, waiting to grab her. "Wait just inside the door. I'll come around and pick you up."

"Okay." Her voice trembled.

Good; she was taking the threat seriously. "Get your stuff and wait for me. I'm calling 911." He grabbed his bag, threw it in the truck, shoved his pistol between the seats so he could draw it fast, and dialed 911 before he started the vehicle.

"Marcus County Emergency, what's the nature of your emergency and the location?" A male voice drawled.

He started the truck, hoping he didn't blow up. "I'm at Deb's Bakery on Main Street, and I need the bomb squad. Someone shoved a putty-like substance into the back door and I think it's C-4 explosive. I'm ex-Army; I've seen and smelled it before." Putting the truck in gear, he drove around the bakery, survey-ing the area carefully. No running vehicles, no vans without windows, no fancy cars, just Deb's outdoor tables.

"Understood. Is there anyone in the building?" The voice was no longer bored, and held a distinct snap.

"I've told Deb Boulanger, the owner, to evacuate. I'm picking her up, then we're going to a secure location. We'll coordinate with you via phone." He stopped in the bakery's front parking. Leaving the truck running, he put in one ear pod, shoved his phone in a pocket, pulled his weapon and stepped out. He walked to the door, his head on a swivel, inspecting everything around, above and below his position.

"Deputies and city are on their way, and I've notified the bomb squad, but they have to come from Missoula. Law enforcement would prefer you remain nearby for questions."

He crooked his fingers at Deb, then turned away from her, scanning for threats. Sirens wailed in the distance. "Understood but refused. The substance is shoved between the frame and the door on the north side of the back doors. I scared off the guy doing it. Looked like a meth head. We'll get you a picture from the surveillance. I've got to get Deb now." He turned his head. "Deb, stay right behind me, one hand on my back. If shooting starts, we'll retreat to the side of the building. Understand?" He jerked his head towards the abandoned lumberyard.

"Got it. Go."

Her hand landed on his lower back. He strode through the outdoor tables to the street, watching everything, and opened the truck's passenger door. Deb climbed in. He circled around the front of the truck, got in, and slammed the accelerator down while shoving his pistol between the seats again. Being a work truck, the tires didn't bark, but they flew down Main Street. The flashing lights of the cops passed them going the other way. He pulled his cell out and threw it to Deb. "If 911 is still on, can you talk to them? If not, call Wiz. Even if they are still on, call Wiz. We need to get you someplace secure."

Deb's phone rang and she pulled it out of her jacket pocket. "Hey, Wiz. We're heading your way. I'll put you on speaker so Michael can tell you." Wiz must have an alert set for anything concerning Deb's address. Deb fumbled with her phone, then his. He repeated what he'd already told law enforcement.

"Get up here ASAP. I'll open the gates for you. Drive into the garage. I'll send copies of the surveillance to the city and county. Running facial recog, but you're right, Michael, this guy looks like a meth head. Probably just an errand boy who knows nothing."

"Dead man walking." Deb gasped and Michael wished he'd kept his mouth shut. "I know you live in the Sapphires, Wiz, but can you direct me?"

"Deb can. She's been here. But wait," Wiz said. "Crash on the highway. I'm not sure you can get here safely directly from Marcus, and going around will leave you vulnerable without a good alternative. Go somewhere else."

Michael wasn't sure where he could take Deb, but if he figured it out, he didn't want it broadcast. His place was easy to find, and all his friends lived in Marcus or far away. "Deb, if 911 is still on, hang up. Got any ideas on where to go, Wiz?" He pulled over, checked the road, and did a U-turn.

"This is Tom. I'm texting you directions to a friend's hunting cabin. You might have to walk the last part if there's still snow up there. The place is winterized, so you'll have to clear the water lines and all that, but I'm sure you know more about that than I do. There should be propane and canned goods. We'll bring you some stuff in a few days."

Relief unknotted the back of Michael's neck. "Great. Thanks, Tom."

"We'll bring more weapons, too. After you get Tom's text, turn off your phones," Wiz said. "And I mean all the way off. If you know how, remove the battery. Don't take them to the cabin. We'll bring you a burner phone. Smart watches, too. Check the truck for Air Tags or Tiles."

"Shoot!" Deb raised her hands to her forehead. "I've got to tell my employees."

"Do it right now, Deb, then turn off the phone," Wiz said. "Tell them there was a threat, and you're closing for everyone's safety for at least a week, maybe two. Give them paid time off so you keep them. I'll front you the money, no rush on paying me back. And don't say no. This is an emergency. I'll contact Sam. She can talk to the police and the press. We'll all keep an eye on the bakery. I'll tell Nic and Kim what's going down. Deb, take this time to decompress. A mini wilderness retreat. We've got your back. Go now. Wiz out."

Deb's phone chimed. Probably the address. He checked their surroundings again—nothing but dark farmland—pulled over and grabbed his phone off of Deb's lap, checking that she'd hung up with 911. She was typing; most likely, a group text to her employees.

Tom had sent him directions, not an address; he was fairly certain it was high in the mountains above the West Fork of the Bitterroot River. As a bored teen, he and his friends had cruised the dirt roads of the Bitterroot and Sapphire mountains, drinking, smoking and building bonfires, but it had been many years since he'd been in the area. He pulled his contractor binder and yanked a blank page from it, scribbling the directions by hand, using the top of the metal binder, so his writing wouldn't leave an impression on the pad for someone to find later if they had to abandon the truck.

Then he turned off the phone, removed the case, the backing, and then the battery. Deb was struggling with her phone's case, so he took it from her and did the same, then handed her the phones, still in pieces. "There's an old metal tool box on the floor behind your seat. Put both of those in there, along with your smart watch. I'll put the batteries in the console, here." He slid the thin rectangles into his binder pocket, then put the whole thing back in the console. He didn't bother wearing a watch.

Deb hung over the seat, and metal clanged. He looked away from the tempting sight. No sense in making his life more difficult. When she flopped into the seat, face flushed, he put the truck in gear and drove at four miles above the speed limit. "I've got a few things with me, but not a lot. I'll get gas on the south side of Marcus and look for hidden trackers. You run inside and get the stuff you'll need for a couple of days, like a toothbrush, comb, that kind of stuff. Do you have your purse?"

"No. I've got nothing but the clothes I'm wearing and my keys."

Shifting to his left, he yanked his wallet out of his back pocket. "See how much cash I've got in there. We'll need a full tank, but I can probably risk putting that on a card, as long as we're moving out right after that."

Deb shook her head. "How is this my life? I'm not a criminal, but I'm on the run like one."

"It's not fair, Deb." He put his hand palm up on the truck's middle seat console, and she put her much smaller hand in his. "I'm sorry your ex got you into this. Or Sharlene Murphy, or whoever else is at fault." He squeezed her hand lightly. "But it really doesn't matter why or how. What matters is staying alive. We think about the here and now, and planning for the future. Multiple plans. Don't think about the past." He was used to planning for the worst case scenario, then doubling down, but Deb wasn't.

She pulled her hand away, and he let go, reluctantly. She pulled bills out of his wallet. "You've got sixty-seven dollars."

That would barely fill the tank. "Okay, we'll stop in the middle of Marcus, where the main roads cross, and fill the tank with my credit card. Stay in the truck. Then we'll stop on the outskirts of town, where fewer people will be around, and get supplies. We'll use cash, so get only what you need. If it was later, I'd go to a thrift store for clothes, but it's too early. I've got another jacket and some raingear in here, so get a t-shirt and if they've got any, some underwear." Heat rose in Michael's cheeks. "We'll hand wash and make do with what we've got. I'm sure Wiz will bring you clothes."

Deb scoffed. "Wiz won't think of that, but Sam will."

"Point." They entered Marcus, driving just above the speed limit. "Look for anyone or anything out of place."

"Like what?"

"Like the TriWestCo guy's Mercedes. Or a gathering of vehicles, especially if they're all the same make and model. Or vehicles flashing their lights while parked." There were undoubtedly other examples, but none came to mind; he'd know it when he saw it. At one of the main intersections, he pulled into a gas station, stopping at the last pump in the row. "Keep an eye out, Deb." He turned off the truck, but left the keys in the ignition, ran his credit card and filled the tank. He surveyed his surroundings, then slid under the truck, checking for trackers. Then he ran his fingers across the many nooks and crannies of the truck, but found nothing. When the pump clicked off, he finished and drove away, pulling behind a station at the edge of town with a larger store.

He put on his coat, slid his weapon into his coat pocket, and led Deb inside the brightly lit store. He gathered canned goods, bread, coffee, energy bars and a case of bottled water, because starting the water pump might not be easy if the cabin was snowed in. He joined Deb; she had toiletries, some clothing, and small packages of flour, sugar, and baking things. He tapped the baking powder. "Is that necessary?"

She scowled. "Unless you want to die, yes. Baking is stress relief."

He held up both hands, palm out. Surrendering to her needs for non-security issues didn't bother him. Maybe because everything she made was delicious. "Got it. Don't want to get smothered in my sleep." Not that she had a prayer of doing that, even with her unusually strong hands and arms. Her sweet smile bloomed, making him feel like a superhero.

He paid, putting it on his card after all. If the bad guys could track his purchases, they'd know he was going south. But from here, they could go farther south into Idaho, or east into southwest Montana, or into the Bitterroot or Sapphire mountains. And he'd have a little cash left for bribes if necessary.

They carried their supplies to the truck and drove into the darkness. Light glimmered beyond the Sapphire's heights on his left, but he kept a sharp eye out for wildlife. They drove through the tiny town of Darby. Michael was ready to turn off the highway if it was blocked, but they made it through. Rather than taking the quickest way to the West Fork, he drove on, and took the next turn. There were no houses or stores at that intersection, so it was less likely someone could track their travel on a surveillance or doorbell camera. He'd feel better if he'd found a tracker; he had no way to look for an electronic signal. He continued along the tree-lined two-lane highway, the darkness fading into overcast skies.

He turned onto a dirt road, and began the long, slow drive up into the mountains. Initially, the road passed practically through the front yard of three houses; he hoped they didn't have doorbell cameras or other surveillance. As they climbed, the road became rutted and roughened; the spring rain and snowmelt had run fast and hard. Deer bounded in front of him twice. As the road climbed, snow appeared on the sides, then the middle of the road, the tracks narrowing; probably ATVs.

Spotting an opening in the brush to the right, he turned, bouncing and jolting over the even rougher surface of the partially snow- and ice-covered road, ending in a circular clearing probably used for camping. Or teen bonfires. "This is where we leave the truck." He circled the area, pulling to the side of the clearing, where it was shielded from the road by brush, and pointed the nose of the truck out for a quick getaway. "I'll put the truck keys under the driver's side door. There's a ledge where the step attaches. That way, we won't have to carry the keys. Come around and I'll show you." And if he got taken out, she could still drive away. Hopefully.

Deb's plastic bags rustled and she joined him, grimacing at the squishy mud below their feet. She wore flimsy tennis shoes decorated with sunflowers; something else to take into consideration. They'd have to find shelter soon, or her feet would freeze. He moved his concealed weapon to the front of his waistband, pulled his big duffle bag out of the back, threw his extra clothing and emergency gear into it, then slid his arms into the handles, making it into a makeshift backpack. It wasn't comfortable, but it was easier than carrying it in one hand, and allowed him to carry the case of drinking water. And it left both hands free to fire, if he dropped the water. He locked the truck, stowed the keys, checked that the back utility boxes were secure too, then set off for the road, Deb following. Where the camping spot's access track met the dirt road, he scuffed the tire tracks with his boots, and kicked some snow across the entrance.

Deb tried to help, so he held up a hand. "Don't. Your feet will get wet enough in those shoes. Walk in the dirt tracks as long as you can, then get on top of the snow." He looked at the sky. The clouds were heavy but not dark. "Hopefully it will rain or snow."

"After we get there, right?"

"Right." He waited, listening and watching, but nothing moved, so he walked up the road. Hopefully, it wouldn't be too much farther. His back couldn't take the big load for very long, and Deb didn't seem like a hiker. But the farther they went, the less chance they'd be spotted, so they trudged onward.

Chapter 8

THE HEAVY PLASTIC BAGS cut into Deb's hands, and despite her best efforts, she fell behind Michael. Her shoes were perfect for the bakery's sealed concrete floors, but they provided little traction on the icy drifts covering the road. She hadn't gone down, but she'd come close, slipping and sliding over and over.

The sun had risen, but that deepened the shadows in the ruts and reflected off the ridges in the snow, making it even more difficult to stay on her feet. She'd worry about bears or mountain lions, but she didn't have the energy. If an animal jumped her, at least she'd get to rest for a few seconds before she was put out of her misery permanently. Michael hadn't even glanced back at her; he didn't care if she got eaten.

A thud and a groan made her look up from the unending white expanse. They'd reached the cabin! Michael put his hands just below his waist and stretched backwards, his face a rictus of pain. If she had been able to raise her arms, she'd smack her forehead for her uncharitable thoughts. Michael hauled a heavier load; his injured back probably hurt. He undoubtedly cared, but could barely manage to endure his pain.

Michael had done more than enough getting her away from the threat. She had to pull her own weight and more. She trudged faster so he wouldn't come back. But he didn't even glance at her. He turned to the front door and lifted a padlock. Pulling a sheet of paper from his pocket, he did something to the lock, pulled out his gun, opened the door, and walked into the darkness beyond.

Deb took the opportunity to stop, pant, and inspect their hideaway. An unimpressive hut of bare plywood, topped by a steep, slightly rusty metal roof, with a small window beside the front door, it didn't inspire confidence. She plodded on. Wire mesh covered the windows and door frame—probably to keep mice and rats out—and the tiny front porch planks looked rotten. When Tom had said "cabin," Deb had pictured a cute log house. But a nicer structure would probably get broken into; no one would bother a beat-up shack.

She reached the porch and dragged her feet up the wobbly steps to the porch and peered into the dim interior. A card table with two chairs sat in front of a plywood counter supported by plain lumber. The counter held a bar-style sink, with bare pipes showing below, and a two-burner propane stove, the kind that used small canisters. Clear plastic bins filled with canned food, paper plates, and other camping gear were stacked below the counter. Plastic plates and a few mugs, along with more canned food and gas canisters, rested on shelves above the counter. The floor was bare plywood, too. Michael stood with his back to her in a doorway beside the counter.

Deb stepped inside, dropping her bags on the dusty table. To her right, a metal futon frame held a large black bag; hopefully it contained the cushion. A lantern sat on an end table next to the futon, and a small rickety bookshelf held a few paperback novels under the front window. A larger window let in light above the futon, and the rising sun highlighted a beautiful view of the valley below. A black wood stove sat in the corner on a small tile platform. The wood rafters above them were dusty and cobwebbed and cheap wood paneling covered the walls.

Michael turned. "Better than it could be. I'll have to clear the solar arrays I spotted out back before we have enough power to run the water pump and clear the winterization, so don't use the water. I hope there are larger propane tanks behind the house, but they could be empty. There's no refrigerator, but it's cool enough that we can hang things outside at night or maybe there's a bear box. Or maybe Tom and Wiz will bring us an ice chest." He walked to the end table and picked up the lantern, looking at the top. "Solar. I'll put this outside, then we can use it tonight." He ran a finger over the bed frame. "I think there's some cleaning stuff in one of those bins under the sink. You can clean while I get the water going." He left, taking the lantern with him.

Deb crossed to the doorway Michael had been standing in and shivered; the back room was colder and darker than the main area. On her left, a tiny window let in enough light to see the toilet with pink liquid in the bowl below. Directly in front of her, a pressure tank for well water, a bank of batteries, a breaker box mounted on the wall above, and a larger box containing an on-demand water heater next to it. On her right, a small shower enclosure with a rust-stained white curtain; in front of it, a shelf held another black plastic bag, with hooks screwed into the wall below. The bag might have linens and towels.

She returned to the kitchen area and found a bin containing paper towels and cleaners. Taking a disposable duster out, she started on the bed frame. She'd like to get the rafters above, but she couldn't reach them. While she'd hoped for the cute log house, a shack with no running water and an outhouse had been more than possible. Still, the shadowed box was rather gloomy. It would brighten as the sun rose.

Michael stomped on the front porch, then entered. He strode to the bathroom and opened the breaker box, then returned with a broom. "Before you do that, let's dust the beams above a bit. Take those bags back outside." He raised the bristles over his head.

"Sure." Scowling, Deb grabbed the plastic bags and dropped them on the porch next to Michael's duffel. Saying please, or even asking rather than demanding must be against his personal code. At her feet, the bag of flour mocked her. Half the things she'd bought were useless without an oven. Maybe she could make pancakes.

The swish of the broom was interspersed with sneezing. Deb rubbed her arms. When she stopped moving, it was chilly. She marched in place to stay warm. Michael emerged, still sneezing. He closed the door, and trotted down the stairs, bending over to brush dust out of his hair, then pulled off his shirt, shaking it off.

Intricate decorative lettering in elaborate patterns interspersed with colorful military patches covered his upper arms and chest, but he was too far away for her to read them. He pulled his shirt back on, covering his impressive musculature, and dusted off his pants. She'd like to see what hid beneath those…

Michael stood, raising his brows at her stare. She turned away to hide the heat rising in her cheeks, gripping the duster like old lady Cust clutched her pearls. She should know better; she didn't like men gawking, either. Although if Michael's glare ever turned to a more pleasant expression, she wouldn't mind his gaze. But that would never happen. And it didn't matter, she had work to do.

"Don't go inside yet. Let the dust settle. Are you cold?" His voice got closer.

There was no point in denying it, even if there was nothing she could do. "Yes, it's chilly."

A zipper sounded, material rustled, then a jacket settled over her shoulders. "I told you I had a jacket for you. Why didn't you get it?"

"I'm not digging in your things." That would be rude, and she didn't want to see his personal items.

With his hands on her shoulder, he turned her around. "Look, Deb, I know this is all new to you, and you don't want to be here. But modesty, manners, and niceties take time and effort. Get past it. Our lives are at stake. My things are yours, and yours are mine, because we'll have to work together to stay alive. This valley isn't that big in the scheme of things. If these people coming after you are organized crime, Russian or American or whatever, they have money and resources. They can hire a plane and look for us, or launch drones, and then send people out on ATVs. We should probably stay here until Wiz and Tom come, then go on to Idaho or Wyoming if it's still dangerous."

Despite the jacket warming her shoulders, Deb shuddered. "But we can't run forever."

"You're right. Eventually, they'll stop looking, but by then, you won't have a business to return to."

She closed her eyes. She'd worked so long, so hard, and was finally tasting success. Then some selfish jerk tries to take it all away, simply to hoard more dollars, influence and power.

Michael growled, then arms closed around her, holding her close. "I'm sorry, Deb. It's not right, but it's reality. Your friends are working on a solution. None of them hold a lot of power, but they all have strengths, and they're working together. They'll come up with a plan. Even if they don't, we'll come up with one, okay? You have to believe. Nothing will kill you faster than giving up. Despair isn't helpful. Determination makes survivors."

She sagged into his comforting embrace and wrapped her arms around his waist. "I'm sorry I got you into this."

"Don't be. Nic can handle the business. I'm uniquely suited to help you survive, and I'll do my best." His arms dropped and he stepped back.

Deb closed her eyes for a moment. Sympathetic Michael was too appealing, but he'd offered the hug out of practicality, not because he was attracted to her. "Well, I'm sure your best at survival is better than mine. The best I can do is offer free cupcakes."

He scowled. "Stop putting yourself down. You're a smart business woman. Don't let your past prevent you from using your best asset." His mouth twisted, probably because she'd glanced down at her body. "Your brain. Negativity kills."

Deb nodded. As a bubbly blonde, she was used to being underestimated. Since she was also curvy rather than waifish, she got ignored, too. She'd heard "she'd be so cute if she lost some weight," more times than she could count. So if someone, usually a man, was dumb enough to believe she was stupid or naïve, she didn't bother to tell them otherwise. And if they were distracted by her body, good or bad in their eyes, that was on them. She couldn't control another person's thoughts, and she wasn't to blame for them, either. Lust was an emotion in the eye of the beholder. She never attempted to create such a feeling, but she'd taken advantage of it occasionally. It was a way to level the unfair playing field a little.

But that wouldn't work with the mob. It might make things worse—organized crime was into trafficking people. She didn't need to make herself a bigger target. Either way, Michael might be blunt, but he was right. She was smart and determined. And while she was thrilled to have helpful friends, the problem was her responsibility to fix, not theirs. "You're right. I am smart and determined. I'm going to fix this."

"With a little help from your friends." He turned to the door and opened it. "Unfortunately, right now that means cleaning this place enough that we don't sneeze constantly. Bring your duster, let's get going."

Deb rolled her eyes. Friends were helpful, but she still wasn't entirely sure she could call Michael a friend.

Chapter 9

MICHAEL

Michael unzipped the bag containing the futon's mattress, pulled it out, and placed it on the frame. When flat, it would barely hold the two of them, but they had to share. Nights would be chilly, they only had his sleeping bag, and they couldn't afford to burn all the firewood, because he had no way to cut more. He wasn't Paul Bunyan, chopping down whole trees. Sharing body heat was the only way to survive. Unless he stayed up nights, watching, and let her watch during the day. But he'd rather rely on staying hidden until there was some indication they'd been discovered.

He was kidding himself. He wanted to hold her close and comfort her. And more. But that was dangerous. He pulled the futon into the couch configuration, and draped his sleeping bag across the back. The toasty scent of pancakes drew him around.

Deb stood at the plywood counter, pouring batter into a pan, a foil covered plate next to her. "Breakfast will be ready shortly. Wish I'd thought to grab some good bread on my way out."

The woman had zero self-preservation. "Better alive and hungry than dead and covered with bread crumbs."

She spun, glaring at him. "I'm not an idiot. I know what evacuation means. But that doesn't mean I can't wish for something better."

He held up both hands in surrender. Again. He simply couldn't keep his foot out of his mouth around her. "I'm sorry. I know you're not stupid. I'm just worried."

Her shoulders drooped and she turned back to the hotplate, flipping the pancake. "I found some syrup if you'll grab it and get some plates and forks."

"Sure." He dug out the requested items, kicking himself for making Deb feel even worse. He should stick to practical things, and stop trying to make conversation, because he was lashing out rather than comforting her. Because he wasn't sure how to keep her safe against organized crime. He had to stop taking his insecurity out on her. She deserved better.

She flipped another cake, then brought the stack to the table, giving him all but two of the flapjacks. Then she grabbed the butter, and two mugs with steaming dark liquid—coffee. "It's only instant coffee, but I'm sure we can find a way to filter some real coffee soon." She placed a small container of milk and the bag of sugar between them. "Eat."

He waved a hand at the other chair. "You first."

Deb picked up the syrup, pouring a generous amount over her small serving, and handed it to him. He frowned at his much larger stack. "Don't you want more than that?"

She shook her head. "I don't usually eat a lot of refined flour. I have to taste too much, so more just piles on my hips and they're wide enough."

He blew a raspberry. "That's ridiculous. You're perfect. And you should enjoy what you make, because it's all delicious." He cut a forkful of pancakes and ate. Sweet and fluffy. "These are great, and we're going to need the energy. We need to clear snow from the woodpile, start the water pump, and find escape routes out of here. All of those plus the cleaning we've already done will burn a lot of calories." He ate more, savoring the stack. "I don't usually eat a lot of refined products, either, but survival demands a lot." He hoped his words were true; he didn't need a migraine slowing them down, and so much sugar would normally push his body into overload.

Deb nodded but kept eating, her eyes on her plate. Someone had really done a number on her confidence; if Franks wasn't already dead, Michael would love to take him down, and smack Deb's parents across the back of their selfish heads. "Finish up, we'll clean up, then go clear snow. Wrap your feet in some of the grocery bags before you get into the snow. It's not going to keep them perfectly dry, but it will help. The minute you feel wet or cold, come inside. You've only got one pair of shoes, and we need those dry if we need to leave in a hurry. Understand?"

Deb nodded, but kept her gaze on the table, rather than looking at him. He'd have to watch her, make sure she didn't overdo it.

They ate the last of the flapjacks and drank the coffee, then put the waste items in a plastic garbage bag. Michael carried the garbage to the shower stall, hanging it from the shower curtain bar. If there were mice or rats in the cabin, they'd have to work for their meal.

In the main room, Deb zipped up his jacket and sat, a few grocery bags in her hands. He crossed to her, took the bags from her hands, and wrapped them around her feet, securing them with painter's tape he'd found in the bathroom-slash-utility room. "It's not perfect, but hopefully it helps." He led the way outside and around the cabin, stomping down the snow drifts where he could. Unfortunately, his tracks would show someone was here, and as the sun rose and set, the snow would melt and refreeze, making the path slippery. But there weren't any good alternatives; the snow was too icy and deep to shovel.

At the woodpile, he and Deb uncovered the bottom of the tarp, then worked it off. It was an old tarp, and it ripped apart more than it pulled off, but they finally uncovered dry wood and carried armloads to the front porch. By then, it had warmed enough for both of them to shed the outer layers, and Deb had to remove the plastic bags, because she was sliding too much. She fixed a simple lunch of soup and sandwiches while he drained the winterizing liquid, then started the water pump. It took a while, but eventually, the pressure tank filled and he was able to flush the system. He checked the batteries; charging, but still low, and using the water pump wasn't helping.

He joined Deb at the table. "It's all working, but charging the batteries will take hours. We might be able to take quick showers tonight."

Deb smiled. "That would be amazing. I'm really not a fan of roughing it."

He chuckled. "I'm not either. Not anymore. But if I have to, I'd rather rough it here than some lousy foreign country."

She drew invisible patterns on the table. "I guess my complaints seem pretty petty."

"No. You didn't sign up for this. I did."

She glared at him. "You didn't sign up for this!"

He shrugged. "No, but I signed up for the Army, and they taught me how to deal with this kind of survival situation. And I'm happy to help you, Deb, because you don't deserve any of this. It's not fair."

She huffed. "Life isn't."

"But what you're experiencing isn't just life, it's criminals taking advantage. I'm not going to stand by idly when I can help. It wouldn't matter if it was you, or Sam, or Wiz, or Erin."

Deb's mouth quirked. "But the guys can help themselves?"

He smirked. "Or Ryan or Tom or whoever. I'm more than happy to help the good guys." He stood, knowing anything else he said was likely to get him in more trouble. "Come on. We've got more work to do before we earn those showers."

Michael opened the front door and peered out. Nothing moved. "We're going to explore, and find some alternative routes away from here. Some will go back to the truck, but others we'll just have to slog on foot. We'll create some traps behind us, too, so if someone's following, they won't for long. Let's go." He left the porch and walked back down the long, rough road, looking for game and hiking trails. He'd do everything he possibly could to make sure Deb survived the wilderness so she could win the coming legal battles. Anything less than complete victory was unacceptable.

Chapter 10

Late that afternoon, Deb panted, trying to keep up with Michael as he sauntered across the steep, rocky hillside on the non-existent trail. She wasn't built for adventure or stealth, especially outdoors. She was made to bake, to sleep in a comfy bed, and bake some more, while tasting her product. All this clambering, skulking, and marking trails in code was hard on her feet, legs, and brain. Even if she had time to look for Michael's codes made of broken branches or groups of stacked rocks, she'd never remember what each variation meant.

He turned back to her, a neutral expression on his face while he waited for her to catch up. It wasn't fair; he wasn't even breathing hard, and there was no sign he was in pain. But his work was more physical than hers. Still, she was concerned. If he was hiding his limitations, his body might give out when he needed it most, and she had no way to help him.

"Do you think you can find the way here in the dark?" Michael pointed at the ground below his sturdy boots.

Deb shrugged, wishing she had boots rather than cushioned, smooth-soled tennis shoes. "I doubt it. I've lost track of how many paths we've gone down or how we got to each one."

Michael shook his head. "So far, this is the only time we've gone away from the truck rather than towards it."

She grimaced. "I know that much, but if I have to run back here in the dark, I'm toast." Turning, she looked at the path to the cabin. Slippery snow, crumbling dirt, and lots of rock; it was a recipe for a twisted ankle and frozen feet. Something dark flashed at her right, and she spun to look up the hill. "There's something up there. Is it a bear?" Dealing with wild animals was way outside her capabilities. She may as well surrender.

Michael shaded his eyes with his hand. "I don't think so. I keep catching glimpses of a person above us. Woodland camo clothing, long beard and hair, moves fast, like he knows the area better than the deer do. I'd bet he's a mountain man, someone who just wants to be left alone. I noticed an old mountain bike hidden off of the lowest trail I showed you. The trail that was a real trail, not just a game trail?"

The paths blended together in her head. "Maybe?"

"It had footprints, and rocks stacked for steps in places." His brows rose as he looked into her eyes. "If you're on that trail, can't get to the truck, and I'm not there, the bike was hidden about fifty feet up the hill behind some boulders and bushes. Take it and ride. You can bring the bike back when it's all over."

"Right." Deb couldn't see how it could ever be all over. Those evil people weren't going to give up.

"Come on." Michael turned around, walking away. "There's a bit of a trail here, too. I'm pretty sure it leads back to the road eventually, just down a switchback or two."

At least there wasn't any snow below them on the south-facing slope. Deb followed, stepping carefully, and after a hundred yards, the path joined a more defined trail.

Michael stopped, scanning the hillside above. The trees were large, but sparse, then thickened into a grove high above. Below, the trail was fairly defined, crisscrossing the rocky slope below, until it disappeared into thick brush, the sound of water rushing implying a stream hid below. He walked up the trail.

Deb sighed and followed. If he'd gone down, they'd need to come back up at some point. But her feet and legs ached. She trudged up the trail, almost running into his back, because she'd been looking at her feet and panting rather than watching him.

Michael crouched, looking at a log with rocks piled behind it, then twisted to look up at her. "Well, isn't this interesting." He turned back to the log. "I was going to set a trap here, but it's been done already." He pointed at a thin twig below the log, and followed a shiny wire up the slope. "A deadfall trap. You pull the wire, and the stick breaks or yanks away, then the log and rocks roll down the hill on the people below." He moved his finger to point at the switchback below them. "That's where the trail from the cabin joined this main trail." He stood, dusting off his hands. "I'm not messing with someone else's trap, nor do I want to go farther, invading someone's territory. Let's go back down, and hope that person doesn't use it on us."

Deb followed Michael down the hill, then back to the cabin and inside. He strode straight to the bathroom, while Deb stopped in the kitchen, inventorying their canned goods. The cabin cooled as the sun set, so it seemed like a good night for chili. She'd bought cornmeal, so she could make corncakes to go with it.

As she pulled the cans out of the plastic bin, Michael joined her. "Batteries are charged, and the water heater lights, so if you'd like a shower tonight, you can have one."

Deb smiled. "Thank you, I'd love that." She was sweaty and smelly; a warm shower sounded like heaven.

He took the can opener from her and attached it to a can. "The pressure tank is pretty small, and the pump very slow, so you'll need to do a Navy-style shower. Wet down, turn the water off, soap up, rinse off."

"Better than being stinky." She was grateful for warm water even if she couldn't stand under a deluge to relax.

Michael chuckled. "You don't stink. But I agree that being clean feels better." He dumped chili in their pot and put it on a burner.

Deb mixed cornmeal, baking powder, salt, a little sugar, oil and water together, then heated the frying pan with some butter. She dropped spoonfuls on the sizzling surface, frying the cakes quickly. Too bad she didn't have her phone; she could make a video about "baking" on a hot plate. She snickered. Neither the recipe or the surroundings would fit into her bright, cheerful "make your day better by overloading on sugar and fat" branding.

They ate in silence at the table, the bland corn-cakes complimenting the zingy chili. When they finished, she cleared the table, and Michael lit a fire in the wood stove. The crackle and pop of burning wood was warm and comforting. He took the pans from her, putting them in the tiny bar-style sink. Water whooshed and metal clinked. "I'll wash these. Go shower."

Deb searched through the few clothes she had, and found sweatpants and a t-shirt to sleep in. She could wash her undies while she was in the shower. In the tiny bathroom, she found a wash cloth, towel, and some soap. While the initial blast of water was breathtakingly cold, it heated in seconds. She let it pour across her head, and down her body for a few moments, then reluctantly turned it off, soaping up quickly. She washed her undies, then stood under the cascade of hot water, rinsing, and turned it off long before she wanted to. The towel was rough, but dried her effectively. She pulled on clothes, wishing she'd had time to pack her usual facial routine and conditioners. Or anything from her normal life.

But Michael was right; dwelling on anything but the present and planning for the future was a waste of time. A shiver ran down her spine. Her future included sleeping on a small futon and huddling close to Michael under the single sleeping bag. If his dislike wasn't so obvious, it could be comforting for both of them. But as it was, she'd have to worry about keeping her distance, both physically and mentally. She'd have to fight her attraction and let his grumpy disdain remind her he didn't feel the same.

Deb wrapped the towel around her hair, and left the bathroom. With the wood stove crackling, the cabin was pleasantly warm; her hair should dry quickly. Probably into a frizzy halo, but she couldn't do anything about that, either.

Without a word or a glance, Michael entered the bathroom, carrying his toiletry kit and some clothes. A big pill container sat on the table; only three of the days and four of the nights contained medication.

She draped her underwear across the back of a chair and moved it closer to the wood stove, then plopped down on the futon and gently worked the tiny travel brush through her hair. That pillbox gave them a deadline. Either Tom brought Michael's prescriptions with him—hopefully, Nic was talking to Wiz and Tom—or they had to return to Marcus. Both options worried her.

No matter what, she had to reopen her bakery soon, or go broke, and she'd worked too hard to give it all up. She had to fight. The problem was, she wasn't a warrior like Wiz or Erin. And she couldn't rely on others forever. They had their own businesses to run, their own lives to live without the threat of violence. With his medical issues, Michael needed his comfortable bed, and access to all his medications. If he fell sick or got injured because he didn't have those things, she wouldn't be able to take care of him or protect him if the bad guys found them.

"Hey." Michael stood in front of her, and put a fingertip under her chin. "Positive thoughts. We'll figure this out." He pulled away and drank a glass of water, his throat moving as he swallowed.

Throats shouldn't be attractive, but Michael's was. Deb flopped back against the hard, rather lumpy futon cushion. "While I appreciate your help, this really isn't your problem. You have a business to run. You should go home tomorrow. I'll be fine here. Tom can come get me in a couple of days." Unlike fictional heroines who investigated and then got in trouble, she'd read and rest, staying quiet and unobtrusive. No one would notice her.

"Not going to happen, cupcake queen. You have no way to protect yourself." Michael shook his head.

"Sure I do." She scowled at him. "Just like a bunny, I'll hunker down, and stay still." She shrugged. "I'll burn wood only at night, go to bed with the sunset, and get up when it rises. I'll read and rest. No one will even know I'm here."

He frowned fiercely. "You really do live in a fantasy land, don't you? This is temporary. They'll find us eventually. We have to be ready to move when that happens, and protect ourselves as we go."

She raised her chin to prevent the hurt from showing in her wobbling lips and sniffed, trying to make it sound derisive. He'd made his disdain perfectly clear. "I'll stay here for a couple of days, then Tom will come get me. I'll go back to Wiz's, and we'll figure out a plan of attack. I can't close my bakery forever and you can't leave Nic to do everything, either."

He plopped down at the other end of the futon, rubbing his forehead. "Look, can we talk about this in the morning? I need to take my meds and sleep."

"I'm sorry. I didn't mean to give you a migraine." Deb whispered and got up to turn off the remaining lights. Bright lights made migraines worse.

"You didn't and it's not a full-blown migraine, just a headache. I didn't drink enough water today." He smirked, but the expression seemed self-deprecating. "I'm making up for it, but I'll apologize now. I'll be up at least three times tonight. You should drink too, or you'll get leg cramps."

Deb chuckled. "Oh, I'll get charley horses, it's a guarantee. I'm not a hiker, I don't work out, and I don't do sports. I'm completely unsuited for all this." She waved her right arm around, trying to indicate the mountain environment.

He captured her hand in his much larger palm, squeezed, and pressed her hand down on the futon, then removed his. "You're doing fine. I know you're not a survivalist or an outdoor enthusiast. If even part of what we did today sticks in your mind, we'll be fine." He gazed into her eyes. "But only if we stay together. I'm not leaving." He got up and held both hands out, palm up. "Come on, let's make this into a bed and get some sleep."

She sighed, placed her fingers into his warm hands, and got up, wincing at the soreness in her legs, while enjoying the clasp of his strong, rough hands around hers.

"Go get some water." He let go, and moved behind the futon.

Grumpy and bossy, too. She had to kill her attraction; she didn't need a bossy guy in her life. She grabbed a glass and filled it, drinking deeply, then refilled it and put it on the card table so she could have some in the middle of the night without a lot of fuss.

Michael put his water bottle next to her glass, opened the pill box, and shook out a rather large number of pills. He swallowed them down, then turned back to the futon. "I've put the woo-bie—that's a poncho liner to you civilians—on the bottom, and we'll have to huddle together under the sleeping bag. Don't be shy, just get in close so we can keep each other warm." He shrugged. "Don't overthink it, it's simply survival." He flipped back the sleeping bag; his sweatshirt and jacket had been rolled into pillows. "You're on the side farthest from the door."

Of course it wasn't anything but survival. Like usual, she was nothing but a burden. The extra girl nobody wanted. But despite that, she'd be just fine. She'd taken care of herself all these years, and looked out for her sister and nieces, too. Sharing a tiny bed with Michael was nothing in comparison.

Deb rounded the futon and sat, then laid down on her side, turning away from Michael. She shimmied to the far side, giving him the majority of the room. His massive shoulders needed the space.

The futon sagged and bounced. Michael's sigh warmed the top of her head. "I'm not going to bite and you'll need the warmth." He wrapped his powerful arm around her waist and pulled her into the curve of his body.

She stiffened. While his warmth appealed, cuddling with someone who disliked her so much didn't.

"Relax. Go to sleep." Michael slid his other arm under her neck, and curled his legs behind hers. "Count sheep. If you don't sleep, I won't and I need it."

"Fine." Deb closed her eyes, and concentrated on the warmth radiating from Michael, rather than the comfort of his embrace. She deliberately blanked her mind, thinking about heated, weighted blankets, and counted the cupcakes drying into inedible lumps on her cooling racks in the bakery.

But what let her fade into sleep was knowing Michael would keep her safe, no matter how he really felt about her.

Chapter 11

MICHAEL WOKE TO MOONLIT night, warmth wrapped around the middle of his back like a snug sweater, easing the pain of overworked muscles. But thinking about Deb in tight, fuzzy knits was a big mistake. Regardless, he closed his eyes and enjoyed Deb's softness tucked in tight against him for a few more seconds before his bladder made it impossible. He slid out, tucked the sleeping bag around her, grabbed his weapon off the floor and trod softly to the back. Goosebumps formed; the cabin had chilled in the night.

After going to the bathroom, he peered out all the windows, the three-quarters moon bright enough to show nothing moved. Time to brave the bed again.

Deb sat upright. "Ow!" She reached for the back of her thigh. "Ei-yi-yi-yi!"

As predicted, her muscles had cramped. Michael sat on the edge of the bed next to her. "Straighten your leg slowly, and rub toward your heart." He was going to regret it, but he couldn't stand to see her in pain. He put his hands around her thigh, and kneaded her hamstring, interspersed with long strokes. Medical treatment, not caresses; that's all he was doing. But neither his body or his brain believed him. Deb's knotted muscles smoothed under his touch, and her pinched expression faded.

"Oh, that's so good. Don't stop." Her voice was breathy and she ended on a moan.

Michael forced his fingers to release her. If he kept stroking, and she responded like that, they'd be doing something more dangerous, because he'd like to hear those words in a different context. And while she might admire his body, a beautiful, successful woman like Deb deserved someone better. Someone whole. Someone who didn't struggle with chronic pain. He rose and fetched her glass. "Here, drink."

"Thank you." She took the glass and swallowed half of it, then got up and padded to the bathroom, closing the door behind her.

She was too beautiful, too tempting. But that changed nothing; he had to keep his distance. She wasn't for him. He drank some more water, checked out the windows again, and plopped down. They'd figure out a better solution in the morning, because holding Deb for another night was bound to end badly. The only reason he hadn't done anything stupid was his physical limitations; he was too tired and worn to act on his base impulses.

Deb returned and drank more water. "Thanks for your help."

"Of course." He wanted to say more, but he couldn't. "Let's go back to sleep."

She slid on to the futon, and curled into a ball. He sighed, then followed her, wrapping around her shivering form.

"Thanks for being so nice. I appreciate it."

"Of course. You're family." It was true, if not in the sense he wished. But wait a second—what was he thinking? She was family; his sister-in-law. Anything different would be weird. No matter how much he wanted to hold her romantically, he couldn't. Anything more wasn't right.

"Of course. Family." Deb sighed and relaxed.

If she sounded disappointed, he'd ignore it. Attraction was simply physical and it wasn't enough for him. He pictured bounding sheep and counted, ignoring the soft warmth of the bubbly beauty in his arms.

When light woke him, he stretched and realized Deb was missing. The delicious scent of toasty, buttery bread and hiss of propane reassured him; Deb must be cooking pancakes again. While he wouldn't normally eat so many empty carbs, they'd worked it off hiking up, down, and around the mountainside. He got up, moved the futon into the couch position, and grabbed his work clothes. He'd wash up and they could talk about the next steps.

As he left the bathroom, Deb jolted. "I hear something. Maybe a motor?"

Michael grabbed his weapon and ran to the window overlooking the road climbing to the cabin, staying out of sight. Their footprints were still obvious if someone knew how to look and most all-terrain vehicles could make it up the snow and ice covered road. They needed a backdoor in the cabin; the bathroom window was too high for Deb and too small for him to get out. Standing to the side of the small front window, he darted a glance. Deb was right; a two-seat side-by-side ATV was headed their way. "Deb, get in the bathroom, crouch behind the toilet if you can."

The whine of the motor increased, then decreased. Michael risked another glance. The driver wore a helmet and the passenger seat was empty. The engine noise faded to an idle, and Michael crouched, then popped around the window frame to look at the ATV stopped fifty feet from the cabin. The driver climbed out and removed his helmet—it was Tom Borde. Michael's tense shoulders sagged, and he holstered his pistol.

"It's okay. It's Tom." He opened the front door, surveying the area around the cabin before waving at Tom. He waved back, climbed into the ATV, and drove to them, snow flying from his tires.

Stopping near their door, Tom climbed out, stretching into a back bend. "I'm not used to doing that many miles in one of these anymore."

"Rough ride?" Michael stuck his hand out.

Tom shook firmly with a smile. "Yep, and I'm getting old and lazy. But we wanted to throw off any followers, so we left the truck miles from here and I took some really sketchy back trails." He shrugged. "And some non-trails, too."

A buzzing noise drew Michael's attention to the sky overhead. Tom waved. A drone circled lower, then rose almost out of sight. "Wiz is watching my back." He opened his neon orange hunter's jacket and pulled a thick black rectangle out, handing it to Michael. "Satellite phone. Keep it on. Wiz will text alerts if she sees anything, but the drone's night vision isn't very good, and it needs charging a lot. I've got a small battery pack and solar array in case you have to move out fast, too." He turned to the back of the ATV, and thrust a rifle at Michael. "AR-15. I've got another pistol and body armor for both of you. And food, all your medications, a couple of backpacks, hiking boots for both of you, clothing and some other gear you might need." He picked up a box and handed it to Deb, then grabbed another and followed her inside the cabin.

Michael picked up the last box, glancing up when movement caught his eye. Their watcher was back.

Inside, a phone buzzed, the vibration coming from Tom's jacket. He put the big box on the floor and pulled another sat phone from his inside pocket, listening intently. "Got it, hold on." He pointed toward the top of the mountain behind the cabin. "Wiz says someone's watching you. She hasn't gotten a clear view yet; the person is concealed in the bushes and rocks above us."

Michael nodded. "Yeah, I've caught glimpses, and there are traps set all over the hillside above us. I think we've got a mountain man." He shrugged. "I'm not worried about the guy."

Tom nodded, then spoke into the phone. "Michael's noticed. Thinks he's a non-issue, maybe an old-school survivalist. There are more than a few around here." He listened, then laughed. "Exactly. Love you, see you soon." He hung up and put the phone back in his jacket. "I'm not staying long, because I don't want to draw attention. We're going to park this ATV in a plain grey box trailer down the hill a few miles by road, but less than a mile if you can walk straight down the mountain. I'll strap a bag of survival gear in the back, with a tent, stove, dehydrated meals, and a water filter. Wiz has dropped a pin on a map on your sat phone already along with the lock combination in a text. You should be able to reach the trailer fairly quickly by going around the back of the mountain, then down. There's game trails crisscrossing the hillside, so it's not impossible, but will be difficult at night, even with these." Tom reached into the box at his feet and pulled out night vision gear; a monocle mounted on an adjustable strap.

Michael chuckled, but reached for the headset greedily. "I've never been so grateful for smart, paranoid, wealthy friends."

Tom laughed. "She'll take that as a compliment."

"It is." She'd gotten the good stuff, too. If he tried to buy these, his credit card would scream and die a horrific death.

Deb stacked more cans on the counter, along with boxes and bags. "Please give her my thanks. I'm so lucky to have friends like all of you." She smiled, but it was slightly pained.

Tom shook his head. "We're sorry all of this happened to you, but I've got to tell you, Wiz loves this stuff. She's diving into all kinds of databases, buying specialty gear, and doing a bunch of probably technically illegal things. But she's grinning and giggling when she's not concentrating madly. You've given her the opportunity to make a difference and she loves doing that. Plus taking down horrible, evil people is our favorite thing to do." He laughed. "She's really happy right now. Come on, we'll get the last of this stuff, and I'll get going. I've got cameras to set on my way down. They're set to send movement warnings, then we'll warn you."

Michael followed him outside. Tom handed him a big, fancy ice chest. "You'll probably get a couple more days here, then have to move. Wiz is looking for the right place, and we're all working on the bigger problem." He grimaced. "Eventually, Deb will need to return. Wiz has an idea for a trap, but Deb will need to play bait."

"No way." He glared at Tom.

"Yes way." Deb's voice overrode his. "It's my business and my problem. Besides, Wiz isn't going to put me in a fatal position."

Michael spun. "You can't know that."

She raised both brows at him. "No one is safe one-hundred percent of the time. That's not how life works."

"We'll run the plan by you when it's ready. We're hoping the FBI will step in, but so far, they've said 'thanks for the info, but stay out of our business.' The idiots don't seem to understand what they're turning down." Tom put his helmet on. "Got to go. Don't call unless you have to, like you need something or you have to move. Text if you can instead of calling. Be careful." He climbed into the ATV and started it, turning around and zipping down the mountain.

Michael carried the cooler into the cabin and closed the door behind Deb, then put the heavy plastic box down. "We'll have to organize all this. We're running out of room."

"Nice problem to have." Deb stacked the rest of the non-perishable food on the counter and in the plastic bins below. "We can use this box as a storage bin, or a table."

Michael opened the larger box Tom brought. As he said, there were bullet-resistant vests for both of them; his was rigged with a harness, a retractable attachment for the rifle and double holsters for the pistols. Deb's held a taser and a container of bear spray; wise choices for someone who wasn't comfortable with guns. Underneath the vests, a bandolier containing ammo for the AR-15 and the nine-mils. The AR was a high-end model, with a red dot targeting laser, a flip-up scope, and a suppressor. He whistled. "She's not skimping on anything, that's for sure."

Deb laughed. "No kidding. She's sent expensive meal kits, high-end canned meat, fish and veggies, and only the best spice mixes, oil and vinegar. I don't think she understands baking isn't the same as cooking." She pulled out a smaller box. "Or maybe she does. This is a camping oven and there's baking pans, too. Wiz thought of everything."

Michael pulled two heavy daypacks out of the box. Outdoor clothes were in the main bag, along with rain gear, and water bladders were already filled and in the proper slots. Water filters, first aid, fire starters, and emergency shelters were in the lids, along with maps of the local area. He pulled the maps and spread them on the table; two of the area around the cabin, one showing the southern end of the valley. Wiz had drawn pins for the cabin and the trailer, plus highlighted two alternate routes down to the trailer; the code for the lock was on the back. He'd check the routes on foot later. He folded the maps and put one local and the wide area view in Deb's, and put the other local area map in his. If he wasn't here, and she had to go, she'd need the bigger map more than he did.

Deb put a hand on his back. "Did she send clothes?"

"Yes." Michael turned back to the box, forcing Deb's hand to fall away, and pulled out a huge pink tote bag. "This looks like yours, and there's some clothing in the backpacks, too. Make sure you leave some extra socks in the backpack in case we have to run."

Deb took the tote and opened it. "Oh, bless her." She sniffed. "Actually, bless Sam. She must have packed for me. I doubt Wiz would have thought to add my moisturizer, shampoo and conditioner."

"Maybe, maybe not. She's smart. But she's also smart enough to know that Sam entering your business is a whole lot less suspicious than anyone else going in. I'm sure the organization has people watching the building."

Deb wrapped her arms around her waist. "I suppose that's true." She turned back to the kitchen counter. "I'm so grateful she sent my e-reader. And we've got real maple syrup to go with our pancakes, plus local bacon and luxury coffee." She held up a coffee press. "She really thought of everything."

They ate a delicious meal, but Deb said little and shifted uneasily in her chair. She was probably sore and dreading another day of hiking, but he had a fix for that. "Let's split up the chores. If you can organize all this stuff, I'll go check more trails, and mark them. Wiz sent special pens for nighttime, too. If anyone is chasing us at night, they might be able to see the marks, but I'll make coded marks." Deb scrunched up her nose. "Simple stuff. Trail by number and if it leads to the ATV, it will have a V; if it leads to my truck, an A for Acer. And some additional codes as decoys."

"Okay." She sighed.

"Hey, this is temporary. We'll spend a couple of days hiding, and by then, Wiz and Sam will have figured something out." Unbidden, he reached out, putting two fingers under her chin. "It will be okay."

She smiled, but it looked forced. "Sure." She stood and returned to the counter, stacking dishes.

He'd give anything to hug her, but that would only bring heartache for both of them. He pulled two pouches of ammo off the bandolier—one for each weapon—and put those in his pockets, then took the extra clothing out. Deb handed him a big plastic bag with a sandwich, fruit, and snacks. "Thanks."

She nodded. "You'll need the energy. If you don't stay out until lunch, you can bring it back and eat with me." She gave him a closed mouth smile and a sharp nod, and turned to the counter again, putting away the sandwich makings.

She was such a catch. The single men in the area were idiots for not pursuing her. But he hadn't met anyone worthy of her. She was too good, too smart, and too beautiful for the knuckle-draggers around the valley. Including him. He shouldered his backpack, adjusted it, then placed his weapons. He needed to sight in the new pistol and AR-15, but couldn't risk drawing attention by firing a weapon. Maybe he'd find a secluded hollow where the blast wouldn't echo down to the road below. The suppressor on the AR would help, but firing it would still be obvious to anyone familiar with the sound. Although, he'd seen plenty of these around, so perhaps most people would assume it was target practice.

He checked the windows, and opened the door, then turned to Deb. "Be careful. Lock the door behind me. If you hear anyone coming, grab that bear spray and taser. If they get the door open, use the bear spray, then retreat to the bathroom and use the taser if they keep coming. I'll leave the sat phone with you. If Wiz warns you, grab your backpack and head downhill to the trailer. Okay?"

She nodded, lips clamped and wrapped her arms around her waist again. She wasn't okay. But he was doing all he could. He nodded in return and left the cabin, determined to keep Deb safe, no matter what. She brought so much joy to others and deserved the sweetest life possible.

He hiked to the trail behind the cabin, marking the way with the low-light paint, then followed the game trail down the hill. He stopped when he barely spotted the silver trailer's roof a few hundred feet below. Just in case the bad guys found the trailer, there was no sense in making the trail to the cabin obvious.

Which meant he didn't want to return on the same path. Stepping carefully across the loose, flat shale, he found another faint animal trail, and plodded up. Gradually, the trail became more defined; almost a real trail. A faint glimmer stopped him, and he crouched. A trip wire. He surveyed the slope above; no sign of a log holding rocks, but it could be a different kind of trap, or perhaps a warning. He stepped over the wire, and surveyed each step before moving ahead. The trail entered a group of large pines, and he stopped. The wires could be at any level or even be fishing line, which would be harder to spot.

"Who are you?" The voice was rough, like the man didn't talk much.

"Michael Acer. You are?" The sound was probably coming from above, but it was hard to tell.

"None of your business. Why are you on my mountain?"

Michael chuckled. "Didn't know it was yours. Map says it's Forest Service."

"Only part of it. Why are you skulking around?"

The man was definitely above him, maybe slightly ahead. Michael's tinnitus made it hard to pinpoint sound directions. "I'm not skulking. Just exploring. Do you live up here year around?"

"This is my home. I don't like trespassers."

Michael's instinct was to trust the man was what he seemed, but he'd been wrong before. "Look, did you see the blonde?"

"Yeah. Deb's Bakery, right?"

"Yes." He shouldn't be surprised; most locals would recognize her. "Her business is being threatened, and we're hiding until we figure out how to move ahead."

"Who's after her? The scumbag she married is in jail."

Not surprising the guy knew about the ex, either. Dealing drugs to kids drew a lot of publicity and death threats. Michael had no problem with that. "Actually, he's dead. We think the mob got him, as a warning to her, but we don't know for sure."

"Good riddance." A man in woodland camo, with a long, scraggly gray beard and a black watch cap appeared next to a large rock about twenty feet above Michael's head. He'd either been waiting for a long time, or gotten very close without making a single sound or sending any rocks sliding down, an amazing feat on the very steep hillside. "That guy was dirt. But Deb's a sweetheart. She sends a lot of stuff to the shelter and the food bank. I'll watch for strangers." He shrugged. "I do it anyway, but I'll be looking for idiots who don't know the woods. That ATV was a friend, though, right? The tall guy? And the drone?"

The guy had been paying attention. "Yeah. Tom Borde. He and his Dad own the Rocking B Ranch in the Sapphires; Pete's a Vietnam Vet."

"Knew Pete back in the day. His kid's married to the girl who shot the fire-starting rapist, right?" He spat to the side.

The man was very well informed, but the local paper was free. Maybe he went to town more often than his appearance implied. Or he had a friend helping him with supplies and news. "Yes, Wiz."

"She's a smart one and got a raw deal in the papers." He nodded sharply. "I'll help you out however I can. Be careful. I've been hearing a lot of helicopters to the north, and they're moving this way. Lots of circling, like they're looking for something. I'm guessing it's you two. Make sure you stay inside or far away from the cabin during the day, and don't use lamps at night. When you get back, try to hide the tracks you left in the snow. Be ready to run, all the time. If I'm close, and I spot someone headed your way, I'll slingshot rocks onto the cabin roof to warn you."

"I'd appreciate it very much." Another set of eyes could only help.

"Not doing it for you. Keep that girl safe, you hear?" The man shook an admonishing finger at him, then disappeared.

"That's my number one mission." The man was a ghost. He must know every rock and tree surrounding them. Michael sighed and plodded onward, watching for wires and traps. Just because the man agreed to help Deb, it didn't mean he'd make things easy for Michael. Which meant it would be even harder for some mobster from the city; a very good thing.

Michael sped up, despite the slope and the possibility of traps. If there were helos up, he had to erase the evidence of their passage sooner rather than later, and make sure Deb remained safely hidden. She'd never be his, but losing her was unacceptable.

Chapter 12

Deb sat on the futon and tried to lose herself in a book boyfriend, but her worry for Michael kept her from relaxing. She'd organized their hideout, eaten lunch, then cleaned and reorganized, baked cookies in the back-packing oven and planned dinner. But the sun was sinking, and he hadn't returned. The satellite phone rested on the futon next to her, but Wiz hadn't sent anything, so she had to assume Michael was safe. Unless Wiz's drone was down for charging, all the motion sensors quit working *and* the bad guys had already captured him. Or, more likely, he could have twisted an ankle, or got eaten by a bear, or gotten jumped by a mountain lion, or fallen down the mountain side, or been attacked by the mountain man.

She got up and paced. Worry wasn't useful, but she couldn't help it. She went from window to window, peeking out, over and over. An odd crunching noise, followed by swishing, made her grab the bear spray and taser, and listen again. The crunch, swish, swish, swish, crunch, swish, swish, swish pattern repeated, growing louder, and it might be coming from behind the cabin. A bear digging through the snow?

Deb padded to the bathroom and stood on the toilet to look out the tiny window. Michael faced away from her, holding a bunch of thin branches in his hand. He'd take a step and then sweep the branches across the snow, explaining the noise. He must be trying to remove their tracks.

She laced up her new hiking boots, grabbed the broom, and left the cabin.

Michael pointed at her. "Get back inside. I've got this. You need to hide. There's helicopters looking for us."

"But I can help and we can get done faster." She wasn't useless.

"No. Your hair shines like a beacon. Inside." He returned to his task.

Deb rolled her eyes and stomped inside. Men were so infuriating. She might not be woods-wise or a sniper, but she could put on a hat and sweep with the best of them. She marched back and forth, shaking out her hands each time she clenched them in anger. She couldn't allow him to affect her. He'd shown her, over and over, that he thought she was a helpless idiot. She couldn't change his mind; she could only change her reaction.

But that was hard.

Finally, the door opened and Michael stepped inside, closing and locking the door behind him, then pulling a chair over and untying his boots. His mouth was clamped, and a line formed between his scowling brows.

Well, if he was pointing out her deficiencies, she could do the same. "Sure you want to take those off? The bad guys might be right outside, and you don't want to run down the mountain in your socks, do you?"

He pulled off a boot, placing it by the door. "No, I don't. But I don't want to track snow all over the floor either. Especially after you cleaned it all so well." He looked around the room. "Nice job."

Deb squeezed her eyes shut. Of course he'd be pleasant, just to put her in the wrong.

"I'm sorry if I was abrupt. But there really are helos to the north, and your hair is bright. Even a hat won't hide who you are. Our mountain man recognized you right away."

She spun to face him. "You met him?"

Michael shrugged. "Met might be too strong a word, because I don't know his name. He knows yours, though, and he's a fan. He confronted me and I told him why we're here. He's going to help if he can. If you hear something hitting the roof, and I don't wake up, shake me hard. He said if he saw anyone suspicious, he'd slingshot rocks at the roof. He's the one who told me about the helicopters, and told me to brush out my tracks. We can't use a lamp at night, either. Wiz sent some headlamps; they have a red light mode. Use them as little as possible, though. Got it?"

She sighed. "Yeah, sure. Sit here, doing nothing quietly." Staying busy was the only thing keeping her from worrying to death.

"I'm sorry, Deb. I'm not a fan, either, but I am a fan of keeping you alive."

"Okay." She had no other choice, so she turned back to the counter and started dinner. Wiz made it easy. All the food was prepped, she only had to heat it up. They ate at the table, Michael recounting his encounter with the mountain man in more detail, then they cleaned up and sat at opposite ends of the small couch.

She grabbed her e-reader and turned the light on it to the minimum, catching Michael slamming his mouth shut out of the corner of her eye. At nine, she turned it off and got ready for bed. It was a good thing Wiz sent another sleeping bag; she'd like an inflatable mattress, but there really wasn't room in the tiny cabin. But deep inside, she'd miss the warmth of Michael's arms. She climbed in the bag and turned away from him.

Michael shifted in his bag, next to her. "Sleep well."

After a fitful night, Deb rose with the sun, leaving Michael to sleep. He'd tossed and turned like she had, but she didn't have a migraine problem. The least she could do was help him avoid unnecessary pain. She heated water and made coffee, then settled into a chair to read.

Knowing he was near and safe allowed her to sink into the Lia Huni romcom set in a fictional Bavarian-style town in central Oregon. She stifled her laughter, snickering into her knit hat to muffle the noise, but the description of the gluten-free bakery—and the hero, a yummy baker who kind of reminded her of a nicer, funnier Michael—made her long for her home, and hungry, too.

She couldn't create elaborate German pastries or Stollen with the backpacking oven, but she could probably manage a streuslkuchen. She rose, found most of the ingredients and figured out substitutions for the others, mixing it quickly, and setting it to bake while Michael snoozed.

After she checked it the first time, Michael's nose twitched, then he sat up and rubbed his eyes. "That smells amazing. What is it?"

"German Streusel Crumb Cake. I hope it turns out as good as it smells, but I've never baked a cake in one of these ovens before." Deb checked the time; she didn't want it to burn.

"Why did you let me sleep so late?"

She sighed. Grumpy Michael had woken with a vengeance. "Because you needed it? You've been working really hard, and you need sleep or you'll get sick. I'm not working so hard, so I can do without. I'll take a nap later."

He scowled. "I was going to get out of here in the dark, when no one could notice. Now I'm stuck here all day." He threw back the covers and stomped to the bathroom.

More like *she* was stuck. She had to put up with his moody self in a tiny cabin with next to no entertainment. *Wonderful.* Pulling the oven lid off, she pressed the center of the cake, and it bounced back, so she pulled it off the burner, and after loosening the edges with a spatula, set the cake aside to cool. By the time she made more coffee and cut the cake, Michael had returned. She put a slice by him, and took a smaller piece for herself.

Michael reached out and traded her pieces. "If I'm sitting all day, I can't eat that much sugar."

"Oh." Deb swallowed her hurt feelings, but she couldn't tell him it was okay. Baking was her love language. She took a bite and concentrated on the flavor and texture. A little toasty on the bottom, but it hadn't burned. This would make a good morning muffin, and the German name might be a selling point. If she had her phone, she could have made a really cute video. "Baker goes wild" or "Success in the Rough" would be awesome titles and might bring a new audience.

She dropped the fork, her appetite disappearing. It seemed like she'd never enter her bakery again. She poured another cup of coffee and returned to the futon. She'd just read and ignore Michael. Sizzling drew her attention—he was cooking eggs. She should have done that—of course he'd need protein after all the hiking. Maybe she should create more low sugar versions of her cupcakes. Michael couldn't be the only one who couldn't handle the sweetness. Frosting might be harder, but perhaps monkfruit or stevia would be good substitutes. She reached for her phone to make a note, but it was in the truck along with her smart watch. Wiz had probably sent notepads and pens, but she didn't feel like getting up. Besides, it was a stupid idea. She was known for sugary, fatty treats; changing her brand was a bad idea.

Michael ate his eggs, but checked out the windows every few minutes. Deb tried to read, but each time he got up, she got distracted. After an hour of pacing, he left the cabin, remaining on the tiny porch. Eventually, she learned to ignore the squeaking boards, and immersed herself into the adorable story.

She made salad for lunch, and they ate in silence at the table. She didn't want to break the standoff, and it seemed he wasn't willing to either. Which wasn't surprising. When Michael finished, he got up, and her mood dropped farther, despite the sun shining through the windows.

He put his boots on. "I can't stand sitting around doing nothing. I found some planks and a saw next to the cabin's back wall under a tarp. I'm going to fix the porch. I think I can get to the pile without leaving any tracks in the snow."

Deb dropped her e-reader on her lap. "Won't nailing be noisy?"

He shrugged. "I won't replace anything. I'll mark the bad boards, then measure and cut new boards by hand. Maybe there are screws rather than nails. That wouldn't make too much noise." He opened the door, then turned back. "Besides, with the beard and hat, I look like every other guy in this valley. If you stay inside, no one will notice me."

Deb rolled her eyes. "I'm sure they've got pictures of you. Plus, that helicopter probably has the latest and greatest cameras."

He held up a hand. "The minute I hear a helo, I'll come inside. Warn me if you hear one." He closed the door firmly.

Typical man. Make all the rules, then break them and ignore the woman who points out the hypocrisy. Deb returned to reading, trying to ignore the sound of snow

crunching, nails screeching, saw rasping and muttered curses coming from outside.

The light through the windows softened and her
tummy rumbled. Then the thump of a helicopter
sent her running to the door. Flinging it open, she
peered out. Michael wasn't on the porch. "Michael!"
She kept her volume low, but tone urgent. She crept
out on to the porch, peering around the ends of the
house. "Michael!" He couldn't have gone far. Sprinting to the bathroom, she climbed on the toilet and
tried to look out the tiny window, but saw nothing.
It didn't open, so she tapped a finger nail on it, just
in case he was out there.

"What are you doing?"

She spun, too fast, and her stocking feet slipped on
the toilet lid. She fell, but Michael caught her, stag-
gering back under her weight to slam into the doorway. Her stocking feet slipping on the vinyl flooring,
Deb clung to him. Michael's arms wrapped around
her, holding her tight against him. They both fell
to the floor outside the bathroom, Deb landing half
on him, and half on the floor. "Oof." She sank into
the comfort of his embrace, enjoying the strong arms
and solid chest pressed against her body.

But he'd made it clear; they weren't anything but
friends. Her feet scrabbled for traction. Remaining
pressed against Michael was very dangerous; she
might be tempted to do something stupid, and he'd
reject her again.

"Wait. Just stay still." He squeezed her tighter. Deb
stopped moving and his arms fell away from her.
"Now roll away rather than trying to get up."

How practical. She did as he suggested, and climbed to her feet. "Are you okay? I'm sorry, I was trying to warn you about the helicopter." The thump-thump of the aircraft grew louder.

"Thank you, I think." Michael grimaced, then rolled to his front, slowly pushing to all fours, then getting up, one hand on the doorframe.

She'd injured him. Shame churned her stomach and heated her cheeks. She was too fat for any man to pick up, let alone one with back problems. "I'm sorry. You should have let me fall. I'm too heavy."

He turned to her, scowling. "Not going to happen, cupcake. Besides, us falling had nothing to do with your weight, which is definitely not too heavy. It has everything to do with slick floors, stocking feet and physics." He scanned her from head to toe and back again. "You're perfect."

The heat rolling through her changed from shame to desire, but he turned away. Striding to the side window, he stood just outside the window frame and looked up. "They're circling. Shoot. They're going to send someone here to investigate for sure. At least it's too late in the day for them to land safely." He turned and pointed at the box by the door. "Get your boots and body armor on. I'll adjust the straps. Then check that you've got everything you need in your backpack." He stepped to the table, grabbing his medications and dropping them into his pack. He pulled energy bars and other items from the shelf, loading those as well. "Deb! Move it."

She shuddered and ran for her boots. Even in the cabin, she couldn't do anything right. Surviving a run down the mountain and an escape in an ATV seemed impossible. But she couldn't stay, because the too-honorable Michael wouldn't leave her behind. She had to try, despite knowing the outcome would be terrible. She tightened her laces, shrugged into the stiff, uncomfortable body armor and tried to adjust the side straps. As Michael predicted, the thump of the helicopter moved away and quieted. The red glow of sunset shifted the cabin into an unfamiliar landscape of gray lumps.

"Stop." Michael batted her hands away. "It's hard to do this by yourself. I should have fitted this to you last night."

As Michael's hands brushed against her side rolls, heat rolled down her face and into her chest. He adjusted both sides, then stood in front of her, grasping the vest on either side of the front piece, and shifted it back and forth. "Good enough. Put your jacket and hat in the backpack, and anything else you'll need. Take nothing optional."

She took her coat and hat from the hooks by the door, stuffing them in the small pack, then grabbed her toothbrush, toothpaste, hairbrush and sunscreen from the bathroom and added a set of undies and a sweater. On her way to the door, she grabbed the e-reader too.

"Leave it. It will only slow you down." Michael barked the words while shoving energy bars in his pack. "Got meds?"

"I don't have any." She forced a smile. "Except chocolate." She shoved the e-reader in her bag despite his command. He tossed a rectangle to her, and she almost dropped it, but managed to catch it. Dark chocolate—guess he thought she was serious. But she dropped it in her pack regardless, and slid her arms into the straps. It wasn't too heavy, but she felt unbalanced since it rested against the back of the stiff vest rather than her back.

He plopped a strange headband contraption on her head, adjusting the fit. "Look down. Does it fall off?"

She looked at the floor. "No, but it's not comfortable."

"If it's painful, we can loosen it. But you don't want it falling off or pulled away by brush." He slid the same headband on his head, then grabbed the big, black rifle and fastened it to his vest, and gripped both pistols, sliding them half out of the holsters, then back in.

She put both hands to the headband and tried to move it. It slid against her hair, so she probably couldn't loosen it. "It's okay."

"When it gets too dark for you to see the trail, flip the eyepiece down." He put a hand on the cylinder fastened to the top of his head, and rotated it. "It's a low-light monocle."

"Night-vision goggles?" Wiz really did think of every-thing.

He nodded, but his mouth twisted to the side. "Yeah. It amplifies low light. If it's too dark, it won't help."

"Okay." Not much of a difference to her, but clearly the distinction meant something to him.

He scanned the cabin, threw his backpack on with a grunt, and trod to the door, then spun back, almost crashing into her. "Almost forgot the sat phone." He picked it up from the side table and slid it into a pocket on the front of his backpack strap. Reaching out, he put a finger under her chin. "Stick close to me and we'll be fine. It will take time for them to get anyone here and we'll be long gone. Let's go."

He turned and walked out the door. Deb swallowed hard and followed him into the fading light, the sunset staining the landscape red as blood. Hopefully, that wasn't a bad omen.

Chapter 13

MICHAEL

MICHAEL CURSED WHEN HIS feet crunched through the snow. Their pursuers would know exactly where the two of them had gone. But they were better off leaving; setting false tracks would take too long. The warm day had melted a lot of the snow, and it wasn't long before they reached the rocky, south facing slope. He started down the barely-there game trail, hoping Deb wouldn't trip and fall. His back ached, sharp pains shooting randomly too, probably from the work he'd done on the porch and the tumble he'd taken with Deb. Maybe he was a bigger fall risk than she was.

A few minutes down the trail, a voice hailed them. "Ace!" He looked up the hill where the hail had originated, but couldn't see their mountain man friend. "Saw the helo. Think they're sending someone?"

"Yeah. Almost certainly." He wanted to run, but knew better.

"Okay. You get going. I'll put down some additional tracks in the snow, and when they leave, I'll trigger some traps. Try to slow them down."

"Don't put yourself in their sights, man. They're dangerous." He'd always hated having others at risk for his benefit, and the older man deserved a quiet retirement.

The man barked a rough laugh. "Naw, this is fun. Haven't gotten to do anything like this for a long time. Besides, I can't think of a better person to help than Deb. Love your cupcakes."

"Thank you. You're welcome to anything we left in the cabin. We won't be back." She sighed.

She was right, but it was still generous. The food alone would be a huge treat, if the mobsters left anything. "We've got to go. Thanks again."

"You're welcome. Take care."

"You too!" Deb called, too loudly.

But he wouldn't bother saying anything, because it was done. They scrambled down the slope, both of them slipping and sliding. At the halfway mark, he flipped the monocle down, the landscape shifting to shades of green. Deb fell against his back, but pulled away immediately. "You might want to flip the eyepiece down."

"Oh, yeah. I forgot. Thanks."

His feet and legs twinged along with his back by the time they reached the trailer. Deb leaned against the side, panting. He undid the lock, and pulled the back ramp down, exposing the ATV. A big black bag covered most of the cargo area, with a five-gallon fuel can strapped behind the seats, and the license plate was covered with something black. He yanked his backpack off, then pulled Deb's off too, sliding them under the webbing holding the bag in place. "Come on, hop in the passenger seat. Strap in. This will be rough, dusty and noisy." He held out a hand to help her up the ramp.

Deb placed her small fingers in his, and he led her to the front. She pulled a helmet off the seat and climbed inside. He pulled the harness across her body. "It fastens on both sides and between your legs." He clicked the side buckles, letting her get the one on the seat—dangerous territory there. He gently pulled the headband from her hair, and slid it into her backpack.

At the driver's side, he unfastened the rifle from his vest and clicked it into the vertical holder between the seats. The helmet didn't have an attachment point for the low-light monocle. Better to squint into the wind than drive blind. He put the headband back on, put the helmet between the seats, buckled the five-point harness, and examined the straightforward controls. The only issue would be turning the lights off; a lot of these machines were designed for safety and that meant always-on lights.

He grabbed the bottle of earplugs from the front console, handed a pair to Deb and inserted his own. The only remaining question was where they were going. He undid the harness, got out and grabbed the sat phone from his backpack—a stupid mistake. He should have let Wiz know they were leaving, but the mountain man distracted him.

On the phone's screen, a series of texts from an unknown number rolled by until he clicked on the one labeled "Safe House." He pulled up the entry, finding coordinates and directions. They'd backtrack up the

Nez Pierce Trail—the most dangerous part of the drive because they could be easily spotted on the main road—and then turn south on the highway, passing Painted Rocks Lake and entering a ranch just to the south. He enlarged the map, then handed the phone to Deb. "Hang on to that!" Her hands clenched around the black rectangle.

He started the machine—a deafening roar in the confines of the trailer. Backing out, he slid it into drive, turned the lights out, and put the hammer down. Bumping and jerking, they careened along the narrow road, then he slid around the corner on to the slightly wider forest road to the cabin. He didn't know where the bad guys were on the road. If they spotted an ATV with no lights, they'd be likely to turn around and follow. Especially if they had more than one vehicle.

But if he turned the lights on, looking more like joyriders or hunters, they'd definitely be spotted as they drove down the switchbacks, and the bad guys would set up an ambush. They'd shoot out the tires, and probably shoot him, too, assuming Deb would be the passenger. And if the ATV contained hunters, the mobsters wouldn't lose any sleep over killing innocents. He was better off keeping the lights off and hope the enemy drove good vehicles with modern soundproofing.

If a vehicle turned and followed them, he'd have to take side roads and throw them off, hoping the road didn't end at a cliff, and going around any gates in their way. Driving illegally was better than dying, and it was unlikely Mr. Ranger would be patrolling at this time of night. They'd have to catch him first, anyway, an equally unlikely event since Forest Service law enforcement drove pickup trucks, and would have to open the gates.

He drove fast as possible down the dirt road, slowing for the blind corners—hitting a deer or elk was their biggest risk. Reaching the pavement, he turned north and turned the lights on. Hiding on a well-traveled road was practically impossible.

He turned on to the West Fork Road towards Painted Lakes, breathing a sigh of relief. But seconds later, headlights appeared in his rear view mirror, quickly growing larger and brighter. He sped up, trusting his reflexes to keep them from hitting animals, and tried to remember a good side road. Signs flashed, showing the lake was just ahead. At the lake's head, the road forked, snaking around both sides of the lake. Michael smiled, knowing exactly where he could go. Remaining on the highway, he slid around the left-hand turn and the lights in his rear view mirror disappeared. He turned off the ATV lights, put his monocle back down, and stepped on the gas.

Deliberately turning the ATV from side to side to raise dust, he drove a half a mile, then turned left, leaving the highway, and onto Little Boulder Bay Campground Road. The road would take him above the lake, then reconnect at the boat ramp. With any luck, the vehicle following him would keep going on the road, and they'd return to the highway long after their pursuers had passed. Towards the end of the road, he'd stop and search the highway for vehicles before returning to the road. If the enemy knew the area, they could easily figure out where they'd gone and ambush them, or turn around and follow them, but the road wasn't as straight forward as the maps made it look.

The road grew rougher, bouncing and jolting them against the harnesses. He was sure Deb was squealing, but he couldn't hear her over the engine, and didn't dare take his eyes off the track. He held his left eye shut as much as possible, but both watered with the dust and high speeds. If they'd had more time, he'd have rigged the monocle into the helmet with duct tape. He careened around the corners, and pulled onto a long driveway that ended at a hay shed. As a bored teenager, he'd spent a lot of hours driving the backroads in the area with friends and that experience was paying off big time. He drove around the back of the hay shed, turned off the motor and took out his earplugs. Engines growled, and vehicle lights flashed, then passed on the road below them. Another set of lights rolled along the highway around the lake. Both vehicles disappeared, continuing south. Michael waited.

Deb put her hand on his arm. "What are we waiting for?"

"They might come back, or they might keep going. Twenty minutes should prove it either way." He held out his hand. "Can I see the phone?"

"Sure." She gave it to him.

He checked; no new texts had come in. He typed, "Left cabin. Chased on way to safe house, but will lose them before arrival."

A few seconds later, a text came back. "Ack. Overhead not available. Move when safe."

"What does that mean?" Deb pointed at the screen.

"The drone can't fly right now. We have to rely on stealth."

Another text came in. "Another lollipop loop available on Hughes Creek. Contacting the ranch for secure alternatives."

Before Deb could ask, Michael explained. "That means we can take Hughes Creek road, farther south, and run in circles for a while if we have to. And Wiz is trying—probably through Tom and Pete's connections—to get us on to a ranch, then they'll lock the gate behind us. Locks can be cut, but no one wants to mess with ranchers." He shrugged. "Although these guys might not be smart enough to know that."

On the highway below them, two vehicles drove north. One turned off on their road, the other continued along the lake.

"Time to go." He handed the phone back to Deb, made sure the lights were off and fired the ATV, and then bumped along a rough track under the power lines that generally paralleled the Forest Road, then crossed it. Technically, he was trespassing, but he didn't think anyone would care; the track was well-used. Reaching the highway, he pulled off the monocle, put on the helmet, turned the lights on and sped down the road, hoping no critters popped out in front of him. Even if their pursuers turned around when they met at the head of the lake, the two of them would be too far south to catch and safely at the new place.

Michael grinned. He loved it when a plan came together. They flew down the highway, Painted Rocks Lake glimmering slightly in the scant moonlight. A few miles past the lake, he slowed. If he remembered correctly, the turn on to the ranch was next, then across the valley and up the hillside to their new safe house.

He pulled on to a dirt road and stopped at a gate, turning the lights off and hopping out. The gate was fastened with a chain, but the lock was undone. He opened the gate, drove through, closed and locked it, then put his monocle back on and drove the bumpy road across the big meadow. He kept his speed low so he wouldn't have to use the brakes—red lights would shine like a beacon out here. He wanted to watch the rear view mirror, but he couldn't. Watching for cows and elk was more important. They crossed the meadow, and the road entered a narrow valley. Cut into the north hillside, the track rose parallel with the valley's floor, tall pines crowding around them, making it less likely they'd be spotted from the highway.

The road made a hair-pin turn at the head of the valley, then continued upward, switching back and forth across the mountainside. The trees thinned, but didn't disappear. Finally, the road emerged into a small meadow, with a log cabin at the far end. Michael blew out a sigh of relief, and continued ahead to the cabin. Rather than parking in the clear area in front, he drove around the structure and stopped in the back, slamming the ATV into park to minimize the red flare of taillights.

"Are we there, yet?" Deb's tone wobbled.

"Yeah. We're here. I think we lost them, but no guarantees." He took the ATV keys, unfastened his harness, grabbed the rifle, slung his backpack over one shoulder, and grabbed the big bag. His lower back screamed from the long, rough ride, and his mouth was drier than the

Afghanistan mountain tops, but they'd survived, and that's what counted.

Deb took both backpacks and preceded him to the cabin's back door, the sat phone clenched in one hand. She entered a code, the lock beeped, and they were in.

She reached for the light switch, but he stopped her, pulling the headlamp from his backpack and clicked through the modes until he turned on the red light. They stood in a small mudroom, with hooks for coats and a bench with slippers underneath. The kitchen was on their left, open to the living room taking up the front half of the cabin. A door to the right was probably a bathroom, and the ceiling overhead was probably a bedroom loft.

Dropping the bags, he gripped the AR-15, and put the ATV keys in Deb's hand. "Stay here." Padding through the small cabin, he cleared each room and the larger cabinets, then returned to the back door. "It's clear. The bathroom is there." He pointed to his right. "And the bed is upstairs. I think you'll be safe to use the light in the bathroom once the door is closed, but use the red light on your headlamp for everything else, okay?"

"Sure." She skittered for the bathroom and shut the door. Light shined below the door, but not too brightly. The sprint wasn't unexpected; the ATV's rough ride was tough on the body.

Michael explored the kitchen; it had been stocked with groceries, a welcome surprise. Back in the mudroom, he opened the big black bag from the ATV. Inside, a second bag held freeze-dried backpacking meals and a stove, which he left. Two smaller bags contained clothing. He dropped the pink bag outside the bathroom. "Deb, there's a bag with clothes outside the door."

"Thanks."

He continued into the living room. The cabin was maybe twenty by twenty feet; a love seat and two chairs faced a TV over a fireplace, with two stools under the kitchen counter. The front door was locked, and he drew the shades over the front windows, leaving a small gap to peer out at the bottom. At the top of the steep stairs—almost a ladder—a king-size bed took up the majority of the loft's far end, with two chairs flanking a small table at his end, and a wood chest at the end of the bed. Floor lamps stood on each side of the bed, but since the loft was open to the living room below, and an uncovered window near the roof's peak provided him a view of the meadow in front of the cabin, they couldn't use the lights.

A fan turned on and water sprayed below him. Deb must be taking a shower. Michael checked the chest—extra blankets and pillows—then dumped his clothes on top, finding sweatpants and a t-shirt. He'd take a shower after Deb finished, but he had to stay busy—thinking about hot water sluicing around her was a very bad idea.

Taking his backpack back downstairs, he lined up all his medications on the kitchen counter and took his evening doses, adding an over-the-counter pain reliever to reduce the inflammation in his back. He couldn't afford to take the stronger stuff—they might have to leave at any moment, and his decision-making skills and reflexes had to be perfect. He filled the empty days of the pillbox, and swept the individual bottles back into his pack. Normally, he wouldn't fill the daily organizer until he took the last day's doses, but with their current predicament, preparation was critical.

Deb emerged from the bathroom in a pink t-shirt and loose pants, with a towel wrapped around her hair, carrying bags. Michael wanted to turn on the light, but he couldn't, and it was just as well; increasing his longing for her would be dumb. But when it came to Deb, his brain short-circuited. He cleared his throat, trying to cough away his desire, too. "Leave as much as you can near the back door. If we have to leave in a hurry, we need to grab and go. Take the vest upstairs, so you can put it on immediately if bullets fly."

Her shoulders drooped. "Right. I guess it was silly to think we'd be safe here." She carried her bags to the back door, then went back for her boots and backpack.

Michael wanted to comfort her, but grabbed the black bag instead, and took it outside, webbing it in place on the ATV. Back inside, he put his backpack and boots next to Deb's, and entered the bathroom. Citrus and Deb smacked him in the nose—and the rest of his body. Grimly determined to control his reactions, he disrobed, carefully placing the weapons where he could reach them from the shower, and got in, sighing at the relief of hot water on his tight back.

The citrus shower gel didn't smell the same on him, fortunately, so he cleaned up and finished his night-time routine. After checking the doors and windows, he climbed the steep stairs, placed his weapons, and gently slid into bed next to Deb.

The large bed gave him no excuse to hold her close—a very good thing. She deserved better than a broken-down old man dependent on a dozen meds to get through the day and more to sleep well. He concentrated on his breathing, ignoring the siren call of the warm, lovely woman beside him, and fell into an uneasy doze, ready for any indication that they'd been found.

And if Deb starred in his dreams, no one else had to know.

Chapter 14

Deb woke, squinting at the sun shining in her eyes from the east-facing window at the peak of the roof. The far side of the bed's covers were wrinkled, but pulled into place; Michael must be up already. Too bad; she liked cuddling with him. She stretched, wincing at the ache in her overworked muscles. A back rub would be even better. But he wasn't interested—she had to stop thinking about him that way. He was a protective friend, but only a friend. She was fortunate to have him, because without him and the rest of her friends, she'd probably be dead. Or worse; a captive.

Despite her longing for romance and comfort, Deb threw back the covers and scooted out of bed, changing into her "tactical" clothes. Or as close as she could get. Gathering the bulky protective vest and her sleeping clothes, she carried them downstairs, repacked everything neatly and dumped the vest by the back door.

The bathroom was empty, and there was no sign of Michael other than his bags. The dark, rich scent of coffee lured her into the kitchen. A pot gently steamed, with cream and sugar waiting next to it. She poured a cup and doctored it heavily, then plopped down on the love seat, sipping and staring into the empty fireplace. But she couldn't sit for long, wondering and worrying about Michael. They had bad people after them, plus there were wild animals, and whoever owned the cabin. But he was smart and a trained military man; he wouldn't do anything stupid. If she went outside looking for him, she'd end up inviting the bad guys inside and serving them breakfast.

To forget her concerns, she explored the gorgeous, luxury log cabin. The pale, exposed logs brightened the inside, and the shade-covered windows were large for a log structure. The kitchen cabinets were beautiful knotted hickory, with dramatic white and gray-veined marble countertops and high-end appliances. The living room furniture was Stickley, and small bronze statues of cowboys tastefully nodded to the ranch's working status. The bathroom mirrored the kitchen's scheme, and Deb hoped they'd be there long enough that she could use the shower's multiple spray heads. Last night, she'd been too tired and sore to do anything but get clean and plop in bed.

She peered into the lower kitchen cupboards. A big set of expensive pots, baking pans, and small appliances would make it easy to cook and bake whatever her heart desired, and if she dared to make a video, it would look fabulous. In the pantry, staples were plentiful, plus expensive jams, jellies, pickles and imported canned food along with two loaves of her competitor's bread.

She chose the sourdough and carried it to the counter. By now, her bakery would be full of rock-hard loaves. Hopefully, one of her friends threw everything away so she didn't have a rat problem when she returned. *If* she returned.

No, she had to stay positive. Inside the fridge, fresh veggies, meat, eggs and fruit, along with a selection of premade salads and meals. The owners or Wiz had thought of everything.

She pulled eggs, shredded cheese, carrots, onions and celery from the crisper. Since Michael wasn't a fan of carbs, she'd make omelets. Before she finished chopping, the back door opened.

Deb ducked and peered around the end of the counter. Near the entry, Michael unhooked his rifle and vest. She stood, feeling ridiculously jumpy. "I was going to make a veggie and cheese omelet. Do you want some?"

"Thanks. That sounds great." He sat and reached for his boot laces, grimacing.

Deb frowned. The ATV ride had been much rougher than a car. His back must be hurting. After breakfast, she'd offer a massage with no strings attached. Separating her feelings from her actions might be difficult, but she had to help him. He was sacrificing so much for her; a back rub was nothing. Besides, putting her hands on him wasn't exactly a hardship.

She returned to chopping and tossed the veggies in a pan, the hot olive oil snapping and crackling, and then beat eggs with a little cream, salt and pepper, pouring them over the veggies and stirring. She put bread into the toaster. Michael might not eat bread, but she couldn't do without it—her pudgy waist proved that. Once the omelet was set, she added cheese and folded it, sliding a third of it on a plate for her, and setting both plates on the table. "Michael, breakfast is ready."

He shuffled to the chair, lowering into it slowly. "Thanks, looks great."

"Coffee or tea?" She filled her cup.

"Coffee, black, please." He picked up a fork, cut off a bite and chewed. "Perfect."

Deb poured a second cup of coffee and carried both to the table, placing his near his right hand, so he wouldn't have to reach. She sat, and they ate in silence. After Michael took his last bite, she steeled her resolve. "It looks like your back is hurting." She raised her hands. "I have strong fingers from baking. Would a massage help?" She winced, anticipating his refusal. "It's purely a medicinal and survival offer, nothing more." Maybe if she said it enough, she'd believe it.

Michael shook his head. "No, thanks. Manipulation doesn't help." His brows wrinkled above his nose.

He wasn't telling her what he needed. "But?"

"There's a hot tub around the side. Alternating heat and cold helps, but there's a possibility of making it worse, and that would leave you unguarded." He shook his head. "I can't take that chance."

"But if you don't do something, it will get worse, right? And that would have the same result, without the possibility of making it better." She might not be a mom, but she had nieces; she could play a mom when necessary.

He grimaced. "Yes. You deserve to know my limitations. The pain can be intense, but I can work through it."

"But there's no need to." She shrugged, while searching her heart. She could act for others, if not herself. "Can you teach me to use the rifle or a pistol? I don't want to shoot anyone, but I will if I have to."

He scowled. "Killing isn't something to take lightly. It leaves a stain on your soul."

"I'm sure it does. But these people are after us. They're going to extremes to get what they want, including deadly violence." She shuddered. "Maybe I can't do it. But I need to know how to use those guns, because I'm pretty sure I will shoot to protect you." She forced a chuckle. "Probably not to protect myself, but someone else? I'm pretty sure."

Michael shook his head. "Pretty sure isn't good enough, Deb. If you're going to pick up a gun, you have to be absolutely certain you *will* shoot to kill. Trying to scare someone or wound them will *not* work, especially with contract killers. And that's what these guys are. People who kill for money." He captured her gaze and held it, his tone intense and sincere. "The movies portray mobsters in a romantic light. But they're the farthest thing from that. They use people, enslaving, addicting, and killing them with as little emotion as exterminating rats. People are assets, like cash or drugs. They won't hesitate to kill." He reached, putting his hand over hers and squeezing gently. "These are strong, but your heart is soft. You use live traps at your bakery, even for mice." His grimace twisted. "I can't let you harden yourself like that."

"Let me? You're not my father. I can do whatever I want." She yanked her hand away.

He sighed. "You can, but I'm not helping you with this. You want to practice with bear spray, a taser, or hand-to-hand self-defense? Fine. But I'm not putting a deadly weapon in your hands. You want a teacher, ask Wiz or Erin, but I'm betting they'll tell you the same thing I did. This isn't the right thing for you. Please don't go there." He rose. "I'm taking a shower. I'll bring my weapons with me. If someone's coming, open the door and yell. I have no problem shooting in the nude." He hobbled away, picking up the rifle and pistols, and closing the bathroom door with a final snap.

Deb cleaned up, fuming at the overbearing man making decisions for her. As she worked, she considered his unusually passionate declarations. She picked up a spatula, gripping it in both hands and raising it to eye level. Squinting down the length of the handle, she imagined the suited man who'd threatened her pointing a gun at her, then Michael. If she squeezed the trigger, John Scott would fall dead at her feet, bleeding to death.

She dropped the spatula into the sink, her hands shaking. Michael was right. She couldn't kill, not even for him. She was destined to be a victim.

After she finished the dishes, she paced the living room, but she needed space, a chance to drown her defeatist attitude. Quietly, she put on a dark stocking cap, shoving her ponytail up inside, picked up her backpack and slipped out the back door, locking it behind her. She had the code, so there was no reason to leave Michael more vulnerable than he already was in the shower, whether he was willing to charge ahead stark naked or not.

And that was an image she didn't need taking up space in her head. Longing for someone who didn't want her wouldn't help.

She scanned the backyard. Beyond the firepit surrounded by Adirondack chairs, birds called and flitted in pine trees swaying in a light wind, but nothing else moved. She trod to the corner of the cabin, and peeked around the side. Three deer grazed in the meadow in front of the cabin and no dust rose from the dirt road. Turning back, she noticed a trail leading up the hill from the firepit. She could hike up the hill, burn off energy and nerves, and maybe find an overlook to survey the valley below for danger.

She should leave a message for Michael, but if she went back inside, she'd either plop down in a chair or get in an argument with him, or do something extraordinarily stupid, like try to kiss the man. She had to clear her head; start thinking, not reacting. She'd walked and thought a lot after her ex got arrested; she'd gotten lazy since her bakery turned a profit, relying on her creative abilities rather than analysis. She couldn't afford to be emotional. But she was also used to moving all day. The hiking they'd done had been more strenuous than baking, but the exercise had kept her from panicking.

Deb walked up the needle-laden trail, the pines whispering secrets in the soft breeze, and the sunshine baking a hint of vanilla from the bark. A few minutes later, the trail ended on a rocky ledge overlooking a narrow valley with a small creek running through the middle. Black cows dotted the emerald green of the meadow far below. A log bench to her left invited Deb to sit, so she did.

She watched the cows graze and tried to simply enjoy the scenery, but she couldn't stop thinking about her situation. Hiding was a short-term solution. She had a business to run, and so did Michael.

Oh no! She *had* to return—she had a huge wedding cake to bake! She trotted back down the trail.

At the cabin, Michael stood in the back doorway, protective vest on and rifle raised. He stepped from the doorway, toward the corner of the cabin, scanning his surroundings through the sights of the long, black gun.

Deb froze. She didn't want to startle him—getting shot would make it very difficult to bake. Was she better off staying still, moving forward, yelling, or maybe speaking loudly? "Michael."

He spun, pointing the rifle at her, but lowering it immediately. "I thought they got you! Where did you go?"

Deb grimaced and walked down the hill. She really should have left him a note, but she'd thought he'd stay in the shower longer. "I needed a walk. Sorry." She wasn't really sorry, but she didn't want to get in a fight either.

Michael scowled. "I thought you were smarter than that. They're looking for us with helicopters, remember? We're not that far from where we were yesterday, and they followed us to this area. Wandering around outside with your head in the clouds will get you captured or killed."

"I was paying attention, I'm wearing a hat, and I had to leave, or attempt to smother you with a pillow." Deb pushed past the annoying grump. Inside the door, she found his backpack and pulled the satellite phone from the strap. "I have to return today or kiss my business goodbye. I have a wedding cake to bake. The bride is probably panicking. If she's already gone with someone else, I'll have to return the deposit, and it was a big one." Michael slammed the door behind her. She jumped. "Hey, this isn't our house. Take it easy."

"I'm not taking it easy when you're determined to get yourself killed. Do you not understand your life is at risk?" He swiped at the sat phone in her hand.

Miraculously, she pulled it away before he could grasp it. "I do understand that. I also understand I can't keep running or I won't have anything left to run to." She put the sat phone behind her back, and poked her forefinger at Michael's face. "You have the same problem. We have to find a better solution." She stomped away from him and into the living room, plopping into a chair, then texted Wiz. "Need to return. Big wedding order."

Seconds later, a text replied. "Saw it on your calendar; contacted customer with reassurance. Sending transport. ETA 1.5 hours. Luggage allowance of 1 small bag; leave everything else. Have retrieved work truck; monitoring both cell phones."

Deb put a hand over her aching heart. She should have known Erin, Sam, and Wiz wouldn't have left anything to chance. As small business owners, they knew how hard it was to survive, let alone thrive. They'd do everything possible to support her.

Michael yanked the sat phone out of her hand. "You've got to be kidding me." He stomped away, clicking the phone's keyboard.

She chuckled. The man had to be in charge—but he was doomed to disappointment. With this change, he'd undoubtedly be even grumpier. She rose to pack. At least she'd learned what items were important and what she could leave behind, although Michael probably wouldn't agree with her priorities. But he didn't agree with anything she said or did, so why bother trying to please him? The attempt was doomed to fail and she was so over head-strong, bossy, grumpy men trying to make decisions for her.

Michael had saved her business from literally blowing up, and kept her safe when the bad guys chased them. But she made the decisions about her life and her business, not him, and she wouldn't allow her attraction to overcome her common sense. Head, not heart. That's how she'd survive the next few days, not by relying on an overprotective grump who couldn't see the bigger picture.

She added her toiletries and a change of clothes to her backpack, and checked that the headlamp, water filter, and other emergency gear was still inside. Then she went through the tiny cabin, checking for any personal items that might give their identities away, but found nothing.

"I'm patrolling the grounds. Stay inside." The door didn't slam, but it wasn't quiet, either.

Deb got a glass of water, a snack and a magazine, and plopped into one of the comfortable chairs. She hated to leave the beautiful cabin, but she was more than ready to return to her business, even if she had to adapt to a new way of life.

She could return to baking custom requests only, and maybe the farmer's markets. Closing her dining room and retail space wasn't ideal, but it was better than going under. Perhaps a drive-up window, open only in the mornings. Wiz and Michael had installed metal security shutters on her apartment window that shut with the press of a button, so she could have something similar done for take-out. A sliding drawer like a bank, only larger, and maybe a separate drawer with cup holders for drinks? Or she'd stop offering beverages entirely. The coffee was more hassle than it was worth, and offered only to appease her regulars. The older men and women who gathered at her shop would have to find another home, but there were plenty of coffee shops in the valley, including Erin's. She could easily sell more cupcakes to those businesses.

A thumping noise drew her to the windows and she peered out the gap. A helicopter dropped into the meadow below the cabin. The bad guys had found them. Deb grabbed her pack and ran for the backdoor. She'd run up the trail, and hide.

Michael opened the back door. "Come on, our ride is here."

"What?" That made no sense.

He frowned. "That helo is for us. Come on." He grasped her wrist, tugging her from the cabin. "Got everything you need?"

"Yes, but I'm not getting in that spinning death trap!" She stopped walking. Michael didn't let go of her wrist, and she stumbled forward in his wake. He wasn't gripping her hard, but he wasn't letting go either. "I'm not getting in that thing!"

He turned to her, scowling. "The enemy is literally at the gates, cupcake. If we use the ATV, we'll get caught. Same with hiking out of here. We'll be lucky if we don't get shot down." He tightened his grip and marched forward, towing her in his wake.

Deb surrendered to her fate. If they fell out of the sky, all her troubles would be over, quick. She followed Michael to the helicopter, the thump of the blades deafening, the wind whipping her hair around her face. Michael slid open the back door of the aircraft and pointed at the seat. Deb swallowed hard and climbed in, sitting on the very comfortable cushioned bench. Michael slid her door shut, then entered the other side. He took her pack and put it on the seat between them, along with his, and looped a seat belt through the straps. He pointed at a headset in front of her.

Deb picked it up and put the ear pieces on, the thumping roar lessening. "Please fasten your safety harness. We'll get going after you're strapped in." The woman's voice was calm and authoritative. Deb found the harness on both sides of her body and clicked the straps together over her chest, then fastened the bottom buckle between her legs. "Excellent. Sit back and relax. To avoid any unpleasantness, we're taking the scenic route over the mountains, so enjoy the ride. If maneuvers make you ill, there are air sickness bags in the pocket in front of you. Welcome aboard."

Before Deb could ask questions, the thumping noise sped up and the volume increased. As they rose, the meadow below them dwindled. She clenched the seat with both hands and hunched, expecting to fall from the sky. They flew over the cabin and into the mountains as the pilot said.

Michael's big hand reached across her body and grabbed the wire leading to her headphones, clicking a small controller. "Now you can hear me and the pilot. If you need to speak, push the big button."

They skimmed above the treetops, rising and falling with the hills, then flew through a valley, surrounded by tall, snow-covered mountains. The pilot had a death wish; they were going to crash!

"The flight should take another twenty minutes, but if we have to avoid aircraft, it might be longer. Ever used that rifle from a helo?" The pilot's voice held an undercurrent of amusement.

Michael tilted the weapon, looking down at it. "Not this particular rifle, unfortunately, but the military version? I've fired from helos a lot, mostly in the desert."

"Army or Navy? You don't look like Air Force." The helicopter swooped and dove.

Deb hung on, her hands aching. How could they talk so casually?

"Army. Got injured, but I can still shoot." Michael pulled the big black gun away from his body, stretching the tether to his vest.

"The window opens, or you can lock the door open if you have to, but that induces some drag if we're at higher speeds."

Open the door? They were nuts! She was going to die!

Chapter 15

Michael glanced at Deb—eyes and mouth wide, face pale, knuckles white—yep, she was terrified. Good thing he'd left her microphone on push-to-talk, because she'd be screaming soon and he needed to concentrate.

Besides, he was having fun. He grinned. The excellent pilot sped just below the mountain tops and popped over the passes. Hopefully the avalanche danger was low, because flying so close was sure to knock a few loose. Spring was a bad time to be in the backcountry, but there were always a few thrill seekers, ignoring the risks, desperate for those last few turns.

"Gunner, incoming helo from the east. I don't think we've been spotted, but I've got to cross a pass soon."

He'd hoped to escape without notice, but that was asking too much. "I can't fire unless we're fired upon."

"Agreed. Hang on, 'cause it's about to get a little wild."

He checked Deb's harness—tight—and cranked his down. The pilot would be twisting, turning, dropping and rising unpredictably to avoid getting shot. His chances of returning fire successfully were pretty low unless she straightened out and flew right; there wasn't any sense in being thrown around the cockpit for no reason.

They dropped like a rock and rotated left, skimming a high, rocky ridge rising from the side of the mountains on their left, while rolling side to side. When the granite spine ended, the copter dropped, Michael's stomach rising, then they leveled off above a flat, snowy plain. Probably a frozen lake. A wall of rock rose in front of them, and the helo's nose went up. They skimmed the rock face, popped over the mountains, then dropped again.

Deb was still white-knuckling the seat cushion, but she wasn't screaming. Her expression seemed like a mix of terror, incredulity and joyous amazement. Michael grinned. Maybe she was more of a thrill seeker than he'd thought. Or she'd believed.

They flew into a narrow valley, following the twisting river below. "Gunner, they've fired at us several times. I've recorded it and reported it to local air controllers, but I can't contact them down here. This is a box canyon, but the river turns abruptly to the west at the end. We'll scream around the corner, then I'll sling her around so you can fire. Three shots, then we go."

"Three shots, then move. Got it." He opened the window, loosened his harness so he could slide to the edge of his seat, and stuck the rifle's barrel out the window. Frigid wind chilled his face and fingers. He braced his left foot against the front seat attachment point and his right leg against the back seat. The pilot turned often and unpredictably, flipping them half upside down occasionally, staying close to the mountainside. A hard turn to the right, then she spun the helo in a flat circle.

Michael aimed at the corner they'd just flown around, but kept his gaze unfocused, looking for movement above and below his aimpoint. The vibration of the helicopter made his sight picture shake. Rotors emerged from the cliff wall above his target. He crouched, raising the end of the rifle's barrel and waited, stabilizing his breathing. The helicopter's dark gray nose appeared; Michael released his breath half-way and pulled the trigger. Once, twice, three times, and the helo dove, turning away. "That's a Huey. One of the local logging companies uses them."

They turned, climbed, and dropped again, following another valley. "Yeah, I know them. I warned them off on a private channel, but didn't get a reply. Pilot's probably at gunpoint."

Michael pulled his rifle back, closed the window, and tightened his harness. "Most likely. This is such a mess."

"Feds will be involved now, for sure. The FAA doesn't take running gun battles in US airspace lightly."

"No kidding. The FAA I don't mind. The other alphabet agencies?" He sighed. "Some are better than others."

She blew a raspberry. "The Feds will have reams of paperwork for me. I won't be flying for a week. This sucks."

"We'll pay you for your time." She deserved every penny.

Deb grabbed his hand and pointed at her chest. Michael shook his head.

The woman laughed. "Don't worry about it. Haven't had this much fun since I got out. Besides, Wiz gave me hazard pay. She has the best jobs."

Michael chuckled. Pilots were crazy, especially combat pilots. But that made him equally crazy, because he was having just as much fun. "Which service?"

"Coast Guard, then Customs."

Michael's brows rose so fast his forehead ached. "So you're used to being shot at inside the US."

"Yup. Drug runners and coyotes are bad news. This is just another day at the office, with better scenery."

He laughed. She was something else. "Happy to provide entertainment."

"Sure. We'll be in line-of-sight soon and I've got to talk to air control. Despite their orders, I'll drop you at Wiz's, then I'll go to Missoula. I'm not going to tell them you were here, so police your brass, please."

"Wilco." Michael found two of the brass shell casings ejected when he fired the AR-15 at his feet, but couldn't find the third. Then the last one landed in his lap. Deb smirked at him. He smiled his thanks and she looked away, a faint pink tinging her cheeks. But that could be from the cold wind.

They crossed the Bitterroot Valley north of Hamilton, then flew north along the Sapphires, dropping into Wiz's property precipitously. The intercom buzzed. "Thanks for flying Amiga Airlines. Stay safe out there and let me know if you need another ride."

"Thanks for getting us here. Safe skies." They landed with a tiny jolt. Michael unfastened his harness and slid open his door. He jumped out, slammed the door shut, and ran around the nose of the aircraft, saluting the pilot on his way. Deb was already out of the helo, so he shut her door and grabbed her hand, tugging her to Wiz's paved driveway and through the gate to the house. The front door of the majestic post and beam mansion was open, but every window was covered by metal shutters. Tom rested a rifle against one of the massive log and rock pillars holding up the portico roof, pointing it at the road to the house.

Once they reached the front door, Michael turned to watch the helo fly away. It shot ahead at top speed, going straight north. Tom lowered his rifle and walked to the door. "Come on in. Deb, you know where the guest house is. Pete's watching from the top deck, so you two can drop your gear out there, freshen up if you want to, then come back for lunch. And talk strategy. Erin and Sam gathered supplies from your bakery for the wedding cake, so you can bake that here and we'll deliver and set it up."

Deb followed Tom inside. "Thank you so much. I can't tell you how much that means."

Michael stopped in the doorway, gripping the frame. He'd been expecting a soaring two-story interior with exposed beams, but got a small room, already crowded with Tom and Deb inside. Coats and hats hung from pegs and boots were placed neatly below a bench. Despite the obvious use as a mudroom, it looked like a trap.

"Keep your shoes on." Tom shook his head, probably at Michael's panicked expression. "The entryway is a security measure. Keeps the heat from getting out in the winter, too, but the inner door won't open until you close that one." Tom raised his chin with a quirked brow.

"Right." Michael forced his feet to step inside and closed the door with a solid thud. The door into the house opened, and they emerged into the space he'd expected. A huge open living room, with a massive rock fireplace dividing two seating areas from a dining table and a kitchen with commercial appliances. Luxurious living room furniture created comfortable seating areas to his right; on his left, an enormous flat screen TV surrounded by several smaller screens were mounted where a window would normally be. Gaming chairs waited in front of a low table with a plethora of game controllers.

Tom led them through the dining room—the table sat fourteen—and kitchen, to the back door. He checked his phone, then held open the door. "Take your time. Maybe take a nap and shower? We'll have lunch in an hour and a half. Erin, Ryan, and Sam are joining us."

"Thanks, Tom." Deb hugged the tall cowboy. "But I'll be right back; I have cakes to bake."

Michael followed her out the back door. They crossed a flagstone patio, with a full outdoor kitchen, a fire pit, and two outdoor seating areas, one of them under a covered post and beam portico. "I guessed Wiz was well off, but I didn't realize she was a multi-millionaire."

Deb showed him the code for the guest house. "I'm really lucky to have her help, in so many ways." The

house was a smaller version of the mansion, but equally well decorated. Michael followed her through the
open plan living room to a short hallway at the back.
"There are two bedrooms, both with full bathrooms. I'll
take this one if you don't mind." She didn't wait for his
agreement, but entered the door to the right and closed
it.

Michael didn't mind, but he didn't understand her
reactions either. He shook his head and entered the
room on the left. A king-sized four poster bed with a
dark blue and silver comforter took up the majority of
the room. A closet held drawers on the left and open
shelves on the right, separated by a rod with empty
hangers and two hotel-style white robes. The bathroom
had a double sink, with a dark gray solid surface top,
and the shower was also solid surface material with a
heavy glass door. Dark blue and gray towels were neatly
folded on a towel rack, and the sink cabinet contained
an extensive collection of luxury toiletries for men and
women.

Michael lined up his medications, and grabbed a
t-shirt and track pants. A shower and a nap sounded
like a winning plan. Then he could decide what to do
next. He cleaned up, then alternated heat and cold on
his back until he couldn't stand it, dried off and dropped
into the cloud-like bed.

Muffled voices woke him; he recognized Deb, Erin
and Sam's. He'd slept twenty minutes; the perfect
amount to get him through the day and still let him
sleep through the night. He felt too groggy to face the
trio of intelligent women in the living room, but he'd do
it anyway.

He splashed water on his face, brushed his teeth, and left the sanctuary of his room. In the living room, Deb wore her trademark pink apron with yellow sunflowers, facing a phone on a stand with an LED ring light. Alarm shot an arrow of pain down his spine. "What are you doing? No phones. They'll track you."

"None of us are idiots. I know how to prevent that if we wanted to, but we don't." Wiz stepped forward, frowning.

He hadn't noticed her, sitting in the corner beyond Erin and Sam. He was slipping and he couldn't do that or Deb wouldn't be safe. But they were in Wiz's compound, and she was far more expert with computers than he was. Once again, he'd stuck his foot in his mouth. "Sorry. I guess you do. But why risk it?"

"Strategy." Sam drawled the word and raised her brows. "You may be an expert in the whole 'escape into the woods' thing, but you don't know squat about social media. Your website is pathetic and your branding non-existent."

He put a hand over his heart. "You're right, but ouch." He could and would admit when he was wrong, but he didn't understand. "So can you explain the strategy, please?"

Deb rolled her eyes. "Look, I'm known for bright, cheerful videos of delicious cupcakes. I make one every night, showcasing the next day's specials." Her cheeks pinked. "I have fans all over the world, even though they'll never taste my products. After three days went by without a video or an explanation, my supporters were asking where I'd gone. They even started a hashtag called 'WhereisCupcakeWoman' of all things." Her blush intensified and she looked at the table top.

"Since organized crime thrives on secrecy, we're going to make a fuss." Sam buffed her fingernails on her shirt. "We're not getting any help from law enforcement, so we'll embarrass the heck out of Mr. John Scott and advertise what's happening in Marcus. With enough publicity, the organization will pack up and go, because we're not worth the risk. There's not enough here for them." She shrugged. "If we were a larger town, or the businesses more competitive, then this approach might not work. But once we start putting out videos, other businesses around Marcus will join us."

Michael nodded. "I get it. But until everyone else joins in, it might put Deb in even more danger."

Erin, wearing a pink t-shirt with a sunflower and the words "Team Cupcake Woman!" on it, put an arm around Deb. "That's why Ryan and I already recorded a video. We're not nearly as good as Deb, but we're better than nothing. And we've set up a store to raise money for Deb, selling t-shirts, stickers and mugs." She pointed at her chest. Michael didn't look; he didn't want Ryan on his case.

"I'll be doing a video, too, exposing Scott's background and what he's done to other communities." Wiz grimaced. "His name isn't John Scott. It's Igor Kozlov and he's got ties to the old Soviet State Security, the KGB. He did financial analysis on enemies of the state, both foreign and domestic. When the iron curtain fell, he saw an opportunity and built a fortune. He's an evil man, and he's only gotten worse over the years since then."

Michael's sense of danger deepened. "That will make you a huge target."

Wiz's mouth twisted. "I'm already on their list. I've turned their requests for internet security services down many times, and I've continued to do so. Besides, if there's any private person who can stand up to them, it's me. I've already bloodied their noses. I'm fairly certain they were behind my ex's lousy attempt to burn my house down. He owed a lot of money and I've tracked emails back to Scott's organization."

"The next attempt might be a lot better." Michael regretted leaving the AR-15 in the bedroom.

Wiz nodded. "It might. More reason to go public with what I know. He'll try to discredit me, just like he did during the trials, but he won't win." She smirked. "One way or another, he'll lose this one."

Wiz was probably the smartest person he knew and he was certain that in her mind, laws were more flexible than Sam might believe. "Let me know if you need help with that last part."

Sam put her hands over her ears. "Please remember I'm an officer of the Court and obligated to report crimes."

Wiz laughed, changing her entire countenance. Her laugh was high and tinkling, like a fairy, and her face turned from solemnly interesting to startingly beautiful. No wonder her ex-husband wanted her back; rich and gorgeous was a killer combination.

But Deb was just as beautiful and her laughter eased Michael's soul. Plus, Deb probably couldn't kill him a dozen different ways with her hands. Although, with her knowledge of baking, she could probably poison him undetected, if such a thought crossed her mind, which it wouldn't. She was too good for a broken vet who couldn't get out of bed some days. She watched the conversation like a tennis match, bouncing from person to person.

Wiz recovered her stoic expression. "Don't worry, I'm not doing anything illegal. I wouldn't do that to you." She winked, but didn't smile.

Sam shook her head. "You're trouble, but the good kind."

"I sure hope Igor 'John Scott' Koslov remembers that." Wiz huffed. "And I hope your ex realizes that too, because if he gets in my way, he's getting run over."

Sam scowled. "Go ahead. I stopped worrying about him years ago."

Erin snort-laughed. "Sure you did." When Sam turned her glare on Erin, she held up both hands. "Hey, I'm on your side. He was an immature ass and still is. He's not worth your time."

Sam stood. "But you know what is? All our businesses. So, do some more videos, and I'll go talk to some other business owners, get them on board." She picked up her leather portfolio and walked to the door, heels clicking on the slate tiles. At the open door, she spun on a toe. "Watch your backs."

"You too, Sam." Michael joined the chorus of concern, and added to it. "You might not be making a video, but by doing the footwork and coordination, you're making yourself just as big a target."

She nodded. "I know, but it's worth it and I'm not defenseless." She snorted. "Far from it, actually. Don't forget to eat." She walked away, hips swaying and the door shut behind her.

Deb locked the door and turned to them, shaking her head. "She's not telling us something, and I'd bet Trevor Mills is behind it. She never could resist him."

Erin snorted. "Pot, meet kettle, Deb." She shrugged. "It might be for the best."

"Mills better not screw up." Wiz scowled at the door. "I don't have a lot of friends, and I'm very protective of them." She turned to frown at Michael. "But I'm sure you remember that."

Michael nodded once. "Oh, I do. Don't worry. I have no intention of messing this up." And he didn't. He'd protect Deb with his life. The world deserved a ray of sunshine and light like Deb, and he'd make sure she was safe.

Chapter 16

AFTER LUNCH, A COSTUME change, and filming several takes, Deb's finger hovered over the garbage can on her phone's screen. She could do a better video. But her new pink t-shirt with the words "Cupcake Woman: Putting the Icing on Happiness" surrounding a cartoon cupcake with a sunflower was adorable.

Erin, sitting next to her on the small couch, captured her hand and pulled it away. "It's good enough. Post it."

"Too perfect and it won't look sincere." Wiz pointed at her. "You know this."

A burly arm reached over her shoulder and snatched her phone from her hand. "Let me see. You need a man's perspective anyway." While they ate, Michael had taken a sandwich outside and had just returned.

Deb blew a raspberry and twisted, reaching for her phone. "No, I don't."

Michael held it high, out of reach. Her voice blasted from the phone. Deb gave up and watched his face.

"Hi there, friends! First, thanks so much for reaching out and your concern. I really appreciate it. The hashtag is awesome!" Deb winced at the sound of her forced laugh. "I had no intention of disappearing, but I didn't have a choice. Organized crime is trying to take over my bakery and the rest of beautiful Marcus, Montana. First, a man name John Scott with ties to the Russian Mob told me I'd better agree to his terrible plans for my bakery or bad things might happen to me. Then two men abducted me, tied me up, and threatened me unless I gave them money I didn't have. My friends rescued me. The next morning, someone tried to blow up my bakery's back door! So I ran."

Deb cringed at the shakiness of her voice. "Good friends helped me hide, but these horrible people hunted us down. We moved, but they found us again. So, we have to go public. I know some of you will think this is a publicity stunt, and others will say I'm faking it, and still more won't care. But I'm not the only one being threatened. In the coming days, you'll hear from other business owners who are experiencing the same pressures. And standby for Victory Security's expose on John Scott and his ties to organized crime. He's done this to other communities. Hardworking small business owners just like me are being threatened, used, and abused to hide money and the trafficking of people. These criminals are bribing officials and misusing the law, too. Please help me stop them by sharing this video. And if you're one of the unfortunate business owners who have been targeted, make your own video. Join us.

Let's shine a light on the darkness, expose the evil, and stomp on it. We've got to kill it or it will kill us."

Even on the phone's tiny speaker her breath sounded tremulous. "I hate asking for help, but I have to. My very best friend, Erin of Coffee & Cars, put together a fund raiser to help keep me in business; the link is in the comments if you can spare a few dollars. If there's extra, I'll help the other businesses in Marcus. Whether you can donate or not, remember that we all deserve to live in peace and thrive. America must enforce their laws, or lose their security. Speak up today."

Michael handed the phone back to her. "Put the link in. I posted it for you because it's perfect."

She scowled at him. "You had no right." But she hadn't been able to push that button; asking for money made her cringe.

"You were going to do it, I just sped up the process." Michael lowered his chin and raised his brows. "You did a great job." He went to the kitchen, and turned, leaning against the counter. "If anyone can make this work, it's you. You're so transparently honest and your bravery shines like a beacon." He smiled, a real smile, not a smirk. "Perfect in every way. Don't forget the link." He got a glass of water and returned to his room.

Deb closed her eyes, gathered her courage, and then pasted the fund raiser link in the comments. She put the phone down; she didn't want to see the replies.

"Deb, make Victoria Montana an admin on your business accounts, please." Wiz lifted her tablet. "I'll check the comments and block the trolls." Her lips lifted in a tiny smile. "Then I'll troll them back."

"You have social media accounts?" Deb was astounded the extremely private woman would have accounts, let alone post anything.

Wiz swiped at her tablet, and showed them a profile picture of a horse. "Only for research. We don't accept personal friend requests or post anything but generic pictures of Montana life, like horses, cows and saddles."

Deb brought up her business manager app and accepted Wiz's request for access. "Done." She clicked on one of Wiz's profiles. "Wiz, you have more than three hundred thousand followers on Instagram!"

She shrugged. "Pretty pictures of Montana plus lots of fake followers. Our account is set to automatically follow back and block certain kinds of comments. I don't post anything but the pictures and hashtags, and I never respond to comments or direct messages. But I'll repost your video and see what kind of traction we get."

"Wow. Thanks. That's a wonderful offer." Deb couldn't get luckier.

"Just like you said. If we hide in the dark, they win." Wiz rose and walked to the door. "And there's enough evil in the world. I'll do my part to bring the light." The door shut behind her.

Erin leaned her shoulder against Deb's. "She's made huge progress, but still has trouble showing her emotions."

Deb put an arm around Erin. "Don't we all? And speaking of that, thanks so much for putting together the fund raiser. I'm so lucky to have you as a friend."

Erin hugged her back. "Nah, I'm the lucky one. Besides, you're right. If we work together, we can drive these people away." She let go and stood. "Despite my desire for a girl's day, you have a cake to bake, and I have a business to run. Ryan's holding down the coffee shop with a little help from some heavily armed friends, but I need to get back." She opened the door. "Hang in there." The door closed with a thump.

Erin was right. Deb would love to stay on the couch, but she had an enormous cake to bake and decorate. And if she didn't have all the ingredients, someone one would have to go get them, so the sooner she took inventory, the better. She got up, washed her coffee mug, and grabbed her already-packed bag. Funny how quickly she'd adapted to the "ready to run" lifestyle. She checked her cell phone for messages then left the guest house, almost jogging to Wiz's mansion.

In the kitchen, she immersed herself in work, her tension releasing the longer she worked with flour, sugar and eggs, the scent of vanilla calming her. After putting the layers into Wiz's double ovens, she pulled up her Instagram account and gasped. Her followers had doubled, and people were sharing her video like crazy, the numbers rolling up as she watched.

The door to the second floor opened, letting Tom and Wiz out. "Deb, have you seen the response?"

She shook her head. "I can't believe it. These are crazy numbers."

Tom grinned. "The fundraiser is even better, and we have graphic artists offering more designs."

"It's stunning." Deb put a hand over her heart. "I can't thank you both enough."

"Just keep me in cupcakes, and I'm a happy man." Tom put an arm around Wiz, leading her toward the front door. "I'll be back this evening. Let me know if you need anything."

"Be careful." Wiz reached up to Tom.

Deb looked away. She didn't need to see the happy couple kissing; jealousy wasn't pretty. She'd plan a return to her bakery instead. Staying at Wiz and Tom's wasn't a long-term solution.

The back door opened, and Michael strode inside with his backpack and weapons. He passed her without a glance. "Hey Tom, can you give me a ride down the hill? Nic's coming to pick me up, and there's no sense in him coming up here if I can meet him at the highway."

Tom let Wiz go. "Sure. What's up?"

"Nic's been working a big job by himself and the timeline is getting tight. He needs help, whether he's willing to admit it or not. Deb is safe here, so there's no reason to stay, right?" He held the big black rifle out to Wiz. "Thanks for this. Really saved our bacon."

Wiz raised her hands and stepped back. "Keep it and the nine-mil. You might need them. You're a target, too."

Michael slung the rifle over his shoulder and walked to the front door. "When Deb insists on going back to her bakery, let me know. I'll help out however I can."

Tom quirked a brow at him. "She's right there, tell her yourself."

Michael spun. "Sorry, didn't see you. Let me know." He entered the mudroom, letting the door shut.

Tom shrugged, kissed Wiz and followed him. Wiz did something on her tablet, then joined Deb in the kitchen. "I'm not always great at interpreting people, but that was weird, right?"

Deb nodded. "Yeah. Very strange." Even for a guy who ran hot and cold, that was odd.

"Tom will get it out of him. He's good with people." Wiz paged through her tablet. "Interesting. Sam says the FBI came to visit her about your video. Now they're visiting other main street businesses while wearing suits that just scream 'junior FBI' and handing out cards like Halloween candy."

"Not Trevor Mills, I hope?" Sam didn't need her jerk of an ex showing up after ghosting her so badly. He'd come back a couple of times, and stayed just long enough to reel Sam in and then leave her heartbroken again. It'd had been a few years since his last visit, but never would be too soon.

"No. These guys look and act like rookies." Wiz glared at the screen. "I'll find out who they are, but they're too young to have any real experience. Figures. Why waste talent on a tiny Montana town in the middle of nowhere when you can send a couple of newbies out to make a scene and scare off the non-existent bad guys since the bakery girl is making it all up as a publicity stunt?" She scowled.

"That's pretty specific." Deb frowned at Wiz. "And insulting."

She huffed. "They told Sam that John Scott is a hard working American businessman who doesn't deserve to be slandered. She showed them the documents, research and videos we've compiled, but they're still pushing back. I wonder how high up the corruption goes." She shook her head. "This might be even more dangerous than I thought."

Deb's stomach twisted and turned like she was still on the helicopter. "Wiz, if this gets crazier, I'll go." She shrugged. "Heck, I'll just sign the papers and close my business. There's no sense in anyone ending up in jail for me."

Wiz shook her head. "If you sign, you can't close. You have to stay in business as the flagship or you lose everything." She put a gentle hand on Deb's arm. "And even if you do exactly what they say, Scott will want revenge because you dirtied his name. It's too late to turn back."

"It's one thing to risk myself, another to risk all of you ending up in jail. I can't do that to you."

Wiz snorted. "You're not doing anything to me. I volunteered, and I knew the risks from the start, probably better than you did. Corrupt officials were guaranteed. I found some obvious ones already, but there had to be more. Scott's got too much power and wealth for it to be otherwise. He's almost certainly using a combination of drugs and sex with blackmail, plus good old-fashioned bribery at many levels of government." She shrugged. "The only question is how high does it go? If it's really high, then we might all end up dead and discredited. But we'll have created enough doubt that they can't erase us entirely. There are still too many uncorruptible people in government for them to win." She put a hand on Deb's arm. "Don't give up. We'll get through this together."

Deb sucked in a big breath, and blew out her dismay and doubts. "And even if we don't, at least we tried, which is more than a lot of people can say. I couldn't bear to let that man win without a fight."

"Good." She nodded sharply. "We'll let Sam deal with the feds, and keep doing what we're doing. We'll have to do more videos—you know the algorithms are hungry. We need to feed them with at least one post a day, preferably three."

Oh, she knew that. "I can do some that are more normal posts, right? Like something on this cake?" She turned the oven light on to check the progress.

"Absolutely. Entertainment and attention first, then sales. That's how it works."

Grabbing a potholder, she opened the oven and spun the cakes. They had to bake evenly or they wouldn't be level enough to stack well, even with copious amounts of frosting. No one complained about extra frosting, but there had to be a balance. She had to balance her needs with the needs of her friends and the community too. She'd promised unlimited cupcakes to her friends, so why not share the wealth? "If you've got a list of supporters in the local area, I could pop in and reward some of them with custom decorated cupcakes. That would be fun, and I'd feel better about asking for help."

"If it's a surprise, we could keep you safe by moving fast and having multiple escape routes. And we could take video while you give out the cupcakes. Or maybe we can get Erin to do it for you." Wiz nodded. "Excellent idea. I'll look up addresses." She jogged out of the kitchen and up the stairs.

Deb looked at her to-do list. Mixing fondant was next, so she could make extra, and create some sunflowers for her reward cupcakes after she finished the wedding decorations.

Getting through the nightmare would be difficult, but she owed it to everyone helping her to be strong. To truly create that light, not just talk about it.

And if she didn't have a strong pair of arms to hold her when times got tough, it wouldn't be the first time. She'd survived and thrived despite her drug-dealing ex; she could survive mobster Igor too. Maybe if she said it enough—and ate enough chocolate—she'd believe it. The timer dinged, and she pulled the cake layers, testing them. They weren't perfect, but with a little work, they would be. Just like her.

Just like the cake, Deb's Bakery would look perfect with a little trimming, frosting spackle, and a little glitz. Or at least good enough for the Russians and the FBI.

Chapter 17

MICHAEL'S TENSE BACK MUSCLES—AND his heart—protested leaving Deb behind. But Nic needed help, and Michael wasn't the right guy for Deb anyway. Too old, too broken, too set in his ways. He had to cut the connection quick or dangle high on a cliff, the rope fraying as he swayed.

He walked down the dirt road leading from the Eastside Highway to the Borde's Rocking B Ranch and Wiz's compound. The sun shone bright, so Michael slid his sunglasses on; he didn't need a migraine on top of heartache. About ten minutes later, Nic pulled up in one of their work trucks. Michael opened the door and jumped in, placing his backpack, tactical vest and rifle on the back seat, then pulled a sandwich out of a brown paper bag for Nic. "Told you I'd get you lunch. It's good stuff."

Nic shoved an Acer Home Improvement t-shirt at him, then took the sandwich, putting it on his thigh. "Wasn't worried about that, bro. I'm worried about you. And Deb." He checked for traffic and pulled out on the highway. "Worried for all of us. You're taking on some powerful people, and those baby feds aren't going to help much."

"You think my involvement will blow back on your family?" Michael pulled off his black t-shirt, and put on the logo shirt. Alarm ratcheted his spinal pain higher.

"It's a possibility. But we knew that from the start." Nic sighed. "Kim's carrying pepper spray and a loud alarm, she spoke to the kid's teachers and daycare and the kids got the stranger-danger talk again. But you know Sophia. She's never met a stranger. Isa will help keep her in check, but..."

"I'm sorry, man, I never meant this to impact you." Michael matched Nic's gusty sigh.

Nic shot him a glance. "Doing nothing isn't an option. Because my kids are at risk every day from these kinds of people. They're adorable and that makes them a target. Standing up to the bad guys might increase the short-term risk, but it's the only way to make a difference. All of us understand that. Neither Kim or I will make a video, but we'll support you in every other way." He chuckled evilly. "And on that note, Kim is scripting a video for you to shoot."

"What? No way. I'm not going on video." Michael side-eyed Nic. "Nobody wants me talking to them in real life. I'd be terrible on social media."

"You'll be fine with a little coaching." Nic laughed. "Actually, you will be terrible. But you're doing it anyway, because it'll be authentic. And our social media presence is better than you think. Kim took it over a year ago, remember?"

"I guess? I don't touch it, so I don't think about it." He probably should; even in a small town like Marcus, social media was key to discoverability.

"Fortunately, Kim is smarter about it than we are." Nic pulled into an alley in the middle of a city block and parked behind a Queen Anne-style mansion. "Her posts look like HGTV stuff. It's great. Especially because it doesn't show us, just our work. But for this video, you'll have to appear." He opened the truck door. "Don't bring the rifle."

Michael huffed. It had become part of him; just like the Army. He slid it behind the backseat and threw his dirty t-shirt over it. "You're carrying though, right?"

"Yeah. Good thing I got that concealed carry license." Nic patted the cargo pocket on his work pants.

"Too many contractors get robbed by druggies. Better safe than sorry." Michael joined Nic at the back of the truck and studied the two-story house. Movement at both upstairs windows caught his attention. "Are the owners living here?"

"No, it's empty."

Michael grabbed Nic's arm and pulled him around the far side of the truck and down into a crouch. "There's people in there, watching." He pulled the nine-mil from the back of his pants.

Nic drew his weapon—just a tiny .380—and duck walked to the front of the truck. "There shouldn't be anyone inside. I'll check. On three."

Michael turned his back on Nic and scanned their surroundings. Nothing unusual. He relaxed his gaze, unfocusing his eyes slightly, watching for movement. "I got your six."

"Three, two—" Nic popped his upper body around the front bumper and returned. "Both upstairs and downstairs windows have movement or shadows. It's an ambush."

Michael opened the truck's back door and slid the AR-15 out, then grabbed his vest, handing it to Nic, and slung his backpack on. Nic tried to shove the vest back. "You've got kids. Take the vest." Nic slid it over his head and tightened the straps. Michael handed him the rifle. "Extra mags in my backpack."

Nic shoved his handgun back in his pocket, and took the rifle, checking the chamber and the safety. "We've been here too long. They'll be sending people out. We can move through the houses behind us or try to drive out."

"Let's try the truck first." A pop, and air hissed; another pop, and the hissing increased—they'd taken out both tires facing the house. "Suppressor. You lead the way." If the enemy was firing suppressed weapons inside city limits, they'd just taken the fight to a whole new level. They'd get a little farther away, then call 911.

Nic sprinted to the small garage just to their south. Bullets thwacked into the wood siding behind him. Nic and Michael waited for the bad guys to run out of ammo, then Nic popped around the corner of the garage, firing the rifle. The AR's suppressor didn't work as well the bad guys' smaller weapon. Nic's four-round burst was louder, but the shattering glass and the screams that followed meant all chances of a quiet battle were gone.

Michael waited for Nic to fire again, then ran to the other end of the garage, cursing his unreliable back when his muscles seized momentarily. He stumbled and almost fell, but made it, bullets spraying splinters around him. He kept moving around the back of the small building, put his back to Nic's, and pulled his phone, dialing 911 with his left hand. "This is Michael Acer. Somebody's shooting at us! They're in the big house under construction on 9th Street. Send help! They shot out our tires. We're running." He hung up and dialed Wiz. "Taking fire. E&E on foot; need a safe house or ride."

"Copy under fire; E&E on foot. Looking for options. Head downtown to Sam's. Will text updates. Notifying all parties including Nic's family. Will secure them ASAP. Wiz out."

Michael made sure his phone was on vibrate and put it in his pocket. He pulled his backpack off and handed Nic two magazines, picking up the ejected empty. Michael waited for Nic to finish his next triple burst. "Sam's office if we can get there. Wiz is contacting Kim."

Nic flattened his back against the garage, breathing hard as bullets thudded into the wood. "Thanks. We can try for downtown, but we're a half-a-mile from there. We'll draw some attention for sure."

Even in Marcus, openly armed people were unusual. But they didn't have much choice. Stay and die, or escape, evade and live—maybe. "We head for that house—" Michael pointed at the one in front of them, another older home "—then across the street and into the next alley if there's no tall fences. Be ready to move left or right. I'll go while you fire, then cover you."

"Three, two, go!" Nic bent around the side of the garage and the AR spat.

Michael sprinted for the corner of the house, spun, and raised his pistol, pointing it above Nic's head. "Go!"

Nic ran to Michael's left, out of his line of sight, so the enemy couldn't see him from the ground level. If they still had someone posted in the upper windows of the construction project, the two of them wouldn't make it. After Nic reached his position, Michael took a step back and spun. As Nic aimed at the enemy, Michael jogged to the end of the house, searching for threats up and down the quiet residential street and the line of houses across the road. "Nic, go!" He turned and covered Nic's retreat, glancing over his shoulder to check Nic's progress.

Nic sprinted past him, across the street, and crouched by the corner of an older log cabin, the perfect material to soak up bullets. Michael turned to follow, but a round smacked the side of the house where his head had just been. He twisted back, fired three shots in return, then stepped backwards, keeping the pistol raised. A weapon appeared at the corner of the house, and Michael fired another three rounds. Eleven remained in his magazine. He backed and slid around his corner, darting out to see if the enemy was following. Nic would watch his six.

Tires screeched and Michael spun to meet the new threat. The driver's window on a huge shiny black SUV lowered, showing the upper half of a man's face. "Come on, get in!" The driver looked familiar, but that didn't mean he was a good guy. "FBI! Trevor Mills, remember me?" The driver shoved a shiny badge out the window.

At a distance, the badge could be a fake, but if there were more than two enemies, he and Nic were dead, and there could be a lot of civilian casualties. Mills was much younger, in the same high school class as Deb, but the face looked right. Michael ran for the SUV, going around the far side. "Nic, come on. It's the feds!" He opened the door and dove in, scrambling across the back seat.

Nic bounded inside and slammed the door shut. "Go!"

Tires screeched again as Mills fled the scene. As they almost slid around the corner, stars appeared on the back windows, but they didn't shatter. He and Nic ducked. Must be an official vehicle with shatter resistant glass.

"Acer, right?" The driver's voice was calm. "Call Sam. We'll pick her up, then Nic's wife and kids."

"You're really Mills?" Nic pointed the AR's barrel over the seats at the driver's head.

The driver threw a flat dark object between the seats. Michael caught the wallet and opened it. "Trevor Mills, Special Agent." The shiny badge glimmered in the dim light the smoked glass side windows allowed. A government access card displayed a solemn picture of the driver. If it was fake, it was a good one.

Nic pulled the rifle away, putting it between his legs with the barrel pointed at the car's roof. "Good enough." He buckled his seat belt.

Michael tossed the wallet back to Mills and pulled his phone, dialing Sam's office.

A female voice answered. "Attorneys at Law, may I help you?"

As Mills slalomed around corners, Michael jammed his feet into the seat supports to stay upright. "This is Michael Acer. Put me through to Sam, it's an emergency. Then lock down the office. I repeat, lock down the office."

"Hold, please." The line went dead.

"Da—" The assistant probably didn't believe him.

"Michael? What's going on?" Sam's voice calm, but there was an undercurrent of tension.

"We got ambushed. We're on our way to you. Lock down your office, and get ready to run for the big black SUV when I call again. We're with Mills." The driver shot a glare over his shoulder, but Michael had just lived through an ambush; he couldn't set Sam up for one.

"Wonderful. I'll be ready." She hung up.

"Is she coming?" Mills pushed a hand across the top of his head. "I don't see anyone behind us, but there could be others heading her way."

"She said she'd be ready, but she wasn't excited about it." Michael sat back and fastened his seat belt.

Mills nodded. "Just want to keep her alive. You've bit off more than you can chew."

Michael snorted. "Oh, and your organization has been so helpful. Those idiots in the bad suits are a joke. We've done what we've had to do. And we would have survived this too."

Mills skidded around a few more corners, then slowed, rolling into the downtown. "Call her."

Michael dialed Sam's cell, which he should have done from the start. "Get ready, we're almost there."

"Okay. I don't see anyone suspicious."

"Like she'd know," Mills muttered under his breath.

Maybe, maybe not. Sam wasn't stupid, and she'd helped Erin and Wiz previously. Wiz wouldn't leave her ignorant or unguarded. A text buzzed from Wiz. "Suspicious car half a block west of Sam's door. Use back door."

Michael put his phone on speaker. "Sam, Wiz says there's a suspicious car near you. Can you get to the back door? And where is it?"

"Yes. Alleyway behind the building." Fabric rustled. "I'm headed there now."

Mills yanked the wheel, cursing. "Always trouble."

Sam scoffed. "Like you aren't, Mills? Save it."

No love lost between these two. Michael examined Mills' expression. Or maybe too much love. Either way, Michael wasn't getting in the middle. The SUV careened around two more corners. Mills slammed on the brakes, sending all of them jolting forward. Michael raised the phone. "Now!"

The door opened, and Sam ran out, jumping into the front seat. Mills peeled out, then slammed his foot on the brake. A car blocked the alley in front of them. Mills threw the SUV into reverse, using the mirrors and the backup camera to fly down the alley, stopped abruptly, and turned into an even narrower alley to their right. Sam struggled to get her seatbelt on, finally clicking it home. At the street corner, Mills eased forward, then peeled out, flying the remaining blocks to the highway. He took a right and sped up, then turned left on to the Eastside Highway.

Once they were steady enough to type, Michael texted Wiz. "Nic's family?"

"On their way here. Kim's ahead of you. Sending overhead her way."

Relief let him breathe. "Nic. Kim and the kids are headed to Wiz's. She's driving, and Wiz is sending the drone to watch her."

Nic put his hand over his heart. "Thank heavens. Does Wiz know where she is and can we catch her?"

"I'm not sure how far ahead she is." If he was driving, he'd make it happen, but Mills was in control.

Mills flashed a glance over his shoulder. "Color, make and model?" The SUV's engine roared and Mills passed the car in front of them.

"Red SUV, big black stallion outlined on the side." Nic grimaced. "Too obvious it's mine."

"That might not be bad." Sam pulled down the visor and patted her hair into place. "If those people tried to stop your car, everyone around would notice and call 911."

"If there's anyone around to notice." Mills passed another car, cutting it close enough that the oncoming truck blew his horn and swerved to the side. The speedometer rose to ninety, and Mills drove his huge SUV like a race car, passing everyone, slowing only for the corners. After squealing around another corner, Mills pulled in behind Nic's SUV.

Nic dialed. "Hey, we're behind you in the black SUV, so speed up and don't worry." He listened. "Yeah, babe, I'm fine. Not a scratch. Michael's got a date with some tweezers, but overall, he's okay too. Just get there. We're with Trevor Mills; he's FBI. He can take care of the cops."

Mills grimaced and Sam shot him a glare. Warmth trickled down Michael's cheek; he swiped at it. A needle of pain shot into his flesh and his hand came away red. Guess Nic hadn't been joking about needing tweezers. Some of those shots must have shattered the wood siding near him and he'd caught a few splinters with his face. Lucky he'd still been wearing sunglasses or he could have damaged his eyes.

They followed Kim up the highway at a too slow eighty miles per hour, and turned on to the Rocking B Ranch Road, then into Wiz's compound, the gates opening and closing around them. Once again, Tom stood behind a porch pillar, scanning the road and hillsides above with a scoped hunting rifle. Both vehicles pulled under the portico, and Nic tumbled out in his hurry to reach his girls, leaving the rifle in the car. He pulled Kim into an embrace, then crouched to hug both girls.

Michael picked up the AR-15, happy to have the security back in his hands. He moved behind the pillar at the other end of the porch to help Tom watch. Sam joined Nic and Kim, then led the family to the front door and inside. Mills stayed outside, glancing between it, the two of them guarding the area, and the surroundings.

After a minute, Tom raised his rifle and turned. "Let's go, gentlemen."

"You're sure she wants me in there?" Mills motioned over his shoulder with his thumb. "I know she doesn't think much of law enforcement."

Tom frowned. "Now that's not true, Mr. Mills. Wiz is just wary of it, and justifiably so. If you're not here to cause problems, you won't have any. Leave the pistols and threats holstered and you'll be fine." Tom smirked. "Probably." He jerked his head toward the door. "Let's go."

Michael let Mills go first, watching his reaction to the unexpectedly small mudroom, which was remarkably similar to his initial response. Tom gave Mills the same speech he'd given Michael, and they entered the main house.

Deb was settling the kids into the seats in front of the TV with a tray of snacks and drinks. She shot a smile at him, then returned her attention to Sophia.

He'd never been jealous of his brother's instant family before, but suddenly, he wished for a couple of blonde girls, or maybe a tow-headed little boy, all of whom looked like Deb, not him. He shook his stupid musings away and joined the adults seated around the long dining room table. Dreaming about things that would never happen wasn't very useful, especially when they had real problems to face.

Sam sat at the head of the table, the rest of the adults joining her. Mills sat next to Michael.

Nic leaned forward and spoke to Sam. "Kim and Deb will join after they get a movie going."

"Deb's giving them the headphones, right?" Wiz tapped her ear.

Nic nodded. "Yep. They don't need to hear this." He waved his hand palm up across the table in front of him.

No, they didn't. It was scary enough for the adults. Michael's nightmares were sure to feature Deb, Kim and the kids tonight.

Chapter 18

AFTER SETTLING THE KIDS with a movie, Deb led Kim toward the dining room table. As she walked, Kim turned in a circle. "This place is huge. And way too fancy for us." She kept her voice low.

"Yeah, I know." Deb bumped her shoulder against Kim's. "But it's also super safe. And Wiz is wonderful, even though she'll seem pretty reserved." She grimaced. "Maybe wary is a better term. But she's been awesome."

"Okay. Must be nice to have all this."

"Staying in her guest house certainly isn't a hardship." Deb grinned, but remembering the reason they were there made her frown. Reaching the table, she sat next to Tom and Kim plopped down between her and Nic. Trevor sat across the table, next to Michael. Way too close to her and Sam.

Sam stood, her emerald green blouse and black pencil skirt perfect despite literally running for her life. "I'm calling this meeting of the Cupcake Woman Protection Society to order."

Deb snort laughed. "You're kidding me, right?"

Sam winked. "Nope. We had to call it something for the fund raiser. Something that wouldn't get us sued for libel and catchy enough to get attention. But that's not important. Getting shot at is important. Attacking people in the middle of Marcus is crazy. There are too many houses and people, even in the middle of the day." She shuddered, seemingly lost for words.

Wiz spoke up. "Mills, I'm almost glad you're here, because we can't deal with that kind of collateral damage."

Mills frowned. "None us can. But I'm not as helpful as you think. I'm not here officially. I'm on medical leave."

Sam frowned, but with a tinge of concern. "For what?"

Deb matched her frown without the worry. Trevor was a rat and not worthy of a moment's distress.

"Nothing critical. Don't worry about it." Mills waved her concern away.

Sam crossed her arms. "Whatever it is, it better not impact our safety."

Wiz leaned forward, a crease forming between her brows. "None of that is true." Mills stared back at Wiz, stone-faced.

He was definitely hiding something. But Deb hadn't seen him for years, and his poker face had improved a lot.

Wiz's head tilted. "You can't tell us anything. That plus all the rest means you're undercover." She raised one brow. "Driving an official vehicle isn't smart, nor is showing us you have active surveillance. Or you're being very smart, and showing us without telling us a thing. One thing you'd better be truthful about—if, despite all my precautions, the feds can listen to this conversation, I need to know."

Mills' lips twisted up on one side. "Nobody can penetrate Victory Security's fortress without military grade hardware blowing a hole in the wall or a tow truck pulling the doors off, Victoria May Meadows Borde. The geeks try all their newest tricks and get nowhere."

Tom lunged across the table and grabbed Mills' tie. "Watch yourself. You're here on sufferance and I'll happily toss you out. Understood?"

Deb put a hand over her double-timing heart. She'd expected a violent reaction, but not from Tom. He'd been the epitome of cool, calm and collected, with the laid-back drawl of the local cowboys. Obviously, Wiz—whose real name must be Victoria—was a tender spot for him, which wasn't surprising. They didn't publicly display affection, but their love for each other shone like a beacon on a rocky shore.

Mills didn't struggle. "Yes."

Michael snorted. "You can quit trying to distract us with emotional tricks, Mills. There's too many of us here with different triggers. One of us will see through whatever cheap tactic you try."

Tom let go of Mills' tie and sat back in his chair. Nic nodded with an ironic smile, backing Michael's play. Wiz smirked. "If no one can listen in, then you can spill the beans."

Mills' shook his head. "My word means something to me."

Sam scoffed. "Your word is trash. You've proven that."

Deb agreed with Sam. Trevor Mills couldn't be trusted. He'd treated Sam like dirt. She could only hope he'd had his heart broken a dozen times while he was away. He was a capital R-A-T!

Mills sat back, crossed his arms, and clamped his lips together.

Wiz leaned a little closer to Mills. "If one of my friends is injured or dies and you could have done something about it, you won't have long to regret it. Your bosses either." Her menacing tone sent shivers down Deb's spine. Mills' expression didn't change, but he swallowed hard, a dead giveaway.

Wiz sat back. "So, we get no help from the feds. I'm sure, though, if we set up a trap, they'll be happy to roll in for the recovery and take all the credit. I've seen that before, and so have you, Mills. I don't care about myself, but don't forget what happened the last time you tried to screw one of my clients."

Mills opened his mouth, then slammed it shut. He knew something. Maybe she could harass him the way he was attempting to annoy all of them.

"Oh, don't worry." Wiz slashed her hand through the air above the table. "I know it wasn't you; you're just the fall guy. Doesn't mean you can't fall farther, especially when no one in your chain of command has your six."

Michael cleared his throat. "Hey Wiz, let's move ahead. We'll plan on the feds making the worst move possible at the worst time, and if we get something better, it's a win. I'll be happy if they just stay out of it." He turned to Mills. "Appreciate the save today. We'd have gotten away, but the chances of collateral damage were rising."

Michael shouldn't be thanking the rat. Helping others was his duty as an officer of the law. On the other hand, Deb admitted she was grateful Michael and Nic were safe.

Nic shuddered. "I expected a little old lady with a tiny dog to walk down the street in front of me every second the bullets were flying. I'll second the thanks, and the warning. Just stay out of the way. You're welcome to any and all credit if my family, our friends, and my town survive." He wrapped his arm around Kim's shoulders.

"And on that note, let's get everyone safe sleeping quarters." Pete tapped the table. "Nic, your family takes the guest house out back of here, where Deb was staying. Sam and Deb can stay at the Rocking B with me. Michael, Erin and Ryan, you can stay at the place across the road. We'll warn our ranch hands and lock the gates at the highway. Mills—"

"I'll be staying at Sam's house." The words resounded in the resulting silence.

Sam leaned forward and glared. "No, you won't. I don't remember offering and I won't. Stay away from my house. And me."

"Fine." Mills nodded. "Don't worry about me. I have accommodations."

Michael grimaced. "Mills, I warned you to stop playing games. I don't care about your former relationship with Sam, Wiz or anyone else. If you can't quit poking, then leave."

Deb was done. Sam had gone way above and beyond for her, and Mills had no right to act like an immature idiot. "Yeah. If you can't be useful, go. None of us wants you here." Mills didn't say anything or change his expression.

Michael tapped the table, the thud punctuating his words. "We need a strategy to push the mobsters out. We've got social media running, but it will take more than that."

Kim raised her hand. "I've been monitoring Deb's and some of the other businesses' channels. I'll push a few more locals to make videos, and I'm chiming in with encouragement and smashing trolls." She pointed at Michael. "You'll be doing a video with Nic right after this." Michael grimaced.

Deb couldn't quite see the grumpy ex-soldier making any kind of video. He certainly wasn't going to dance and lip synch.

"Kim, if you're willing to take the social media on, Sam, Tom and I can work a larger psyops campaign with you." Wiz smirked. "And I'll be truly grateful if you can take that part. It's a pain and takes a ton of time."

Kim's nose wrinkled. "Psyops?" Thanks goodness she asked, because Deb had no idea what it meant, either.

Mills said, "Psychological Operations. Winning hearts and minds."

Kim nodded. "Sure. I'm pretty good at that. I've got a script for Michael and Nic, kind of a knockoff of some HGTV stars. If I can get a few pointers on SEO and hashtags, that would be awesome." Michael and Nic pointed at each other, both mouthing "not me."

Deb snickered and bumped her shoulder into Kim's. "Sign me up. I love doing that stuff." And if she got some tips, even better.

Michael said, "So, that definitely takes psyops. What's our next move, operationally, especially Deb's bakery? Taking out foot soldiers is a waste of time. There's always more. How do we run our businesses *and* get Igor Koslov out of town for good?"

Wiz nodded. "The first part of that is psyops, too. I've put together a documentary-style video on Koslov. It still needs narration, but I've got a script. I was going to check with the feds, but since they're not cooperating—" she glared at Trevor "—we'll put it out tonight or tomorrow, and then we'll push it on a bunch of internet boards along with social media. The preppers and both extremes of the political spectrum will love it, because it will give them a no-kidding bad guy to target. But Igor will push back. He's given a lot of money to big-name charities just to kill these kinds of attacks. The other downside is we're likely to find more people walking around armed in Marcus. Most of them are harmless, but there will be some who aren't mentally stable, and most of them won't consider things like collateral damage. They'll be looking for trouble and trigger-happy, and they won't consider what might be behind their target."

"That's why the FBI would prefer you not release anything like that." Mills loosened his tie. "It often doesn't end well for the people producing the video or those around them."

Wiz sniffed. "It's more that Koslov has a bunch of feds on his payroll. Don't try to tell me otherwise—oh." She huffed a laugh. "That's why you're here. That's why you took the fall. The FBI is cleaning house and you're one of the brooms."

If Deb hadn't been watching Trevor, she would have missed the split-second glare he shot at Wiz. She was scary smart. But she'd better remember Trevor was a rat, and clever like one, too.

"Okay. We'll let you know most of what we're doing, but not all of it." Wiz raised her brows. "And you have no veto power, got it?"

Mills didn't change expression. Compared to him, Sam's face was a study in mixed emotions, until disbelief won. "I'm not buying it. Throw him out and let's get on with planning." She picked up her phone. "I'm closing my office and putting my assistant on paid leave. I'll suggest she take a vacation somewhere else and I'll work from here, if you don't mind, Wiz."

"No problem. The ranch and the neighbors have great internet too." Wiz put her hand on Sam's arm. "But Mills stays for now, sorry."

Michael said, "If nothing else, we can feed info back through him. But back to our businesses. If the organization continues to ambush our projects, Acer Home Improvement is done for. No one will want us near their houses."

Deb put a hand over her aching heart. He'd already taken so much time away protecting her.

"I don't think they'll try that again, Michael." Nic shook his head. "Not when it failed so spectacularly. Unfortunately, we owe the homeowners windows and siding, now."

Michael shrugged. "No big deal. The bigger problem is, we're still targets. They'll at least harass us, and we'll have to replace a bunch of tires and radiator hoses."

"I'll set up surveillance on your trucks and projects to catch the petty criminals," Wiz said. "Easy enough. Deb's is harder. She can bake wedding cakes and other special orders here, but our kitchen doesn't have enough capacity for large scale production."

Oh, to be in her bakery, sweating from the heat, the scents of a dozen different spices making her head light. Her heart ached with the desire for home.

Kim tapped her phone. "Her big customers are starting to whine. They were supportive, and still are, but they also need stuff to sell. They're going to other bakeries." She pouted and blinked. "I'm sorry, Deb."

She put a hand over her heart. Even though she'd expected something of the sort, the confirmation hurt. "I'm not entirely surprised. So, how do we get me back to work?" Deb tried to smile, but she was pretty certain no one was buying it.

Wiz turned to Pete. "Could the hands run the ranch next week?"

"Sure. I'm just the comic relief and since you rustled him, Tom's more trouble than he's worth." Pete winked.

Wiz leveled her gaze on Michael. "How about you? Could you get free next week?"

Michael shrugged and pointed to Nic. "I don't have a clue how my own business is running."

Nic shot a glare at him. "*Our* business. Anyway, there's a couple of things I'll need help with, but yes, for the most part, I don't need Michael. We can hire some part-timers or sub-contract if we have to."

Michael nodded. "We've got some people we use for bigger jobs. We can call them in, but we'll have to warn them what's going on."

"Of course." Wiz put her tablet on the table. "I've already upgraded the surveillance at Deb's bakery and I added some sensors and other tricks in the middle of the night so no one should know. I've also contacted the owners of the nearby businesses and buildings. The owner of the empty lumberyard to Deb's north said we can use his building for anything. We can even make physical changes to it. I suspect he'd be better off if the place burnt to the ground; it's been abandoned for so long."

She shrugged. "In addition, I've upgraded the alarms and surveillance on the bulk fuels place on the other side of Deb's, so he's also happy to let us use his property. With both of those under our control, we've got some good escape options, and we can enforce a clear zone around the bakery. But the fuel supplier is a real danger point because he's got above ground tanks, big ones. A bomb could take out half a block and start a fire that could decimate the town. But that's true of any gas station, to some extent."

Wiz leaned around Tom, looking at her. "Deb, I suggest you leave the dining room closed, and ask Michael to install a drive-up service window. Pete, we'll put you on the roof of the lumberyard next door with your sniper rifle. Make it very obvious you're watching, like a chair with an umbrella, and very obvious when you leave with Deb after she closes for the day. Michael, you and Tom can make her deliveries in the afternoons. After a week or so, Deb will start living in her apartment again. But we'll rig escape routes to both neighbors and keep hidden snipers on the next door roofs all night."

Ryan raised his hand. "I'll help with that one."

Erin nodded. "We both will."

Deb was so lucky to have so many highly skilled and brave friends. And she'd get to be back in her bakery. She couldn't wait, even if it meant sliding down an emergency escape cable again.

"I'll ask a few of my friends to help, too," Pete added. "The ones who are still able to climb ladders."

Michael was shaking his head violently. "But we've agreed that the foot soldiers are unending. So why bother? It puts Deb at risk for little."

She glared at him. They were risking everything for her, she had to do her part.

Sam smiled and flipped her long auburn hair. She must be recovering from her escape. "Ah, but it doesn't. Deb, you're going to narrate Wiz's video on Koslov."

Deb pointed at her chest. "Me? The Cupcake Woman who never does anything serious?"

Sam nodded sharply. "Yes, you. You're already the focal point of the campaign, so we're widening your role. And your previous levity will work in your favor. People will believe the change in tone." She pointed at Michael, rising from his chair with his fists clenched. "Let me finish. Koslov would love to target Wiz, but you heard that one—" she moved her accusing finger to Trevor "—it would take a military operation to penetrate Wiz's security. So we make Deb the face of the larger campaign and we push Koslov hard enough that he's as furious as you are right now." She quirked a brow at him.

Wiz broke in before anyone could respond. "In the past, Koslov has let his temper get the better of him. He's taken on enemies personally. That's what we're trying for here. If we can take out the man himself, his organization will be crippled, at least temporarily. They might target us for revenge later, but if the rest of my plan works, the feds should solve that problem."

Deb wasn't so sure that was a good thing. Michael was right about her defenselessness.

Michael clenched his fists. "You're making Deb into a target. A *soft* target. She can't hurt a mouse, let alone defend herself against a cruel man like Koslov. And even if he comes himself, he won't be alone. She'll die."

"I will not!" Deb jumped to her feet. She could admit her failings to herself but she couldn't let her friends down. Friends who were putting everything, including their lives, on the line for her. "I'm not an idiot."

Sam put both hands up, pushing toward the table top. "Calm down. Of course we're not risking Deb. Because it won't be Deb staying in the bakery."

Michael relaxed into his chair. "Well, that makes more sense."

"No, it doesn't!" Deb pointed at Sam. "You've all done enough. I can do this."

Wiz leaned over Tom and put a hand on Deb's arm. "Hey, we all have strengths. Baking is your superpower; ours is military-style operations. We all have a role to play. Trust me, we've got a great plan."

Deb sat, unable to withstand Wiz's logic. She had to believe in them as a team. Besides, she could admit, deep in her heart, that Michael was right. She used live traps even on rats; defending herself like a superheroine wasn't going to happen. But if someone else got hurt or killed on her behalf, it would be devastating.

Chapter 19

MICHAEL

MICHAEL, LITERALLY SITTING SHOTGUN in Deb's delivery van, sent Erin the "we're here" text and regripped his weapon, ready to fire if necessary. The Coffee & Cars garage door rolled up, Tom drove in, and the door rolled down again. Wiz, wearing a blonde wig, pink shirt and yellow apron, darted to the back of the van and the doors opened. Erin pulled the last two bakery boxes out and Wiz climbed in, closing the doors behind her. Erin checked her phone—looking through her garage's cameras—then raised the garage door.

Wiz buckled into the jump seat Erin had installed in the back of the van and put her tablet on her lap. "Go." Erin had also installed bullet-resistant panels around the jump seat, and they had panels they could pull into place and protect the cab as well. It wasn't an up-armored HUMVEE, but it was pretty good for a low-budget civilian vehicle.

Tom reversed and drove back to the highway, through Marcus, and to the bakery's back door. They were silent. Wiz concentrated on flying the drone and watching the surveillance, Michael looked for out-of-place vehicles, flashing lights, strangers with weapons or other oddities on the streets surrounding them and Tom drove, ready to move at a moment's notice.

After making the run for two weeks, it'd be easy to slack off and assume everything was fine. But they all knew better.

They turned off before the bakery, and drove the dirt roads of the older residential area east of her business, then bumped across the railroad tracks, and entered the narrow space between Deb's and the abandoned lumberyard. On the roof, Pete's sniper shelter was visible, but he wasn't. After taking too many drive-by potshots, they'd built sandbag and plywood bunkers with slit windows on both ends of the lumberyard roof, and added tons of surveillance cameras.

Tom backed the van to the metal double doors, and they opened outward, creating a shield for the rear of the van. Michael slid out, holding the shotgun ready and scanning the small parking lot and both sides for threats. Deb would enter shortly, Wiz taking her place in the bakery for the night. Deb wasn't happy with the arrangement, but the rest of them were. Even Tom believed Wiz was better suited for the dangerous night shift than Deb, but insisted on staying with her at the bakery.

Tom got out of the van and entered the bakery. Pete walked toward them, holding out his hand. "Hey, Michael."

Michael handed Pete the shotgun, then rounded the van to take the driver's seat. The van rocked slightly and the doors thudded shut. "I'm in." Deb's volume was low, but Michael heard her. Pete climbed in, putting the shotgun across his lap and belting in. "Secure."

Michael pulled away, the bakery doors closing behind them. He drove south, through the alley, and turned on to the highway, rolling in front of the bakery. Three hulking men stood on the sidewalk, spitting chewing tobacco on Deb's property. Shortly after Deb returned, he and Nic removed her chairs and tables and installed tall, skinny concrete pillars, stringing chains between them, so the jerks couldn't lounge around uninvited and the trespassing line was crystal clear. When normality returned, the pillars could hold a sunshade and lights, creating an inviting space.

Michael glared, but didn't bother calling and reporting. The Sheriff wouldn't do anything about littering or loitering, even if the men stood on the bakery's property. Shortly after Deb opened her new drive-up window, Koslov had organized a "denial of service" attack. He sent a dozen vehicles, with two men each, to drive around and around Deb's. Each time a new vehicle pulled up to the window, they ordered something Deb didn't have, then yelled about it. It was harassment, but there was little law enforcement could do except ticket minor traffic violations. After three days, the State police showed up. They pulled man after man out of the convoy for outstanding warrants and parole violations, based on the surveillance shots Wiz sent them.

The vehicle harassment stopped after that, but the next day, groups of openly armed men lurked on the sidewalk near the entrance. Anyone who attempted to turn into Deb's was blocked. Customers called the police, and they shooed the men away, reminding them that blocking access wasn't legal, but it wasn't long before Deb closed the window due to lack of use. Most of the people who frequented her shop weren't willing to confront the men, and those who were took it too far, either brandishing their own weapons, or bumping the men out of the way with their vehicles. Two customers were arrested, but not charged, and Deb decided to close the window before someone got killed.

Koslov's men lingered, reminding the town they weren't giving up. If they dared to encroach on Deb's property, one of Deb's guards would "test fire" bear spray, or paintballs filled with the same capsaicin mixture, driving them back. They carefully didn't aim for the men or off the property, but used the wind to their advantage when possible, drifting the peppery cloud into the men who started carrying gas masks.

The enemy attempted to stand in the way of the delivery van between the bakery and the neighbor's properties, too, but after a verbal warning, Pete, Tom, Michael and the others shot directly at them with the paintball guns, driving them off. After three days of that, the trespassing stopped, but the "legal" sidewalk harassment continued.

After Michael pulled onto the Eastside Highway, a motorcycle zipped past them and Michael waved. Another cycle lingered a hundred yards behind him. A friend of Nic's had retired from the same US Air Force RED HORSE squadron, and he'd formed a construction site security company. Since RED HORSE secured sites while constructing airfields in austere and hostile conditions, safeguarding sites on US soil was relatively simple. Copperline Security was happy to help; the defense of Deb's Bakery was excellent training. Plus, some of Copperline's clients had been threatened by Koslov and his organizations, too.

Michael and Nic built a basic bunkhouse in the abandoned lumberyard building. Copperline sent four people, rotating them every week, and since many of the employees were former RED HORSE, too, they made improvements on their downtime; the bunkhouse was quite comfortable. In addition to securing the bakery, and their convoy to and from the ranch, they provided personal security for Sam, Michael, Nic and the rest of them as necessary.

The convoy reached the Rocking B Ranch road without problems. The motorcycles turned back to Marcus, and Michael pulled into the ranch's new garage, built to shelter them from prying eyes and overhead surveillance. It was nothing but post, beams, and metal siding, but it worked, plus it kept snow off the vehicles. He, Nic and the Copperline folks had raised it in a day, with a little help from Pete's tractor.

Inside the house, Pete plopped into the recliner and rubbed his eyes. "Nap time for me. Wake me for dinner, will you?"

While Pete was enthusiastic, he was also older. If he wasn't offering to help with dinner, he needed a day off. Good thing they were meeting to discuss their next steps, because the routine was exhausting. And they all had businesses to run.

"Of course." Deb entered the kitchen, scrubbing her hands. Every evening, she finished dinner—usually a delicious slow cooker meal—and went to bed, ready to do it all over again at o'dark thirty.

Michael followed her into the kitchen like a lost puppy. She deserved a better guy than him, but she drew him like a moth to a flame. He'd happily burn, but he couldn't let Deb get scorched with him. "Deb, are you really okay? I know this isn't normal civilian life and it's got to be stressful."

She stirred the slow cooker—smelled like a spicy, South American-style stew—and pulled potatoes from a bottom cupboard. "I'm fine. I can't change anything, so I'll have to adapt and overcome, just like all of you."

Michael took the potatoes from her. "I can scrub and peel with the best of them. Why don't you sit and relax for a while? Read a book."

"Relaxing really isn't part of me these days." But she plopped into a dining room chair and pulled out her phone.

"Danger does that to you. Adrenaline makes you wired. The problem is, you get addicted to it. You've got to learn how to manage the highs and lows. I work out." Deb wrinkled her nose adorably. "Maybe cooking is the right answer for you, then. But after being on your feet all day, I thought maybe you'd like to be off them."

"Sitting feels good. But I am a little jittery, too." She scrolled, and giggled once, then bopped in her chair to some bouncy pop music.

He prepped the potatoes and put them on to boil with a little salt. Deb's giggles, gasps, and snickers were music to his ears; a little normality after weeks of tension. Too bad her good mood wouldn't last.

Once the potatoes were ready, he put them on the table, carried the slow cooker over and added bowls, glasses and utensils. Deb smiled at him, and woke Pete. After dinner, the three of them gathered in the living room and logged into the video conference Wiz set up. All of them looked tired, including the Copperline security team, nearing the end of their tour.

Wiz scowled. "Sam, Deb, do you want Mills to join us? I can keep him out."

"Up to Sam. She's the boss." Deb shrugged.

Sam's brows quirked, then she returned to professional-lawyer mode. "Sure. Maybe we can get something useful out of him."

"Doubt it," Wiz muttered. "He's using us, not the other way around."

Mills appeared. His professional face was good, but not perfect, and he winced slightly. He must have heard Wiz's comment. "Ladies, gentlemen, thanks for having me."

Sam's expression, already stiff, hardened into a mask. "If you have information to share, please do. If not, be silent." Mills nodded. "We will cut you out of the conversation as necessary."

Wiz sniffed. "Don't try to listen in, either. Neither you or your people will like the results. Sam?"

Sam looked down for a moment. "It's been two weeks of fairly low-level harassment. I'm sure Koslov expected us to break by now. We've upped the social media pressure on him; charities are starting to refuse his donations as dirty money, and his invitations to high society events seem to have stopped, because we're not seeing him on the gossip sites. We've rebuffed every one of his harassment tactics, too, although he's kept Deb's casual income lower and reduced the number of jobs the rest of us can take on, so he's had some success."

Mills raised a hand, and Sam acknowledged him. "Even though I'm on medical leave, my boss has been keeping me in the loop, so I don't accidently stumble into something and blow someone's cover. Koslov's associates and customers are pressuring him to pull out of Marcus, because they're getting too much attention. It's only his ego keeping him here. I think you can expect a more active and probably much more brutal attack soon. I don't know where or when; he's staying off the phone and internet. All communications to and from Marcus are via courier on his private jet. For the last two weeks, he's been staying at a luxury resort south of here, but his satellite internet system is acting up, and if he wants to keep up with business, he'll have to move soon."

Wiz almost smiled. "I noticed some military vehicles camped down there and saw a notice in the local paper of an exercise. How convenient."

"Nothing to do with us." Mills shrugged. "The military can't target Americans on US soil unless they're terrorists, so if there are interference problems, it's probably a poorly-adjusted system, or a training error. But that's why exercises are so important. I understand the terrain is challenging."

"Of course. I also noticed a lot of the people deployed with the unit aren't in uniforms." Wiz raised her brows.

Mills shrugged again. "Contractors, probably. Trying to work out the bugs."

They'd traded semi-disguised compliments long enough. Michael broke up their mutual admiration society. "Well, whatever the reason, making Koslov move is good. That, along with the pressure from his biggest customers, will anger him and force his hand. We can expect something violent, soon. But Copperline's made some great progress on physical security."

"We have." Gregory "Geo" Pappas, Nic's friend who owned Copperline, spoke up. "In addition to the concrete bollards in front of Deb's Bakery, we've installed pop-up barriers across the roads at the surrounding access points, metal shutters on the bakery's bottom windows, and integrated the controls into Wiz's security system. We've installed similar, but simpler gates at Coffee & Cars, and the entrance to the Rocking B Road. We can't do that with Nic's house, since it's in town, but I know Wiz upgraded the security system there."

"We'll remain in Wiz's guest house, Geo," Nic said. "Our lives are more important than a house, and it's insured."

"Mine's a rental, and there's not much there," Michael added. "Koslov probably won't bother. But I do think he's likely to go big. He'll attack everything simultaneously. And soon."

Mills nodded. Geo raised his finger. "I agree. I'm sneaking another team in. They're all new, but the regular replacements coming in are extremely experienced. They'll pair up. Pete, now would be a good time to pull in your buddies for daylight duties. I've got to tell you all, though, that the bulk fuel place to the south of Deb's worries me. There was activity there last night. It's a huge explosion waiting to happen, and could spread a fire through the whole downtown. Koslov would love to see Marcus burn. I'm surprised he hasn't tried it yet."

"He's tried." Wiz put a video up. Two men walked along the alley to the south of the bulk fuel supplier, carrying large backpacks. They reached the back fence, pulled wire cutters and snipped through the fence, squeezing through the hole. Both took off their backpacks, reaching inside and pulling out pressure cookers. Blue and red lights flashed, and the two men abandoned their bags, sprinting away. At the front, they split up, but more law enforcement pulled up and both were taken into custody. "This was last night. I believe, Mills, that those are FBI vehicles, not locals. This is considered a terrorist act, correct?" The video disappeared. "FYI, Mills. I allowed the infiltration into my surveillance. That can be rescinded at any time. Understood?"

Mills nodded. "Understood, but it has nothing to do with me. Yes, the men are being charged with terroristic acts. Tying them to Koslov is harder."

"You didn't alert my people, Wiz." Geo scowled. "They reported police activity, but didn't know why."

"No, I didn't. I shut them out, because I knew the feds were actively watching and planning a response. I didn't want your folks responding and possibly getting injured." A smile flickered across her face. "It wasn't as risky as you thought. The trucks coming in with fuel and log oil last week? Those were empty. They pumped everything out and took it to another location. Blowing up the empty tanks would still cause a large explosion and possibly a fire, but it's less severe. The owner would like to sell the place, but it's been used for decades, so environmental cleanup will be expensive."

"Wiz, I don't appreciate being kept in the dark." Geo glared. "My people are risking their lives here."

"You remember Tom and I are at ground zero, right?" Wiz sniffed. "But I won't do it again. I only did it this time because I knew the feds anticipated this and were ready to deal with it. They were already staged."

"You *knew*?" Mills' tone was accusatory. "How exactly did you know that?"

Wiz shrugged. "Doesn't matter. What does matter is what they, and you, do next. I don't know that. Do you?"

Mills glared but shook his head. "No. As I said, Koslov is using couriers."

"So have the FAA do a routine check on the aircraft, and use that opportunity to search for drugs." Wiz gave him a challenging stare.

"We don't need you teaching us how to do our jobs."

Sam clapped her hands together once. "Evidently, you do. So spill."

Mills glared. "I don't know what Koslov plans. I also don't know what the FBI is doing. I'm on medical leave, remember?"

Sam waved. "Since you can't help, I think it's time for you to say goodbye."

His mouth opened, and then his picture disappeared. Wiz smirked. "Good riddance." She sighed. "Geo, I really am sorry to keep your people in the dark. But I didn't want Mills to know how far I'd gotten in their system and I didn't want anyone becoming collateral damage.

So I showed your people old video and told them the two people were vagrants. Sorry, not sorry.”

“And how are we supposed to trust you now?” Geo glared.

Michael had the same question. Nobody had made Wiz commander, but she was too used to working alone.

“Because she’s doing the best she can with what we’ve got!” Deb leaned into the laptop’s camera. “We’re all tired. We’re all struggling. Let’s give each other a little grace, please. Because while I truly appreciate everything everyone is doing, the last thing I want is for us to turn on each other. That would be the biggest tragedy of all.”

“Except Mills,” Erin said, snickering. “The rust-picker can go pound sand.”

Michael laughed, Pete joining him, and eventually everyone did, too.

Eventually, even Geo cracked a smile. “The guy really is annoying. It’s like he’s trying to irritate us.”

“He is.” Michael remembered Geo hadn’t been in their first meeting with Mills. “Nic can give you the scoop later. The bigger problem is Koslov probably has access to military-grade hardware, at least grenade launchers, maybe anti-tank weapons. Wiz’s place can be defended, but not the rest. Do we pull everyone out for safety?”

Wiz said, “I’m digging into local area surveillance, trying to figure out where Koslov is keeping his people and his hardware. He’s at the fancy resort, but his lieutenants aren’t. I’ve caught a few meetings, more by chance or by watching the feds, but they're grasping at straws, too."

"A lot of the people he's using are day laborers or drug addicts looking for fixes, not mob enforcers," Nic offered. "We use day labor for some jobs. Let me ask around."

"Great idea, just be careful." Wiz frowned. "After last night's attempt failed, he'll be ticked. I bet we can expect another attack tonight or anytime over the next seventy-two hours. Tom and I will work with Geo's folks on escape route alternates; we all need to be packed and ready. Pete, bring the trailer with the ATV, tomorrow, please? We'll leave the trailer in the lumberyard. That way, Geo's folks can take the bikes for a fast get away and Tom and I will take the ATV."

"You got it." Pete tipped an imaginary hat to Wiz.

Michael said, "I'll hang out in your house's sniper perch tomorrow night, Wiz. Deb, you and Pete should sleep in Wiz's house. Nic, maybe you and the family move into the main house, too, in the basement."

Tom said, "There are blow-up beds down there, but I don't think there are enough for six people."

Pete shifted on the couch next to Deb. "I'll bring our camping gear up. But don't forget, he doesn't have to wait for night. He could have folks drive by with shoot and run weapons, hitting all the town sites tomorrow. Your current project, Michael, is a great distraction. It's in the middle of town, and destroying a historic home will upset a lot of people. They'll be scared, and they're likely to take it out on us, rather than the mob, who is even scarier."

A buzzer sounded and Michael jumped. Wiz tapped a few keys and Mills' face appeared. "Koslov's rolling a lot of vehicles south. They're spread out, trying to avoid notice, but with only a couple of routes available and rush hour traffic over, the change was noticeable, but it took too much time. You've got five minutes, tops. There may be others already in the area."

Michael rose. "Time to go. Grab your bags, Pete, Deb, and let's get to Wiz's house. Keep in touch, Wiz."

Deb put a hand on his laptop, keeping it open. "Sam, where are you?"

"I'm in my house. I've got a bag, and I'm leaving now." Her display bounced, like she was running while carrying her phone.

"Too late, Sam," Mills yelled. "Go out your back door and meet me at the back fence."

"What? Why are you in my backyard?"

"It doesn't matter. Move. Vehicles pulling up at your house now. Go!" Mills disappeared.

"Men." Sam's face got larger. "But I'm going. I'll check in later. Be careful." Her face disappeared.

Michael slammed the laptop closed and ran up the stairs, dropping it in his bag. He could only hope Mills would keep Sam safe, because there was nothing else any of them could do. He swept his pill bottles from the dresser into his bag, too, and grabbed his kit from the bathroom. He'd gotten lazy; everything should have been packed. His phone buzzed with a text from the Copperline number. "Deploying barrier at ranch road. One truck got past. Recommend alternate route to house."

Pete waited at the back door with his sniper rifle and his six-shooters strapped across his hips. Deb's footsteps pounded down the stairs. Michael grabbed their night vision monoculars and held one out to Deb. "Vests, both of you." He pulled his headset on, and slid the new earpiece in giving them comms with the group. "A vehicle got past the ranch road barrier. We can't take the road to Wiz's." He put on his bullet-resistant vest, the sound of Velcro loud in the mudroom.

"Michael, Nic. Getting the family in the basement, then I'll take the sniper perch. Got your six."

Michael double-clicked his microphone to acknowledge Nic's information.

Pete fastened his vest, and fumbled with his helmet. "We'll take the ATV out the back. I know a couple of alternates."

Michael took the lead out of the house and into the garage, scanning for movement or weapons. "Clear. Move."

Pete and Deb ran to the ATV, Pete taking the driver's seat. Deb put a foot on the tire, to hop in the back. "Deb, take the seat. I need the back to shoot from."

"Okay." She plopped in the seat and strapped in.

He climbed into the cargo area, bracing his feet against the short tailgate. "Lights off, go!" With the backpack still on, it wasn't comfortable, but secure as possible without a harness.

Pete fired up the ATV, bright flares making him wince for a split second, then green spots danced on the edges of his vision. Good thing Michael had been looking out the back. Hopefully, Pete and Deb didn't put their night vision gear on until Pete turned the ATV lights off.

They rolled forward, across the yard and past the small training corral. In his ear, Copperline reported multiple vehicles incoming to the bakery. Wiz said, "Do not fire until fired upon."

Red flared from the ATV taillights. They should have disabled those. The ATV bounced as Deb got out, opening the gate, and Pete rolled through. Michael said, "Don't use the brakes!" Deb closed the gate, and jumped in. The ATV bounced and jolted across the field, on a rough track. The enemy's headlights flashed when the vehicle pulled into the opening between the new garage and the old barn. Gunfire hammered the garage, metal pinging.

Michael raised his AR-15, but they bounced too much to fire back. The enemy's headlights shone on the ranch driveway, and then on the road to Wiz's house. He clicked his mic on. "Nic, vehicle inbound, shots fired on the ranch house; clear to return fire. We're taking a back route."

"Copy. Almost in place." Nic's panting was loud in his ear, then shut off.

"Shots fired at Sam's," Wiz reported. "Three vehicles stopping. Six personnel; two at front, four going to the back. No sign of Sam or Mills. Drive by shots fired at the lumberyard and bakery. Copperline, clear to return fire if vehicles return. Ranch, personnel cutting locks at south highway gate; two vehicles. Will blow culvert when they're on top."

Of course Wiz had rigged the culverts. Her paranoia was paying off, big time. The ATV's brake lights flared for a split second and they skidded around a turn. Shots zinged around him. He slid down, staying on his side so he could continue firing. With the odd movement, his back screamed and electric shocks jolted through his arms. His hands spasmed, and he dropped the rifle, but the tether to his harness meant it didn't go far.

"Heavy weapons showing at the bakery. Copperline, Wiz, Tom, get out!" Geo wasn't panicking, but forceful.

"Copperline, go," Wiz said. "Right behind you. Shoot." Static buzzed in his ear, and bullets flew by. If Wiz couldn't blow the culvert and he couldn't return fire, they were in a world of hurt.

Chapter 20

DEB SHRANK DOWN IN the ATV's seat. Any farther, and she'd choke herself when they bounced. Bullets zipped by them, but Michael wasn't shooting back. She twisted to the back; he was lying down. They must have hit him. She reached for Pete, but pulled back at the last second. They couldn't stop, or they'd all die. Wiz and Tom might be dead already, and Sam might not be safe with Mills, either.

"Deploying screen defense," Geo said.

Deb had no idea what that meant. The Copperline team briefed her on the concrete bollards out front, and the underground barriers that shot up to block vehicles at the exit and entrances to her property, but not a screen. Didn't sound very tough.

The ATV whined and slowed, the hillside growing steeper and the tires spinning. Pete turned the wheel hard to the right. "Too steep and slick with the muddy ice. Got to find a gentler slope." As they crossed the hillside, the whizzing of bullets stopped. The bad guys must not have night vision.

"I can get out and lighten the load. I'm small, no one will see me."

"No. The load isn't the problem. Hang on." They bumped and jumped, Pete turning around the random boulders in their way, and her body slammed into the straps. In the back, Michael remained down; he must be seriously hurt. They slowed, and rolled to a stop behind a large rock. Pete shifted into park. "Deb, get in and drive. I'm gonna take 'em out from here. Go straight up the hill and into Wiz's basement. Got it?"

But she'd never driven one of these things! She unbuckled and ran around the front.

Pete waited, rifle in hand. "Don't put your foot on the brake or they'll see you. Get Michael help. Drive fast, but not fast enough that you roll the thing. Don't use the brakes. And don't worry about me. I'm good at this." He crouched, running away from them, toward where the bullets had been flying. He hid behind a boulder and turned back to her, waving her on.

Deb was a baker, not a racer. She'd surely roll this crazy machine. But Michael was injured and he needed help. She climbed in the machine and strapped in, then examined the controls. *Don't put your foot on the brake!* That was hard; it was so automatic. She put her foot over the accelerator instead, and slammed the gear shift into drive. They jolted and rolled forward. But she had no idea where she was going, other than uphill. They drove gradually upward, and she steered around the increasing number of large rocks in their path. Ahead, thin vertical lines glimmered; it must be a fence. She turned sharply uphill, but the ATV's front end dropped, then jumped so violently, the steering wheel almost yanked out of her hands. Taking her foot off the accelerator, they crept forward, tilting and tipping back and forth precariously. The pasture was getting really rocky.

Or they just crossed a ditch. Light flared, and Deb pulled her foot off the brake. *Stupid!* She couldn't do that. She tried to turn uphill again, and they rolled on, relatively smoothly. But they got closer to the fence, and eventually, she drove into a corner. But there might be a gate...Deb squinted, but the green and gray all blended together. She took her foot off the accelerator, slammed the gear shift into park, unfastened the harness and climbed out.

Already bumped and bruised, jolting across that ditch meant she'd be aching later. She walked to the fence, but there wasn't a gate. The dark bulk of Wiz's house loomed above her. She returned to the ATV and put a hand on Michael's shoulder. "Michael, can you hear me?"

"Yeah." The word was more of a grunt.

"I can't drive any farther, because there's no gate." A boom made her jump. A second boom, with a flash on the edge of her night vision monocular that made her wince. Smaller, rapid flares from the bottom of the hill near the highway must be the bad guys shooting, but bullets weren't zinging by them. Pete had drawn their attention.

"Pete left? Because that was a large-caliber rifle."

"Yes. He said he was taking them out." Deb hated that the older man, who should be happily retired, was killing to protect her.

Michael pushed into a seated position, groaning. He must be badly hurt to let it show. "He's just taken out the culvert, I'd bet. Glad he knows what Wiz did to it. Open the tailgate so I can slide down, please." He pointed at the rear of the small box on the back of the ATV, his hand trembling.

Deb stumbled to the back, unfastened the latches on both sides, and the six-inch high piece of heavy plastic fell away, dangling below the ATV's bed. Michael straightened his legs and pushed with his arms. He fell, his legs collapsing, but hung on, staying upright. His rifle banged and clattered, Pete's boomed, and a chattering noise came from the bottom of the pasture; the bad guys shooting in return. Louder booms came from far above and behind them. Nic must be firing, too. She wriggled under Michael's arm to help him stand.

"No, don't do that. I'm too heavy."

Men. "Michael, you need help, so let me help. Did you get hit?" She slid her arm under his backpack and vest, gripping his muscular waist. Good thing he wasn't taller.

"No, it's my stupid back. The jolting made it seize. If I can get moving, it will loosen." He tried to pull away.

Deb tightened her grip. "Hold on. I'm stronger than you think."

"You're one of the strongest people I know."

His declaration warmed her heart, and hardened her resolve. His arm draped around her shoulders and she held back an exclamation at the load. The man was all muscle. "Okay, we move ahead to the fence, go through it, then get up the hill. Ready? Go." They lurched forward through the darkness, stumbling on the rough ground, taking tiny steps. Gradually, Michael's stride lengthened, and the weight of his arms across her shoulders lightened, letting her walk rather than shuffle.

At the fence, Michael removed his arm, and leaned toward the barbwire, but stopped. "I don't think I can bend enough to get through or pull it apart for you."

"What do you mean by pulling it apart?" Deb wasn't a rancher, and she'd never been into horses, so her experience with barbed wire fences was non-existent.

"You step on the second from the bottom strand, and pull up on the third, creating a gap. If they're loose enough, you can wrap the strands together so they stay apart." Michael panted.

He was in a lot of pain and it seemed simple enough. Deb stepped on the barbed wire strand, pushing it down to the fourth, and lower. "It's pretty loose. Can you get to your hands and knees, and crawl through?"

"It's the only way I'll get through, so yes." Buckles snicked and his backpack dropped to the ground, rattling. "Shoot. Too loud."

She doubted anyone heard pill bottles rattling with all the shooting. Leaving her foot on the wires, Deb turned to Michael and held out her hands. "Here, take my hands and I'll help you down."

"I think using your torso will work better, if that's okay." His tone was tentative.

"Absolutely." He stepped closer, and his big, strong hands clamped on her waist. She put her hands over his to hold him in place, even though her soft hips gave him a good place to hold. Any bruises would be worth it.

Grunting, he half-dropped to his knees, muttering something under his breath. He released her, and lowered his upper body.

Deb stepped harder on the wire, bringing both almost to the ground, and pulled up on the upper wire. Thankfully, all of them were loose, but the metal fence posts on both sides leaned toward them at an alarming angle.

Michael crawled through at an achingly slow pace. Finally, he was on the other side. The continual chatter and boom of gunfire stopped, and Deb froze. If they'd hit Pete, she'd kill all of them with her bare hands.

"Deb, Michael, Pete, where are you?" Nic's voice in her ear was calm, but urgent.

"Trying to get through the fence," Michael replied.

Pete said, "Hunting wabbits. On my way. Don't shoot me, kids."

Deb sagged with relief. He was okay. She released the upper wires, bent down and rolled Michael's backpack through. It caught, and probably ripped in places, but nothing fell out. She straightened, and jumped when a figure jogged toward her. It had to be Pete. If it wasn't, they were dead. "Pete?"

"It's me." He stopped in front of her, breathing hard, and put his foot next to hers, pulling the wires farther apart than she could. "Go, Deb. Nic, I'll help Michael. Can you open the gate through the horse fence and chainlink fence? Watch our backs, too."

"Copy. There's a vehicle pulling away at the bottom of the hill, but I'm scanning for foot soldiers. Horse gate is open."

Crouching, she maneuvered through, the barbs catching her backpack too, but it pulled free. She should have taken it off. On the other side, she stepped on the fence for Pete, but he shook his head and pushed down the top wires, stepping across. He held out his rifle. "Take it."

Deb gripped the gun, the wood smooth and oddly warm under her frigid hands.

Pete crouched and held out his hands to Michael, kneeling at his feet. Michael grasped his forearms. "On one. Three, two, one."

Groaning, Michael struggled to his feet, and wavered, his hands at his back. Pete grabbed the harness strapped across his vest. "Deb, can you get his backpack and my rifle?"

"Sure." She rested the rifle against the fence, and reached down for the backpack. Something zipped over her head, and she dropped flat.

"Down!" Pete went to his knees, helping Michael to the ground. "Nic, we're taking fire."

A series of loud booms sounded above them, spaced every second or so. "Haven't spotted them yet. Spraying and praying."

"Hard to do with hunting rifle." Michael chuckled darkly. "Need to move. Crawl. Leave my stuff, Deb."

With all his medications inside? Not a chance. She pulled the rifle off the fence and handed it to Pete, then grabbed Michael's pack.

Pete raised his rifle. "When I fire, go."

Michael turned over, used his rifle to get into a seated position, then brought it to his shoulder. "Nah, you go. I'll spray and pray better than Nic." Fire spat from his weapon, hot brass showered her, and the noise rattled her brain.

Pete yanked her arm, pulling her forward. Deb grabbed the pack tighter and sprinted. Pete ran crouched over, zigging and zagging, but slowing as the hill grew steeper. Deb's arms ached, and she could barely breathe, but they reached Wiz's outer fence, then the chain link fence gate, then the lower patio. They hid behind the massive rock pillars holding up the deck above them. Metal shutters covered the lower level windows and doors.

"Nic, Michael, we're safe." Pete panted in her ear. "Michael, go. I'll cover you." He raised his rifle, resting it on a rock protruding from the pillar.

Michael didn't answer.

"Michael, go," Nic said. Still no answer. "Pete, I can't see him. He's not at the ranch fence. I'm locking the chainlink gate."

Deb's heart dropped to her feet. He had to be okay. Her bakery wasn't worth his life.

Chapter 21

MICHAEL EMPTIED HIS MAGAZINE, then collapsed, his back spasming with the effort of sitting upright. He ejected and pulled another magazine.

"Drop it." A man's voice to his right. "Drop it now or lose your hands. Bloody stumps won't hurt your usefulness."

Michael released his grip, letting the AR-15 land on his vest, and dropped the magazine to the ground. They'd known Koslov had to have some smarter guys, and one of them just found him. The faint Slavic accent said the man was Bratva and ice formed at the bottom of his stomach. Probably brutally semi-professional; he wasn't likely to fall for simple tricks.

"Take off the earpiece, too, and the pistols. Slowly."

He pulled the comms from his ear, clicking it three times before dropping it. But he doubted anyone would hear it with Nic firing.

"Where's the girl?"

"Gone." Even if she wasn't, he wouldn't tell the enemy anything. He pulled the pistols, glancing at the man. He was in full battle rattle, including an AK-47, a helmet with night vision goggles and a better vest than his. Making a move would only get him dead, and once captured survival was the only mission.

"Up. Let's go."

Michael rolled to his hands and knees, and forced himself up, electric shocks rocketing through his arms and legs, and his lower back muscles seizing and releasing. The AR dangled from the strap. A knife flashed and the tether was cut, the rifle spinning away when a foot kicked it. He forced himself to his feet, pain rocketing through his body.

"Hands up. No stalling. Go."

"I'm not. Back's messed up bad. If you've got decent intel, you should know that."

A hand shoved his back and he stumbled forward, muscles giving out. Someone caught his harness, yanked him upright, and grunted under his weight. "March." A different male voice, the accent stronger.

Michael shuffled forward at the best speed his legs would make, even with the man behind him half carrying him. But the slower they went, the better, because Nic might spot him. He had to remember where his headlamp or flashlight was, and when he fell, turn one on. But his mind reeled with the lightning bolts shooting along his spine, and his muscles seizing and releasing without rhyme or reason. Escape was a pipe dream.

Nic's firing sped up. No, that was two rifles. Pete must be shooting too. The men around him—three of them—sprinted from boulder to boulder, while his captor/helper shuffled him along in their wake, waiting behind each rock until the three ahead of them reached the next. But as they continued downslope, the number of boulders decreased.

Just before reaching the next stone, the point man fell, the next dropping behind him, both dead still. The third, the man who'd spoken to him, made it to safety, sparks flying from the stone behind his back. He spun to face the two of them, raising the rifle. "You. Call them. You die if they shoot again."

Hands shoved Michael against the boulder, Kevlar whooshed, and a spot of cold hit the back of his head. The barrel of a pistol. He fumbled with the phone pouch on his shoulder strap and pulled out the flat rectangle, almost dropping it when his fingers refused to grip properly. He grabbed it with both hands, holding it out in front of him, face up. He had no way to know if the enemy remembered there'd be a light flare, but it was his best chance of escape. Gritting his teeth, he shoved his monocular up with the back of his hand, hitting the phone's on button at the same time, and launched himself forward into the open space between the two rocks. He landed hard, the phone bouncing out of his grip, the light flashing and tumbling away. A round showered him with rocks and dirt, and he low-crawled up the hill, blind in the darkness, his headgear gone.

Men yelled and rifles boomed and chattered. Michael forced his legs and arms to move, shambling along on his forearms and shins, digging his boots into the ground and shoving. On and up, he wasn't stopping for anything. His muscles quaked and fire sparked along his nerves. He wanted to rest behind a rock so badly, but without a weapon, he had no way to fend off an attacker. All he could do was stay in the open, giving Nic and Pete the best chance at the enemy.

He continued, breathing grass, moss, dung and dirt, his elbows and knees rubbed raw. If he stopped, he'd never move again, so he kept going. The boom and chatter of weapons stopped, and his breath rasped harsh and loud. Either Nic and Pete got them, or they were behind him, too close for Nic and Pete to fire. If the enemy had survived, Michael would be dead soon. He stopped, breathing into a clump of grass to stifle the noise. He had to assume they were still alive and looking for him. But he desperately needed rest.

If the enemy still had night vision gear, he was a sitting duck. But if not, once he recovered, he could move forward with more stealth. He concentrated on his breathing, slowing and deepening each inhale, despite the pain radiating from his lower back with each deep breath.

When his panting stopped, he listened for footsteps, but the gunfire had worsened his tinnitus to the point where the ringing in his ears was all he could hear. Time to move again. He slid his arms up, and shoved his toes into the dirt, thrusting his body forward, his muscles quivering like an aspen leaf in the wind. Even if the enemy was dead, he had to reach the house. There might be more of them, waiting, and putting others at risk to save his broken body was unacceptable.

"Michael!" A man's voice, low and forceful, but he wasn't sure whose. "Michael, it's Nic. Where are you?"

Michael slumped in relief. It really was his brother. He turned his head. "Here." He could barely croak. "Here!" The second try was louder.

A body thumped to the dirt next to him, and rolled him to his side. Nic. Michael flopped to his back, muscles loosening with relief, making the spasms and jerks worse.

"Thank God you're alive. Are you hit anywhere?"

"Close call, but no." He panted.

Nic grasped Michael's forearms. "I know you're hurting and you're not going to like me carrying you, but it's the easiest way to get you into the house with the least amount of damage. Ready?"

"Right on all counts. Go." Michael relaxed as much as possible.

Nic rolled Michael's body forward, putting a shoulder into his stomach, and rose, pulling Michael into a firefighter's carry. Michael tried to ignore the sharp, shooting pains, and the pressure on his diaphragm, and relaxed his body, making it as easy for Nic as possible. Despite that, the trip was painful for both of them.

Pete's voice made Michael raise his head, and drop it again. "If you need to rest, we can put him between us."

"Got it." Nic grunted. "Get the gate and the doors."

White light shined, and Nic lowered him to a lightly padded surface. He blinked up at the bright lights on the ceiling. "Oof."

A body dropped on his chest, arms going around his neck and a head with blonde hair blocked the illumination. Deb. She was safe. Despite the agony of misfiring nerves, he closed his arms around her back.

"You're alive." She snuggled her face into his neck and hugged him tighter, then pulled away again. "I was so scared." She cupped his cheeks in her hands, and lowered her lips to his, kissing him softly, passionately.

He responded enthusiastically, and their kiss didn't stay gentle for long.

Someone cleared their throat, and Deb raised her head, her lips rosy, her cheeks pink, and even more gorgeous than usual. Michael couldn't look away from her beautiful, smiling face.

"Hey, glad to see you two kids finally getting together, but we're not out of the woods." Pete stuck his arm down to them. "Let's go."

Deb kissed him again, quickly, then rolled away and stood. Michael grasped Pete and Nic's hands, ignoring their grins, and let them yank him up. They helped him out of his vest, and led him to a poker table in the corner, flipped to the plain top. Deb pulled out a chair, and he lowered himself into it gingerly.

She retrieved his backpack, flopping it at his feet and opening the top. "Which pills do you need?"

"All of them, probably. But right now, I need the one with the bright orange warning labels." He turned to Pete. "My back is in bad shape. The hard stuff is the only thing that will take the edge off now, but it tends to knock me out. But I'm not going to last without it. So, I'll do my best, but if I pass out, just put me on the workout mat and let me sleep it off. Sorry."

Pete shook his head. "Nothing to be sorry about. You survived. That took a lot of fast-thinking, guts and hard work."

Nic put a glass of water in front of him. "After that, I'd sleep for a week. If you can stay awake long enough to give us some intel and your thoughts about our next steps, that's a win." He brought up Wiz's conferencing program on his phone. The only face there was Geo's. "Erin and Ryan are fine, but we don't know where Mills, Sam, Geo's team, Wiz or Tom are."

"That's bad." He opened the bottle, shook out a pill, and swallowed it, then downed the entire glass of water.

Deb took the empty glass. "I'll bring you some food, too."

"Thanks." He needed something in his stomach to buffer the pills. Glancing at the time, he was amazed at how little had gone by. Action and survival stretched and compressed time oddly. But philosophy could wait. "The guys that had me were almost certainly Bratva. Good English with Slavic accents, carried Russian weapons, were comfortable with keeping a captive at gun point. I don't think they're used to military maneuvers or tactics, but they've had training of some sort. If I really had to push my assessment, I'd say they're not used to people fighting back. Even though they were semi-professional, there was a lot of anger and impatience."

"Matches what I've seen on job sites," Geo said. "At first, they can't understand how anyone can tell them no. Then they either react with brutal swiftness or withdraw. The second is pretty uncommon, and usually, someone higher on the food chain comes back later with the brutality. We've taken the fight to them several times, and that does get them to back down. They've also sent emissaries to me several times, trying to get me to agree to some sort of payment, but I don't talk to terrorists or bullies and that's the message I send back. So far, we're too small to be a real threat, but if we keep growing, I expect they'll try to bring the fight to me." He snorted. "Good luck with that. Anyway, my teams know how this goes. They're probably headed to you, or a safe house, or returning to the bakery. Do we have eyes on the bakery?"

"No." Nic shook his head. "I've tried to bring up the cameras, but I get static, darkness, or nothing, but I'm not an expert, especially on Wiz's system."

Deb put a plate with cheese, crackers, and fruit in the middle of the table, along with a pitcher of water. Michael poured for everyone, happy the pain had decreased, although his arm still trembled under the slight weight of the water.

She plopped into the chair next to his and brought out her phone. "Let me try. You might not have all the permissions you need at the bakery." She tapped away, slid through a few screens, and gasped. "Oh, no."

Chapter 22

"My bakery!" Deb dropped her phone on the table and put a hand over her aching heart. A huge, blackened hole gaped in the side where the brand new drive-up window had been. Fire trucks still sprayed water, and red and blue lights flashed. The room twirled, her stomach heaved, and she put a hand over her mouth.

Michael put his hand on the back of her neck, pushing her head between her knees. "Breathe. Four counts in, four out. In...out...in...out."

"It's not as bad as it looks, Deb." Nic's voice was sympathetic. "It's mostly cosmetic, although your sprinklers went off, so you'll be replacing some sup-plies. And the drive up is probably destroyed."

Deb didn't want to look. So much destruction. Her insurance either wouldn't pay, or they'd drop her. Or both.

"Agreed. It looks awful, Deb, but it's not too bad." Michael ran his hand up and down her back, soothing her. "Stay down there. I don't want you passing out."

"Plus, the net saved the front," Geo said. "Looks like it bounced the rockets back into the vehicles that fired them. I'm using those on every site from here on out."

"Net?" Deb swallowed and straightened, brushing her hair back with her hands. She couldn't afford emotional responses, not with their friends missing. "What net?"

Geo smiled from Nic's phone. "I put in an experimental net made of hardened cable and attached it to the concrete bollards with stiff springs. I deployed the net when I saw the launchers sticking out of the car windows." He chuckled. "And yes, they really were that stupid. Not only did the rockets mostly get caught and tossed back, but the idiots set the interiors of their vehicles on fire, because the back end of the launch tubes were inside the passenger areas. I still can't believe they were so dumb. The warning is clear; it's printed right on the launch tubes: keep the area behind the tube clear or risk incineration." He snorted. "Anyway, using the net was a tad bit risky, because if someone is straddling it as it springs up it's going to be painful and it can send the rockets bouncing across the street into the buildings on the other side. If the rockets are still thrusting, then they could do some real damage. Regardless, the springs flexed enough that each rocket was bounced back into the launching vehicles, just as designed. Perfect." He smirked.

"The cops won't like it, because of the possibility of collateral damage, but I think it's great," Nic said.

"Speaking of, I think your team just showed up, Geo." Two motorcycles rolled into the lumberyard to the north of her bakery, each carrying two people.

"They're calling. I'll check in later." Geo's face disappeared.

Pete's face creased with worry. "But where are my kids?"

There were four Copperline people, so Wiz and Tom weren't with them, and Pete hadn't had time to bring the ATV to the bakery. Which was just as well, since it saved their lives. But if Koslov's people grabbed Wiz and Tom, they were all in trouble.

"We'll keep looking." Nic scrolled through screens. "Good thing I got Wiz to show me a bunch of this stuff last night. Shoot. They got the project house too, Michael." The once-graceful house was a mess. The front door and windows were gone, and what she could see of the bottom floor was blackened. Red lights flashed; the fire department was still on scene.

"Dang it." Michael reached for the phone holder on his shoulder strap, but stopped. "My phone is out there somewhere, so I can't even call." He yawned abruptly.

Nic stood and squeezed Michael's shoulder. "I got it. I'll call the fire department first; we'll need to shore up that entryway. Maybe they'll help for safety reasons. Then I'll contact the owners tomorrow. You get some rest. We'll find your phone tomorrow." He walked away, holding his phone.

Deb searched the inside of Michael's bag. "Here's your laptop, at least." She opened it and slumped. A crack ran across the screen and the display flickered. "I'm so, so, sorry, guys."

"For what?" Michael turned toward her, grimacing. "None of this is your fault. It's Koslov's, for wanting what he didn't earn. He's a selfish ass."

"Well, that's true." Her phone vibrated and she pulled it from her back pocket. Miraculously, it had survived their adventures. A restricted number. Could be good or bad. She answered. "Hello?"

"Deb, it's Wiz."

She put a hand over her heart. "Thank goodness. Are you two okay?" She put the phone on speaker. "Pete and Michael are with me. Nic is nearby."

"We're okay. A little smoky, but fine." A current of amusement ran through her words. "We had to... liberate a vehicle, but we're on our way home. You'll have to lower the barrier at the road. I can't do that remotely from my phone."

"Liberate a vehicle?" Pete asked. "Never mind, just get here. I'll go sit in the sniper perch. The enemies here were pros; there might be a few still hanging around, hoping for a lucky break. I'm glad you're okay, kids. Drive careful."

"We will, Dad. Tom says he loves you, and I love you too."

Pete smiled. "I love you both. Get here soonest." He stood and picked up his rifle.

"I'll second that, Wiz. Be careful." Deb blinked back tears. It had been so close, and they still didn't know where Sam was. But Mills would keep her safe, even if he was a jerk.

"See you soon." The phone call terminated.

Nic returned. "Wiz and Tom on their way? I'll cover sniper duties, Pete, and get the road barrier. Take a load off." He trotted to the stairwell. "Michael, Copperline's folks are setting some beams to hold up the second story on the Victorian until we can get there. By then, the fire department should be done with the bakery, and they'll secure it." The door shut.

She was so lucky to have these wonderful people in her life. If it wasn't for her friends, she'd have been in the clutches of the mob already. But it cost them all so much, and she wasn't worth the pain, misery or money.

Pete put his rifle down. "Well, let's bed everyone down. Nic and his family have the blowup beds in the safe room." He pointed at the back wall of the basement. A faint red glow shone from an opening in the wall. "The love seat down here pulls out into a small bed and there's a big couch upstairs. It doesn't have a pullout, but it's huge and pretty comfy sleeping. Ought to fit you two without any problem. There's a bathroom with a shower down here, too." He crossed to the love seat and walked behind it, opening a storage chest.

Deb followed him, taking the blankets and pillows he handed her. "Thanks. You got enough down here for you?"

"Sure do. I'll help you get Michael up the stairs." He plopped a pillow and blanket on the couch.

Michael stood. "I'm okay. Drugs have kicked in. Tomorrow might be bad. We'll see."

"I'll be right there with you." Pete tipped an imaginary hat. "Old bones take time to recover and I haven't been on maneuvers like that in decades. See you in the morning." He turned back to Deb. "Come here, darlin' and get a hug."

Deb stepped into Pete's comforting arms. "Thanks, Pete, for getting us to safety. You're the best."

"It was nothing. You hang in there. We'll get through this." He squeezed her tight, then released her.

Deb turned, blinking away half-happy, half-sad tears. Her bakery might be in ruins, but her family was strong. She picked up her backpack and Michael's. "Come on. I'll come back for the blankets and pillow."

Michael sighed. "I wish I could spare you the trip, but I'll be pulling myself up the railing on those stairs. Actually, after crawling across the pasture, I desperately need a shower, first."

She smiled at him. "Don't worry about it." She carried his bag to the bathroom and shut the door behind him. Then she carried the bedding upstairs. The L-shaped couch had a double-size chaise lounge on the short end, so she placed a pillow and blanket for Michael there, and put hers perpendicular to his, so they'd be head to head. While she'd love to cuddle with him, she didn't want to hurt him, and with his back in such rough shape, it was an unfortunate possibility.

She trotted back down the stairs, and waited. Michael emerged from the bathroom in a cloud of steam and she took the pack from his hand. She followed him up the stairs, wincing at his agonizingly slow movements. On the first floor, he walked faster, and was soon settled on the couch.

"I'm going to shower, now." She reached out to brush her hand across his bristled cheek.

He put his hand over hers. "A kiss goodnight? Because I'll be out when you get back."

Deb grinned at him, put a knee on the couch and placed her lips on his. Firm but soft, his lips enticed and her heart warmed. She wanted to press harder and deeper, but he needed sleep. She pulled away. "Sleep well. I'll be right back."

"With that kiss to keep me warm? I'll be lucky to sleep at all." Then he yawned.

Deb giggled. "Sleep." She almost skipped across the floor. Even if everything else was going wrong, at least she and Michael were going in the right direction.

Chapter 23

MICHAEL

MICHAEL WOKE TO THE sound of popping grease. *Bacon.* He sat up, then collapsed again, fire shooting up his spine and radiating from his lower back. His elbows and knees burned too, and all his muscles ached. He'd avoided a migraine so far, which was a miracle. But to avoid more pain, he needed his medications. He rolled, gritting his teeth, swung his feet over the edge of the couch and pushed himself into a sitting position. A grunting moan came from his throat despite his determination to not let his pain show.

Deb, lying on the couch near him, raised her head and blinked. The most beautiful smile lit her face, then turned into a frown. She sat up, throwing off the covers. "You're hurting. Stay here, I'll get all your medications."

Crap. Deb deserved someone healthy, not a damaged grunt who'd be old well before his time. Still, he couldn't turn her offer down. She came around the edge of the sofa, carrying his pill box and a glass of water. Setting both down, she left again. He downed his meds and winced. He'd need the strong stuff to get through today. Deb hauled his backpack to him and opened the top, pulling out the correct bottle. "Thanks."

She smiled and opened the bottle. "One or two?"

"Just one. Two will knock me out cold." Although, with his pain level at a nine, it might not. But he couldn't chance it. Koslov was sure to retaliate for the failures last night. And if Koslov didn't, the Bratva guy who'd captured him certainly would.

Deb dropped a pill in his hand and he swallowed it, chasing it with the rest of the water. "I'll sit here for a few minutes until they kick in."

She sat and slid close to his side, but didn't press against him. "Let me know if anything I do makes it worse."

Michael chuckled darkly. "It'd be worth it. You're too good for me, Deb."

She blew a raspberry. "Right. The in-debt-to-her-ears baker who no longer has a bakery and has caused her friends a ton of pain and effort is too good for you. Hardly."

"Hey." He leaned his shoulder into hers. "None of that is your fault. It's Koslov's fault. We talked about this last night. He's a greedy jerk going to extremes to save face. And you, cupcake queen, have brought him to his knees. He's failing, because an adorable blonde baker has outsmarted him at every turn. The attack last night will bring attention he can't stand. The publicity will be overwhelmingly bad, and any politician or cop he's paid off won't be able to support him. Unless the head of every single federal agency is in his pay or under his thumb, he won't survive this intact. I'm sure new investigations have started already."

Clapping sounded behind him. "Nicely said." Nic and Kim sat on the coffee table in front of them, and the rest of the gang gathered around. "Both fires were ruled as arsons, already." Nic smiled wryly. "Obvious, I know, but those determinations usually take time. The FBI has declared it terrorism and they've sent senior special agents to assist the investigation. So has the ATF. Since they used military hardware, the Army is investigating supply chains and logistics. The Sheriff and DA are sweating bullets, and falling all over themselves to be helpful. Guess the threat of prison for terrorism is scarier than Koslov's goons."

"They're not admitting anything, though. Just pretending to cooperate." Wiz scowled. "Jerks."

"The national news has sent teams too." Kim showed them her phone. The headlines screamed "Sweet Baker Barbequed! Burned by the Baker!, Save Deb's Bakery Today!" and a plethora of other catchy titles. "They all want interviews with you, Deb. But the FBI is insisting you need to talk to them first."

"Not without my lawyer!" Deb scanned the group. "Where's Sam?"

Wiz shook her head. "Haven't heard from her or Mills. I'm assuming Mills got a credible threat against her and went dark."

Deb frowned. "I'm not sure I trust Mills that much."

"Don't worry. He's not going to hurt her; he's in love with her, plain as day." Nic raised a brow. "He's got a lousy way of showing it, but he'd do anything for her."

"Not so sure I buy it." Erin plopped down on the couch next to Deb. "And even if it's true, he broke Sam's heart. Shattered it. I'm not sure she can or should forgive him."

Deb nodded. "True. And I don't want to talk to federal authorities without a lawyer."

Tom shook his head, standing behind Wiz. "Then you don't. They don't have any right to compel you. And they've got no standing for a subpoena. You've been extremely open about everything happening, and Wiz has shared more than they can reasonably expect. Especially after everything they've put her through. If they insist, you simply keep telling them no. The law is on your side, not theirs."

Deb twisted her hands together, and Michael put his over both of hers. "He's right. Don't worry about them or the news."

"Hey, no worrying about anything except eating!" Pete bellowed from the kitchen. "Chow's on."

"Awesome. I could use more coffee." Deb hopped up and offered both hands to Michael.

He put his big paws on her small, but tough hands, and stood without putting any pressure on her. The meds must have kicked in a little, because while it hurt, it wasn't agonizing. Hanging on to her hand, he followed Deb to the table and sat gingerly.

They ate a rancher's breakfast of bacon, eggs, hashbrowns and more until they were stuffed. Pete brushed away their compliments, but his smile was clearly pleased.

After they cleared the dishes, Kim settled her girls on the couch with homework and Tom moved to the end of the table. "Since Sam isn't here, and I used to be pretty good at the PR game, I'll chair this meeting of the Cupcake Woman Protection Society. First, we owe the public an update, especially those who donated. Kim, can you work that with Deb?"

"Sure will." She raised a tablet. "Made some notes already based on the publicity."

"Pete, you, Wiz, Nic and Michael, along with Geo, can work on resecuring our house, the Rocking B, the bakery, and the Acer project house."

Michael didn't want to admit it, but he would be worthless today. "The priority order is correct. But, I'm a liability out there. Can't move fast enough."

Nic shook his head. "We'll be surrounded by feds today. It's more important that Deb—and you, supporting her—are seen out there, directing the cleanup. And actually, Tom, what I'd like to do is split our forces. Michael, Deb and I will go downtown. You, Wiz and Pete work up here, with Kim and the kids staying here too. I'll get Geo's folks to help us; he's sending more for the next week or so anyway." He turned to Kim. "And yes, dear, I'll get some video of Deb inspecting her bakery. I know we need to reward everyone. We'll get some shots of Geo's crew, too, since those donations are paying for his services."

Deb raised her hand. "If you need help with the ranch gates and fences, I bet Erin and Ryan would come out."

"Inspection first, then we'll see." Pete nodded slowly. "I think we'll find some bullet holes, but not much else. They didn't use any rocket-launched weapons or grenades here, they just sprayed the place with bullets. Plus, the new shed at the house will have soaked up a bunch of those rounds. The ATV is the only thing that might be done for."

"Use ours, Pete," Wiz said. "It's faster."

"But not as useful." He frowned.

Sounded like a well-worn argument. Michael put his hands on the table and levered his body up. His shoulder and arm nerves ignited, but he made it to his feet. The meds were working. "Nic, you and I can trade off telling the feds and the press "no comment" and blocking them from Deb while she gets a good look at everything."

"Actually, I'd be better at that." Kim grinned. "I can get one of our usual babysitters to watch the kids if that's okay with you, Wiz."

Wiz smiled, a real smile, and once again, Michael was dumbstruck by how beautiful she was. She said, "If they're okay staying here with just us, I'm sure we can keep them entertained for a couple of hours." She reached for Tom's hand and gripped it. "We've been talking about adopting a pair of girls, members of one of the local tribes. It would be good practice."

Michael smiled despite his pain. That would be an amazing gift for everyone involved.

Kim grinned. "That's awesome. Let me talk to them. Isa's easy. Sophia? Sometimes. But if they're okay, I'm okay. Nic?"

Nic chuckled. "You may find yourselves regretting that offer in the future." He watched his wife walk away. "We can always use more help now that Deb's so busy with her business." His smile died. "Sorry, Deb."

She shook her head. "It's okay. We'll see how it all looks. But right now, I'm not sure I want to reopen."

Michael squeezed her shoulder gently. He couldn't blame her. "Wiz, do you have another vest that will fit Kim? Even if the feds are surrounding us, I don't think any of us should be out there without protective gear." He grimaced. It was too dangerous to have both parents out there. "Kim should stay here."

"I'm going." Kim pointed at him. "I've got to get out there sometime and today will be safer than tomorrow."

"She can wear mine. I'm not going anywhere." Wiz shivered.

Tom put his arm around her shoulders. "Nic can wear mine." He huffed. "Still can't believe I've got a bullet-resistant vest at all, especially in the middle of nowhere, Montana. But it's good to be prepared."

Michael nodded. "Agreed. Thanks for buying extras. I hope we can find the gear I lost last night, or I'll owe you a replacement."

Wiz waved her hands across the table. "No, don't worry about it. Just come back safe."

"Will do." After cleaning up, he joined Deb and the bakery crew downstairs, putting on vests and checking weapons. His previous AR-15 was still out on the pasture along with his phone, but Wiz had plenty of extras. He adjusted Deb's vest; survival and not baking had tightened her abs and built some leg strength. Being stronger was good, but he'd be happier when she was back to baking full time. If she wanted to keep the muscle, the gym was a safer way to work out.

Once appropriately attired, they took Nic's SUV to town. Michael warned the Copperline folks they were inbound, and they'd come in from behind the lumberyard. Nic drove through the delivery door and into the cavernous warehouse, parking so they could drive away easily, and they all got out.

Nic strode to a tall, dark-haired man with the face of a Greek hero. "Geo! What are you doing here?" They shook hands.

Geo grinned, his teeth blinding white in his deeply tanned face. "All my other sites are quiet. This one? Not so much."

Michael joined them, and shook. Then Nic introduced his wife and Deb.

Geo kissed the back of Deb's hand. "Finally, I meet the lovely Deb. It's such a pleasure."

Gratitude turned to jealousy. Michael held back his instinctive lunge to break them apart. He wasn't a caveman.

Deb chuckled, but slid her hand from his. "Such a charmer. I am very pleased to meet you. Thank you for all of your help. I know I can't repay you, but let me know if you need custom cupcakes or birthday cakes, or anything else."

"Of course, sweet Deb." He turned toward her bakery and swept an arm out in half-bowing motion. "After you."

Michael jumped in front of her, wincing at the electric shock the movement caused. But Geo's chivalry could get her killed. "Me first. I don't care if the Secret Service is out there, I'm checking it out before you leave the safety of this building."

"My people are already out there. We've got it covered." Geo's voice was desert-dry. "And the Fire Marshall cleared us for entry."

Michael didn't care. He opened the door, emerging onto the expanse of asphalt in front of the lumber yard and surveyed the bakery and surroundings. The stench of burned building and the blackened hole covered by particle board, drew his attention first, but he didn't linger. On the bakery roof, one of Geo's people watched the perimeter with a rifle. Behind the bakery, another of Geo's people faced away from them. An older red SUV with the words "Fire Marshal" on the door sat in the bakery's small front parking lot, along with a couple of big black SUVs with US Government plates. Eight or so people stood in the former outdoor seating area, wearing FBI, ATF, and Sheriff's jackets. Cameras lined the sidewalk, reporters in open coats over fancy clothes yelling questions. He turned back to Deb and Kim. "Lots of reporters and Feds. Are you ready?"

Kim pushed in front of Deb. "Yes. No comment for now."

Michael walked out, holding his new AR-15 pointed down, with his finger off the trigger. Keeping his head on a swivel, he walked to the back of the bakery, ignoring the shouts from the reporters. At the back door, he stood aside to let Deb enter the codes.

"Hey, you can't go in there! Federal crime scene." A heavyset man in a windbreaker wearing a tactical vest and a sidearm hustled toward them.

Nic stepped in to block him. "She's the owner. You can't keep her out."

"Yes, I can. Miss Boulanger, you need to talk to us."

"Not without my lawyer present." Deb's voice was loud and clear; the reporters on the front sidewalk could probably hear. "I don't trust any of you. None of you took my reports seriously. It's only now that the news is here that you care. Since you have Victory Security's footage, you're not going to learn anything new from this crime scene. And finally, it's 'Ms" not "Miss," got it?" She pulled open the doors, blocking the FBI man and not waiting for his sputtered reply. The roar of the reporter's questions had quieted, but when Deb finished, they surged again.

Michael put his arm out, stopping Deb. "Me first. Wait." She nodded and stepped to the side. The bakery was dark, so he pulled a flashlight with his left hand and swept the area. Deb gasped, a pained noise. He wanted to pull her in close, but had to ensure her safety first, and Nic was busy blocking the obnoxious fed.

The bakery was a mess and reeked of burned plastics. To protect their lungs, they'd have to wear masks while working. The wall that separated the customer service area from the bakery was a splintered, scorched pile but the supporting columns appeared intact. Soot covered everything, and puddles shimmered darkly across the floor. The front windows were shattered. The tick-tock of water dripped; probably a sprinkler that didn't shut off completely. Fortunately, since the enemy targeted the drive-through window, the worst damage was confined to that exterior wall and the dividing wall. They'd have to check everything carefully, but the expensive ovens, refrigerators, and freezer may have survived. A few cooling racks were bent, but they could probably straighten those.

He walked farther inside, checking behind the debris pile, inside the walk-in cooler, and bathroom. With that complete, he trod upstairs to Deb's apartment. At the door, he wiped his feet, knowing it was mostly use-less, and opened the door. Pictures were knocked off the walls, and ceramic and glass was shattered in the kitchen. The bathroom seemed intact. He retreated, try-ing to keep his dirty footprints to a minimum, but soot darkened the walls and everything else. Probably just as well Deb hadn't bought a mattress, because cleaning was going to take a lot of time and effort.

He returned downstairs, to Deb's side. Kim had wrapped her in a hug, but Deb's eyes were wide, proba-bly with shock. The vests both wore made the embrace look awkward, but protection was important. Nic and Geo blocked the feds at the back door.

"She already told you. She's not talking without her lawyer present. Period. Now go away, and let the woman mourn in peace." Nic shut the door in their faces.

Michael shoved his emotions away, and looked at the building from a contractor's perspective. "Deb, I know it looks awful, but this is mostly cleaning. The drive-up window is a loss, but you weren't using it anyway. The dividing wall is mostly cosmetic and the load-bearing pillars are intact, so it's a simple rebuild. We can muck it out, get a restoration company for heavy cleaning, then we'll check the equipment. But you can be back in business pretty quickly."

"But only if you want." Kim hugged Deb tighter, then stepped away. "Maybe it's time to move on to some-thing different. Or go smaller, or bigger. See this as an opportunity to change anything you didn't like before."

Deb meandered through the dark, dirty space, touch-ing the scorched signs and charred decorations. She wrapped her arms around her waist. Kim joined her, then shot a look at Michael.

He wasn't entirely stupid. He crossed the debris-laden floor, pushed the rifle to his side, and stepped up next to Deb, opening his arms. "Need another hug?" She pressed her vest to his, and slid her arms around his waist, gently. He wrapped his arms around her upper back, rubbing her shoulders and upper arms, where the vest didn't block his touch, and ignored the jumping muscles between his shoulder blades. "I'm so sorry, Deb."

The beeping of a truck backing up came from the back of the bakery, and the murmur of the crowd increased. Stupid reporters, trying to profit from sorrow. They could all go pound sand. He tightened his arms and laid his cheek against her hair.

"Deb, you need to see this!" Nic laughed. "People can amaze you, sometimes."

Kim trotted to the door. "Oh, wow. Deb, come here. Nic's right."

Michael squeezed a little tighter, then released her. She stepped away, and trudged to the door. In the door frame, she jolted, and raised her hands to her face. Cheers and clapping grew louder.

Despite the pain jolting along his spine, Michael trotted to catch up, and couldn't help smiling. Outside, people lined up, holding shovels, brooms, and cleaning supplies. Marcus Hardware handed out N-95 masks, gloves and hardhats. Erin and Ryan held clipboards, getting signatures from each volunteer. Probably a liability release, which was smart. A huge dumpster waited for debris with a small skid steer in front of it, two people in high-vis vests standing nearby. Local churches set up tables with snacks and coolers full of drinks in front of the lumberyard, and more volunteers put up chairs and tables for people to eat at. A food truck was setting up, and a huge grill on a trailer was backing into the slot next to it. Marcus Fire pulled an ambulance into the area between the food truck and the church group, probably for first aid. Down the alley, hoses and pressure washers rolled out of a local cleaning company's van.

Deb grinned through the happy tears rolling down her cheeks. Erin gave the clipboard to a woman, and jogged to join Deb, pulling her forward. "And here she is, safe and sound. Please welcome Deb Boulanger, Cupcake Woman!"

People whooped, hollered and clapped, while Deb wiped her cheeks. Cries for a speech rang. Deb raised her hands and the crowd quieted. "Thank you all for coming. I can't believe it! I'm so, so grateful and I can never, ever repay you. Thank you so, so much." The crowd clapped and yelled. Deb turned to Erin. "Did you set this up?"

Erin laughed. "No. The county volunteer disaster response coordination group contacted me. They had people willing to help, but someone had to organize the effort, because most of the leaders are busy with flooding in eastern Montana right now. Ryan's had a little training, so he took command. Each organization took a specific job. And the local businesses are grateful you took the mob on."

Deb hugged her. "Thank you so much."

"It's literally my pleasure. I'm thrilled so many people stepped up." Erin hugged her back.

Geo sauntered to them, his hands in his pockets, with a huge grin on his face. "The feds are pissed, but the Fire Marshall and your insurance adjustor released the scene. Don't worry, my folks are staying on overwatch, and I'm directing the downstairs cleanup so no one takes out a support column. That's really why I'm here. Erin's coordinating the apartment cleaning."

Michael didn't like how flirty Geo was, but he couldn't complain. Geo had gone way above and beyond, and especially with cleanup, a thankless chore. Michael was lucky to walk; shoveling wasn't going to happen.

Erin pointed at a canopy with a few chairs set up next to the lumberyard's wall, facing the bakery. "That's where you're staying, Deb." She held up a hand when Deb started to protest. "We need you to decide if we should try to clean items, or get rid of them. If it's obviously destroyed, it's going in the dumpster, and you'll never see it. But you'll have to make a lot of decisions, and we need to know where you are."

Kim led her there, and Michael followed. He'd play bodyguard, while Geo's people took the sniper positions. Kim pointed at a high, director's style chair. "If you can handle it, we'll bring the press here too, singly or in small groups. Invite only and some of them won't be getting the call." Her lips compressed.

Michael chuckled. "Just let me know who to escort away, and I'll be happy to help. I won't be good for much else, that's for sure." He'd anticipated a long day and brought more meds, but he still wasn't up to hard physical labor.

Deb put a hand on his arm. "I'm happy you're here. I need the moral support more than another shoveler. I can't believe so many people showed up!"

"I can. You're a mainstay of the community, and a ray of sunshine in the gloom." He forced his gaze to her surroundings, grateful Deb's chair backed against a sturdy wall. "We should block the street view of Deb with something."

"Not unless we have to. The view keeps the vultures occupied." Kim pointed at the reporters on the sidewalk.

"They make great soft armor," Nic muttered. Kim smacked his arm, but she and Deb chuckled. "Besides, no one will attack the press. Not if they want to survive. It's a bridge too far."

Kim patted the arm of the chair. "But if you get overwhelmed, let me know. We can move inside the lumberyard."

Deb shook her head. "No, let them see. Maybe it will help, but whether it does or not, I'm done hiding. If Koslov and his leash-holders want me, they'll have to come themselves. And I'm not changing my mind, so they may as well stay away."

Michael leaned against the lumberyard's brick wall. Deb was so incredibly brave. But when the publicity died down, the bad guys were likely to return. Their organization looked weak, and they'd have to rectify that or the other wolves might attack.

While a mob war wasn't good for anyone, Michael rather hoped another organization took Koslov out. It was the only way for Deb to remain safe.

Chapter 24

DEB SNUGGLED UNDER THE blanket on Wiz's couch, her throat sore from talking to volunteers and reporters all day. With Nic's family still downstairs, she'd suggested they use the guest house, but Michael and Wiz said no. The couch was comfortable and Michael's presence comforting, but a real bed would help Michael's back. As the day had worn on, he'd struggled with the pain. Most people wouldn't notice, but the tight expression, refusal to sit, and stiff movements told her he was suffering. Nic had spelled him, sending him to rest in the bunkhouse after lunch, but he'd been back within an hour.

Worrying about him helped her deal with inspecting the ruins of her life. Most of her bakery's decorative items, gathered over the years, were destroyed. The customer seating and glass-fronted bakery case were toast, and the windows and doors needed replacements. Most of her equipment seemed to have survived intact, and the volunteers had done an amazing job of cleaning the mixers, racks, utensils, pans, and everything else she needed. Michael and Nic both claimed they could fix the shop and have her baking in less than a week. If she wanted to.

Her apartment had fared better. Marcus Laundry was cleaning her clothes and other home goods, and offers of furniture and other things poured in. Volunteers had swept up the broken glass, cleaned and painted her walls; once the window glass was replaced, she could move in.

But she wasn't sure she could ever live there again.

Nor was she sure what to do next. A Marcus Bank employee brought a letter explaining her initial loan review had been completed without issue, but since she was "connected" to a criminal enterprise, they could no longer service her loan. Invoking the criminality clause in her contract gave her two weeks to pay the loan in full, transfer it to another institution or default and have a lien levied against her for the full amount. It took a lot of gall for Sharlene Murphy to send that letter when she was in bed with Koslov and his bosses and Deb was the victim, not a co-conspirator. Erin was livid.

"Deb, are you okay?" Michael's voice was soft, and slightly slurred; probably exhaustion or the medications.

"Yeah, I'm fine. I'm just trying to figure out what to do next." She couldn't imagine any bank taking the risk and begging made her shudder. But she couldn't live with thousands of dollars of debt and no way to repay it hanging over her head either. The only thing she knew how to do was bake. But bakers didn't make much working for others.

"Unfortunately, figuring that out isn't going to happen tonight. You're going to need time to process everything. Maybe some counseling, too. Tonight, try not to worry too much. Do you know how to meditate?"

That seemed like an odd question from the tough soldier. "Some. I learned some basics from YouTube." Back when she'd first opened, anxiety had kept her awake. Desperate for sleep and without the money to see a doctor, she'd turned to the internet for answers. It wasn't perfect, but it had helped.

"Time to use those skills. I find it's very helpful on nights like this, when my mind won't quit, but my body is exhausted." He yawned.

She chuckled. "I can sympathize with that. Okay, I'll give it a shot. Thanks, Michael."

"Of course." He shifted and looked down at her, then dropped a kiss on her forehead. "Sweet dreams." The couch cushions moved against her head when he plopped back down.

"Sweet dreams." Deb concentrated on her breathing, and eventually drifted to sleep.

After a long night of intermittent sleep, Deb rolled off the couch and padded to the kitchen, turning on the coffee maker and setting the ovens to heat. After everything her friends had done, the least she could do was make them something delicious. At midnight, she'd gotten up and made a pan of stuffed French toast she could bake in the morning. After that, she'd slept better.

She put the French toast in the oven, and made a couple of coffee cakes as well, one of them low-sugar and high protein. Then she put together an egg, sausage, potato and veggie casserole, and slid that into the oven to bake. In an hour, they'd have a delicious breakfast. Deb poured another cup of coffee—her third—and sat at the breakfast bar. If the metal shutters were open, she'd stare out the window, but Wiz wasn't willing to risk it. And Deb couldn't blame her. She scrolled through social media instead. Just like Kim had been doing late into the night, she deleted and blocked trolls, then she "loved" all the supportive comments on her multiple posts thanking everyone for their help and replied when she could.

Her first timer dinged, and she ran to turn it off, but she was too late. At the far end of the house, Michael rolled off the couch with a faint groan. She pulled the French toast and cakes out, glanced at the time, and grabbed coffee cups, cream and sugar, lining them up on the breakfast bar. Even without the oven alarm, the temporary residents of Wiz Manor would show up shortly, drawn by the delicious smell. She poured, and as expected, her friends appeared within minutes, muttering quiet greetings. Michael grabbed the first coffee, raising the cup to her in thanks. She smiled, but didn't reply because Nic and Pete showed up, with Tom and Wiz behind them, closing the door softly to avoid waking Kim and the girls.

The second timer dinged and she pulled the casserole from the oven, putting it on the table. Then she added the rest. Plates were filled, coffee replenished, and gradually, chatter rose as everyone fully woke.

"When did you make all this, Deb? They're delicious." Nic lifted a bit of casserole.

Michael rubbed a hand over his face. "Way too late last night and too early this morning. And no, Deb, you didn't keep me awake. I just wish you could sleep."

Her phone buzzed and she picked it up, bringing up the group chat, a motion copied by everyone around the table except Pete.

Geo: Fire alarm at the old lumberyard. Assessing and preparing for evac.

Koslov's idiots needed to give up, already! Her anger was tinged with fear. She'd learned that an alarm wasn't always what it seemed. It could be real, or triggered to flush people out, or both. But Geo's Copperline people knew that better than she did.

Nic cursed under his breath and showed Pete the warning. Michael shoveled his remaining food into his mouth and stood, his motions jerky. He was probably in a lot of pain this morning.

Wiz swiped at her tablet. "Got incoming. Full battle gear, people. Nic, Pete showed you the tunnel out, right?"

"Yes." Nic shoved his chair back and ran for the basement door.

"You're coded into the system and cleared to use anything in the house. Stay in the safe room unless one of us tells you to leave." Wiz yelled down the stairs, then ran up, Tom on her heels.

Deb jogged to the kitchen and pulled a plastic cake pan out of the back of a cupboard. She loaded it with food, adding spoons and paper towels. The kids and Kim wouldn't go hungry.

Michael yanked the box from her. "Get downstairs. You're with Nic and Kim. Hurry."

Deb hesitated, wanting to do more for the kids. But she couldn't if she was dead. She ran to the couch, grabbing her pack, shoes and vest and bounded down the stairs.

Nic waited at the cutout in the wall, Michael standing next to him with her box of food. Both wore vests, helmets, backpacks and weapons. "Kids are in the bathroom with Kim. Thanks for thinking about them."

"Be right back." She ignored Michael's yell, because she wasn't crawling through a tunnel with a full bladder. She waited, and less than a minute later, Kim and the kids came out.

Kim was between the girls, holding their hands. "Come on."

"But Mom, I'm starving and it smells so good!" Sophia pulled Kim forward.

Deb snickered. Michael didn't understand how bad waiting with hungry kids could be. "There's breakfast waiting for all of you, Sophia. No hogging the French toast!" Deb wagged a finger and Sophia laughed. Kim threw a "thank you!" over her shoulder before disappearing. Deb entered the bathroom, used the facilities and brushed her teeth, ignoring the almost continual buzzing of texts on her phone.

A fist pounded the door. "Come on!" Michael sounded worried.

She flushed the toilet, threw her vest over her head, and picked up her backpack. Opening the bathroom door, she almost ran into him. He grabbed her hand and ran for the vault opening, pulling her inside and closing the door with a dull thud, followed by a quiet sucking sound.

Deb leaned against the wall; the room had to be twenty feet long and ten feet deep. Shelving lined the concrete room, filled with canned and boxed food and other survival gear. Two sets of shelving separated the long, narrow room into three parts; the kid's air mattress in the aisle on her right, and Nic and Kim's on the left. The middle was empty; cork tiles softened the concrete floor. She followed Michael along the middle aisle, gazing in wonder.

At the back of the small room, Nic stood at a safe almost as tall as he was, filled with weapons. Another safe stood next to it, still closed. He handed Kim a taser and a pepper spray, then caressed her cheek. "Go eat. If we have to move, it will be a while, still."

"Okay." Kim took the box Deb had packed. "Come on girls, we'll move the sleeping bags and eat on the air mattresses like a picnic!" Deb could hear the forced cheer, but if the girls did, they didn't say anything.

Nic crooked his finger, then turned, leading them into a narrow concrete tunnel beyond the safes. Lights flicked on with their movement. Nic stopped about ten feet inside the tunnel, turning sideways. A door blocked the way, but it looked more like an old-fashioned submarine hatch, with a circle in the middle leading to bars crossing the door, and rubber seals around the whole thing. The bottom of the door was a foot off the ground, and the men would have to crouch to fit through. A very modern keypad gleamed in the center.

Nic tapped the door. "Pete told me this opens into a long, narrow tunnel, going about two hundred yards, uphill. We'll have to crawl. At the end, you climb a long ladder to a hatch at the top. Monitors are mounted at the bottom of the ladder, showing the surroundings at the top. But the hatch is hidden in the middle of a group of pines, so you can't see that far. Hopefully, we'll still have access to Wiz's surveillance, but whoever's attacking has already destroyed a bunch of cameras."

"Why won't they quit, already?" Deb shut her mouth, aware she was wailing.

Michael pulled her into a hug. "I'm sorry. People are stupid."

Nic snorted. "This one sure is. He's already bringing too much attention to his organization. This could be the last straw."

Michael partially released her but kept one arm around her. "It might be. But if he's successful making a clean sweep of all of us, then he's got one success to bring back to his bosses."

Nic pulled his phone from his back pocket. "Geo and his people have escaped. They're joining Erin and Ryan at Coffee & Cars. Ryan reports a drive-by shooting, but they deployed the road barrier at the right time, and a car smashed into it, the second car rear-ended the first. Deputy sheriffs already picked up the injured occupants; the rest ran. The vehicles were full of weapons. Erin and Ryan are fine; they're in the garage, and they'll plan a counter attack with Geo if we need it."

Michael huffed. "Which we might."

Nic scrolled. "Maybe. Wiz said the fire suppression system is taking care of the fire bombs, and they're having a great time shooting down drones from the covered patio at the top of the house. But they have to let them fly fairly close to the house, so they don't light the ranch on fire. They're worried the drones will deliberately drop on the ranch house, but the roof is metal with modern screened vents. Both houses have sprinkler systems that double as fire suppression, so it should be okay."

"Wait a minute." Deb was dumbfounded. "They're using drones to drop fire starters?"

"Yeah." Nic turned his phone to face Deb. A black, cylindrical drone with four spinning blades on top spit bright colored balls out the bottom. "They're used by firefighters to start back burns in areas that can't be safely reached on foot. Civilians shouldn't own them, but I'm sure they're not that hard to make, steal or buy with enough money."

"It's still spring, and wet, but a fire here could run across the Sapphires, and kill people, livestock, and destroy so many lives!" Deb wrapped her arms around her waist, shivering. "Koslov is evil!"

Nic and Michael nodded. "Yes. The guy is nuts."

All their phones dinged or buzzed with notifications. Deb yanked hers from her pocket and selected the video conference link Wiz sent. For better connectivity, they moved out of the tunnel and into the main bunker, and the two men watched over her shoulder.

Wiz stood on the third story patio, the Sapphires behind her. "As of right now, the fire department has staged vehicles about a mile away from the ranch road, and I'll lower the barrier if our fire suppression isn't sufficient." Her face disappeared, and a view overlooking the Rocking B ranch appeared. She zoomed in; news crews were already filming from the edge of the highway and other vehicles slowed, swerved or skidded to a stop on the verge. "The State Patrol is responding to direct traffic; you can see people are being stupid. I've triangulated the drone controller's location—they're north of us—and sent it to the State Police, the Sheriff and the Forest Service. All are responding and an arrest is expected soon."

"Well, at least the sheriff is smart enough to know he can't let arsonists get away," Michael said. "But we're not out of the woods. They may have a tactical team on their way to attack the house, and we can't tell because they've taken out so many cameras."

Wiz grimaced. "I've still got eyes out there. I sent my drone to the fire bomber's location; there were three large SUVs parked at a high spot overlooking the valley. I found two teams of six people in tactical gear on the Crest Trail headed our way; one of them shot down my drone. But, I'm watching several wildlife monitoring networks. They took down some of those game cameras, but I've accessed a couple well off the trail they didn't find. Both teams were a half-mile down the trail when something happened and they turned around. They're loading into vehicles now, probably to avoid the police."

"Wiz, do you have eyes to the north and south?" Geo asked.

She said, "Some. What I just described was on the north. The south is harder. Most of the game cameras there are individual hunters, and they're not networked. I'm launching another drone, but it's slower. Nic, Michael, if you have to escape, go north. I'm sending a map with trails and landmarks. Obviously, you'll want to avoid the trails when possible, but with kids it will be difficult. If we have to leave, the three of us will hang back and cover your six as much as possible. I called my pilot friend, but the helo is down."

Nic said, "Thanks, Wiz. My first choice is to go right down the ranch road. Kim can call the news stations and talk about how we're trying to get our kids out. Any attack on us would be skewered. But that might not work if a fire gets going or someone mows down the press with a vehicle, or Koslov's been driven to the point where he no longer cares about bad press."

Geo waved on his camera. "I've got some intel from someone watching Koslov. I don't trust them entirely, but they have no reason to lie about this. Koslov is on the move. He's in a convoy of heavily armed vehicles and they seem to be headed for a local private airstrip. About ten minutes after he left, a couple of trucks rammed the front gate of his Seattle area home, then his front door. Men in plain black tactical gear and masks got out, and gunfire was heard. The house is on fire." He smiled. "I think his Bratva customers decided Koslov was a liability, rather than an asset, and they're taking him out. Or trying to. I'm trying to find out where his jet is going, but they haven't filed any flight plans and probably won't."

"That would explain why the teams headed here turned around." Wiz nodded. "But we can't assume all of them are gone. Let's sit tight while I get that drone out. Geo, Erin and Ryan stay alert, too."

"We are." Geo pointed up. "I've got my teams on the roof at Coffee & Cars. I agree with sitting tight for now.

But let me know if you need us to sweep your proper-ties."

Pete snorted. "You realize the Rocking B is three hun-dred and twenty acres, right? And Wiz has almost that much?"

His eyebrows raised. "Okay, the areas around your houses and barns."

"I'll have to replace all the cameras I lost, so we'll do it then." Checking with each of them, Wiz's focus shifted on the screen. "Any questions or concerns?"

Concerns, sure, but Deb shook her head. They were in the safest location possible, so why move?

Wiz's hand reached toward them. "Okay, plan A is wait and see. Wiz out."

Deb flicked off the video conference, and turned to face Michael and Nic. "Do you really think it's over?"

Both men shrugged. Nic spoke first. "We can hope. I think there's still a general threat, but I also think the larger organization will probably cut their losses here. Too much publicity, not enough gain, and they've got someone to blame."

Michael frowned. "There's a possibility of revenge for sure, but probably not immediately. As Nic said, too much publicity. I think you've got time to rebuild and restart, if that's what you want to do."

"I have no idea what I want to do yet." Deb leaned against the wall. "Even with all the help, rebuilding seems overwhelming. And then there's the bank loan. Two weeks of notice? That can't be right. Normally, I'd ask Sam, but now she's missing too. And with Mills, supposedly. But what if Koslov got her? Can we trust Mills?" Kim, the girls, and Erin were all safe, but Sam was alone. Or with her ex. Neither possibility was com-forting.

"Don't worry about the rebuild, Deb, we've got that." Nic squeezed her shoulder. "I'm going to tell Kim what's going on." He walked away.

Michael mirrored her stance, leaning against the wall. "Nic's right. The bakery is easy. Deciding what you want to do will be harder. I'd suggest taking a couple of days to recover before you make any decisions. You can bake thank you cupcakes—because I know you're itching to do that—and read through the bank paperwork. Even if yours burned, the bank is obligated to give you a copy. You can probably find it online." He frowned. "Although, I'm not sure I'd trust Sharlene Murphy. She could have modified the documents."

Deb smiled. "Sam's got a copy at her office, plus mine is in a small fire safe with all my paperwork. Assuming no one took it." She hadn't checked recently, but it was unlikely anyone had looked inside her giant roasting pan, kept on top of her apartment kitchen cabinets. She used the roaster once or twice a year for turkey, and during that time, the fire safe went in her bathroom, behind the towels. She yawned. "Sleep before decisions seems like a good idea, though. I don't think I've slept through the night for weeks."

Michael unhooked his rifle, leaned it against the wall, and spread his arms wide. "How about a hug? That might help too."

Deb grinned, stepped in close, and wrapped her arms around him, below his vest. She didn't squeeze, knowing his back still hurt. He held her tight, and laid his head against the side of her head. "That does help, a lot." Deb pulled her shoulders away, and his hands slid from her upper arms to the vest across her back. She already missed his touch, but they could indulge in even better contact. "How about a kiss, too?"

"Excellent idea." He bent and twisted, wincing.

Deb frowned. "Don't hurt yourself." She pulled away and took his hand, tugging him back to the tunnel door. Putting her right hand on Michael's shoulder, she stepped up, twisted and wedged her heels onto the ledge formed into the submarine-style hatch, and put her left hand on his other shoulder. "Is that too hard on your back?"

Michael grinned and stepped closer, turning his head slightly. "Would I care?" He slid one arm up her neck, into her hair, and touched his lips to hers.

Heat flashed through Deb's chest, and her heart sang with joy. She returned his kiss, gently at first, but it soon turned passionate. She tried to pull him closer, but their vests got in the way.

Michael pulled away. "While I'd like to keep doing that more than anything, now probably isn't the best time. And we need to talk."

Deb's heart dropped from the heights and crashed to the ground. But his smile said she was overreacting.

"No, nothing bad." He smiled and caressed the back of her neck. "I'm done resisting this. I don't deserve you, and I'm probably not the best guy for you. I'm definitely not the healthiest. But I don't want to let you go, either. Maybe we won't make it in the long run, but I want to try, and I'm going for the gold ring at the end, Deb. I'm in it to win it. Does that scare you?"

Deb laughed. "No, silly! I'm in it to win, too. Don't run yourself down. You're a prize. I think we can both win if we're together."

"Together, forever." He leaned in and kissed her again.

Neither of them had said "I love you" but she did. And she was positive he loved her, too. But words weren't important with his lips on hers. Declarations could come later. They weren't necessary when two hearts rose together, baking in the fire of adversity into a beautiful creation, iced with happiness.

Deb returned his kiss with her whole heart, knowing that whatever happened, they'd be together.

Chapter 25

A WEEK AFTER KOSLOV's forces had seemingly left Marcus, Michael balled up the strip of painter's tape and threw it to the garbage can. It landed on top of the others with a slight crackle. "Three points! That's it, the last one. I think. Can you see anymore?" There'd been no sign of Koslov or his men, and all of the businesses in town reported the same. Most were co-operating with the authorities, trying to unwind the web the mobster had woven. Even the Marcus Sheriff was cooperating, although slowly. Marcus Bank and Sharlene Murphy refused to talk, forwarding all communications to their lawyers. The feds weren't saying much, except that Koslov had left the country. They refused to answer any questions about Trevor Mills, and both he and Sam Kerr were still missing. Deb, Erin and the rest of them were extremely worried.

Deb walked the perimeter of the bakery, scanning for blue tape, and stopped in front of him. Running her hands up his chest, she winced when she ran into a glob of tacky paint. But they were both covered in yellow, so a little shouldn't matter. She twined her arms around his neck and he happily bent to kiss her, ignoring the slight twinge.

A metallic crash jolted them apart and the back doors flew open. Michael spun, blocking Deb with his body, and pulled his pistol. The front end of an SUV blocked the back doors. He glanced over his shoulder, but the bakery's front door was intact—so far. There might be someone waiting out there, though. "Back." They should have kept wearing the bullet-resistant vests, but they thought the threat was over.

Deb grabbed the back of his pants and tugged. He walked backwards with her, his pistol raised, waiting for movement. There wasn't anywhere to go, though. The dividing wall was gone, and most of the equipment was in storage at the lumber yard. She towed him to the side; the glass front refrigerated display case stood there. With glass on three sides, and coolant coils on the fourth, it wouldn't offer much protection, but it was better than nothing. They slid behind the tall case, and Michael spun it so they stood behind the black fins of the radiator. He peered around the three-foot wide rectangle, watching the door.

The vehicle's windshield was deeply tinted, but he was fairly certain an airbag had deployed. If they were lucky, that airbag was on the recall list, and it took care of the problem for them by shredding the occupant with metal shards.

"Someone just slammed a car into the back doors of my bakery," Deb's voice was quiet but intense. "No, I'm not kidding. Send help. We don't know what's outside, so we can't go out the front, and there's nothing inside to hide behind." She stopped for a moment. "What? I'm not stupid enough to hide in a walk-in freezer! We could freeze to death before the sheriff bothers to send help."

Michael had considered it for a split second, but he was on the same page as Deb. But they could open the door and that would provide better cover. He grabbed the refrigerator case and pushed it to his left. "Come on. Freezer door." As they walked, he shifted from side to side, checking for the enemy.

Deb muttered something under her breath, and took her hand away. Before he could protest, she leaned against him—her shoulder, maybe—and kept moving.

They were almost there. He took a chance, and ran the last few steps, towing the fridge with him, Deb at his shoulder, helping. He threw the freezer open and moved the refrigerator case to block the door. With Deb crouched behind him, he took a knee, and raised the pistol, resting it on the edge of the frigid metal. Leaning forward to check, he jolted back when rapid gunfire assaulted his ears, the freezer door shuddering with the bullet impacts.

When the shooting stopped, he leaned forward, finger on the pistol's trigger, and peered out. A man loaded a magazine into a pistol. Michael fired, aiming for the heart. The man stumbled back, but didn't go down. He must be wearing a bullet-resistant vest. Michael shifted his sights to the man's head, but the man raised his pistol and fired before Michael could.

Michael retreated, counting the rapid-fire rounds. Knowing he'd have very little time to react, he kept his pistol up, the crosshatched grip tight in his hands and his forefinger on the trigger. He lifted the weapon higher, adjusting for the attacker's height if he was running toward them.

After fourteen rounds, Michael popped out from behind the door. But he didn't shoot. Their attacker sprawled across the floor, a pool of red already spreading beneath his head.

"Sheriff's deputy, drop your weapons," a man's voice bellowed.

Michael could barely hear the words over the ringing in his ears. He lowered his pistol, but didn't put it down. The corruption had run deep, and none of them fully trusted the local police. "This is Michael Acer. I'll lower my pistol and stay here, but I'm keeping it."

"Understood. Is Deb okay?"

She wrapped her arms around his waist, and pressed against his back, shivering. "Yes, I'm fine."

With the immediate emergency over, the icy air penetrated. He'd be shivering soon, too. He peered around the door. A deputy near the front of the vehicle holstered his pistol, and depressed the button on his shoulder microphone. Sirens wailed, getting louder. Pounding sounded on the front door. Michael waited for more law enforcement. With two or three different branches, the chances of all of them being corrupt was less.

"FBI! Weapons down."

He peered around the edge of the freezer door. Sure enough, one of the feds slid over the hood of the vehicle half inside the bakery. Michael put his pistol on the floor and stood, pushing the refrigerator case away. He stepped out from behind the freezer door, but he wasn't moving far from his weapon. Deb stayed behind him, and let the freezer door slam shut.

The fed landed, stumbling a little. He straightened and scanned the room, then holstered his pistol. "Who shot?"

Michael relaxed slightly, but remained wary. They still didn't know who they could trust.

The deputy, holding his pistol between his finger and thumb, turned to the fed and placed the weapon on the hood of the vehicle. "I made the fatal shot."

Michael nodded. "Agreed. I fired, but only hit his vest."

The FBI agent strode to the dead body. "Koslov." He kicked the pistol from Koslov's lax hand and it skittered across the concrete floor with a metallic scrape, stopping near the back door. Kicking the weapon in that direction took effort, and seemed odd.

"Really?" Deb's higher-pitched voice echoed his astonishment. She leaned around Michael. "He's really dead?"

"Yep." The fed shrugged and the deputy joined him, standing over the dead man's body. "Guess he couldn't handle being beaten by the beautiful baker."

If Michael was an eye-roller, that would be cause for an epic roll—or three. The deputy shot the fed a skeptical side-eye.

Even Deb's smile looked weak, but from the way the FBI guy smiled back, he didn't realize how unimpressed she was. "I had a lot of help from my friends." She stepped to Michael's side, but left her hand on his lower back, a gesture he appreciated. Especially when something about the scene didn't feel right.

He put his arm around Deb, gripping her bicep so he could pull or push her out of the line of fire. She shot him a raised brow look. He barely shook his head and raised his shoulders in a tiny shrug, keeping his eye on the two law enforcement officers.

The deputy had reported, but the special agent hadn't. Nor had he introduced himself. Something was definitely not right. Besides, more FBI should have shown up by now. The fed pulled out his phone and tapped, then snapped a picture of Koslov. He kept typing, then stepped away from the deputy and snapped a picture of him.

The deputy raised his hands. "Hey, I don't want publicity for this. I did my job, that's it."

Michael really should have a backup pistol on his body. But he'd believed they were secure inside the bakery. He slid his hand down Deb's back, hoping her phone was in her back pocket. She jolted and shot him a wide-eyed glance, then relaxed when he pulled the phone. But her phone was on facial recognition. He mouthed, "999, Wiz," to her.

Deb took the phone, turned away from him and sank to her knees, sobbing. She should win an Oscar for her performance, but her life was the more important prize.

Michael half-turned toward her, dropping to one knee, and rubbing his left hand up and down her back, but watched the fed. If necessary, he could fling his body across hers and protect her. "It's all over, Deb. No need to cry."

"Oh, there's plenty of reason to cry. But you won't be." The fed pulled his weapon, pointed it at the deputy, and stepped back, toward the back door. He stooped and scooped up Koslov's pistol. "Too bad Koslov got all of you before the deputy miraculously took the final shot."

Michael snort-laughed. "Right. That's completely unbelievable and not supported by the evidence."

"He's right." The deputy shuffled away from Koslov, toward them. "Besides, backup is on the way. You waited too long."

The agent smiled. "It's a federal crime scene, I'll make it look exactly how I want it to look."

Deb laughed, turned and pointed at him. "Too bad. You're on candid camera. And not cameras controlled by law enforcement."

The fed snickered. "Victory Security has their own problems. They're about to go down in flames."

"I don't think so." A man's voice, coming from outside the bakery. "Drop the weapon. We already knew you were dirty, but not how far you were willing to go." Trevor Mills' face appeared on the far side of the SUV's hood, his pistol pointed at the agent. "Murder, Young? That's far more serious than what we've already found. You should have turned on Koslov. Probably would have saved you from a jail sentence."

Young raised his pistol, pointing at Mills. "He's got my family. They're probably dead already, but I can't take that chance."

Mills tsked. "Your family is safe. We got them out this morning. Drop the weapons. Look at your phone."

"You're not lying?" Agent Young's tone rose.

Mills shook his head. "No. Your family is okay."

Young dropped both pistols, letting them clatter on the concrete. The deputy kicked them away. Young yanked his phone from his jacket pocket and poked at the screen. His head and shoulders sagged. "Oh, thank God." Putting the phone back in his pocket, he put his hands behind his head. "You're right, I should have come clean. But I didn't know who I could trust."

"You're not the only one. Deputy, if you would?" Mills kept his pistol pointed at Young.

The deputy strode to the fed, yanking cuffs from his belt, and snapped them on. "Special Agent Young, you're under arrest for attempted murder and corruption. And charges to be filed later..." The deputy led him to the front door.

"Mills, where is Sam!" Deb stomped across the floor, fury written on her face.

"She's safe." He withdrew the pistol, but stayed on the far side of the SUV. Which was smart, because if looks could kill, he'd be dead.

"And I should believe you?" Deb tried to jump on the SUV's hood, but she was too short to get her leg on the crumpled front bumper.

Michael joined her, so he could catch her if she fell, but he wasn't stupid enough to help her. The FBI might decide to charge her with assault, and her lawyer, and best friend, was gone, in Mills' hands.

Mills grimaced. "Fair enough. Look, I've got to go. But she'll contact you. And she'll be back soon. She's already sent a friend to represent both of you, so don't say anything to my colleagues until then, okay? Good job on contacting Wiz, but be careful. Don't let down your guard. This thing goes deeper than any of you know." He walked out of sight.

"Mills, get back here!" Deb pounded her fists on the SUV's hood. "Mills!"

Michael wrapped his arms around her waist and put his cheek against her hair. Strawberries and sunshine, she sweetened and brightened his dark life. "Mills is in love with Sam. He's not going to hurt her."

She turned and slid her arms around his neck. "Are you sure?"

He grinned. "Yeah. You know why?"

"Smiling looks good on you." Deb's small, strong hands cupped his cheeks. "You should do it more often. But no, tell me why you're so sure."

Michael pulled his tiny but mighty baker a little closer. "Because he looks at her the way I look at you. I love you, Deb, with all my heart."

She smiled and blinked rapidly. "I love you, too."

He brought her close and kissed her. Every day was a gift with Deb. They'd built a strong foundation despite the fires of adversity, and their love would only rise higher and grow stronger with each new challenge and success.

Chapter 26

Epilogue

DEB HANDED SOPHIA AND Isabella their favorite cookies. "Enjoy!" The two scampered to the child-sized table next to Deb's new decorating station, custom made by Michael. The station's base adjusted up and down with the push of a button, the top was easy-to-clean quartz, with a built-in turntable, and custom-designed snap-on platforms for larger cakes, plus holders for cupcake trays. It made decorating so much easier, and she'd used it a lot over the last five months.

Michael had made so much of her business easier. The two of them, plus Kim and Nic, had streamlined her cupcake production, and built custom stations and tools to implement that process. Taking out the customer seating and bakery case increased the bakery's efficiency, too. Sometimes she missed interacting with her customers and she no longer got all the Marcus gossip, but she'd decreased costs a lot, too.

Kim sighed. "I guess we'll head to the park after this, or those two will be bouncing off the walls tonight."

Deb grinned. "Sorry, not sorry. I'm a baker, and sugar is how I show love." She handed Kim a small pink box. "Besides, you'll benefit too. There's extra cupcakes in there." She waggled her brows ridiculously.

Her sister laughed. "Thanks. I think. I'm supposed to gain a little weight, not balloon to three hundred pounds."

Deb waved her concerns away. "You're gorgeous, mama. And you're hitting all the milestones perfectly." Kim looked like she'd swallowed a beach ball. From behind, most would never know she was pregnant. Deb was fairly certain that if she ever got pregnant, she would look like a whale, and be as graceful as an elephant seal on land. Still, she was hoping that day might come sooner rather than later.

"So the doctor says." Kim put her hands on her lower back. "But my body disagrees."

The back door beeped—someone had entered the correct code—and it opened, letting Nic inside. He strode to Kim, bending to kiss her. He rubbed her stomach. "You're perfect in every way, just like this little one."

Kim gazed at Nic with a lovestruck, adoring look Deb recognized. The back door beeped again, and Deb turned, anticipating Michael's arrival.

He crossed the bakery, took her in his arms, dipped her and kissed her. She held his shoulders tight, and forgot her concerns about his back, lost in the feel of his lips on hers. Nic cleared his throat, and Michael pulled her upright, smiling. "Hey, cupcake queen. How did everything go today?"

"Perfect." Deb ignored her sister and brother-in-law, giving him one more quick kiss. "Happy six-month anniversary. I made us something special." She grinned.

"It's a good thing I had a demolition after PT this morning." He grinned back. "Got to earn my treats."

After their adventures, Michael's back had worsened. The VA sent him to a new doctor, who worked with a physical therapist, acupuncturist, bio-feedback specialist, nutritionist and a psychologist. The combination of therapies had decreased Michael's pain and given him more tools to handle what remained. He still got migraines, but the frequency had decreased, and he could deal with the severity better.

Deb had worked with the nutritionist to develop a line of low-sugar cupcakes, along with gluten-free and higher-fiber alternatives. While her regular cupcakes were the most popular, the options she offered satisfied a wider customer base and opened up a whole new business. She shipped all kinds of cupcakes overnight in special insulated boxes to customers around the world. But the bulk of her business remained local coffee shops and stores, with a sprinkling of special orders for individuals and special events. She was perfectly happy with that; she didn't need national attention or millionaire status.

Neither did Michael. Acer Home Improvement had more job offers than they could handle, so they took the most interesting projects, including work for those who couldn't afford their services. Over the last few months, three different talent agents had offered to shop home renovation television shows to the networks, but they'd turned all of them down cold. Neither man had any desire to be a star or bring any more attention to Marcus, Montana. They'd all had enough cameras shoved in their faces in the aftermath of the Koslov shooting.

"Hey, where did you go?" Michael rubbed her back. "Wherever it was, come back. We have a celebration to attend."

"We do?" Deb didn't remember anything on her calendar.

"Yeah. You, me, dinner and a cupcake for our six-month anniversary." Michael chuckled. "No need to dress up or go out."

She laughed. Michael had come a long way from the grumpy, gruff, isolated man he used to be, but he still preferred to stay home in sweats rather than dressing up for a fancy meal. She had no problem with that. Her wedding and anniversary cakes got her plenty of invitations to swanky events, so she appreciated the chance to wear slippers rather than stilettos. Not that she wore high heels to set up elaborate cakes; she was a baker, not a gymnast.

"But before our celebration, we have another event, first." Michael swallowed hard and shifted his shoulders, like he was nervous. The back door beeped, and her favorite people in the world streamed inside. Erin and Ryan, Sam, Wiz, Tom, and Pete, plus Geo and a few of his Copperline Security folks, and some of the local business owners.

She waved at all of them, then turned back to Michael. "What's going on?"

"Well, while we'll celebrate privately later, everyone here had a hand in bringing us together, and making sure we survived to make it to this anniversary. Plus, they've all supported us while we got our businesses back on track. So, I figured they all deserved to see this." Michael got down on one knee.

Deb covered her mouth with her hands, keeping her scream inside. But an embarrassing squeak emitted anyway. That Michael, still an intensely private man, would include their friends and family in this event was a testament to his character and his love, especially when Deb loved a party, even if he didn't.

He held up a small blue velvet box with Marcus Jewelers written on the top, and flipped it open. "Will you marry me?" He pulled the ring from the box, and held it up. "Please?"

Deb tried to keep from crying, but her happiness spilled over. She lowered her hands. "Yes, a thousand times, yes!"

Michael slid the ring she couldn't see through her tears on her finger and stood, enfolding her in his warm, strong embrace and kissing her. The safe-for-an-audience kiss didn't stay that way for long. Deb reveled in his soft firm lips, calloused hands, and deep, abiding love.

Cheers and clapping eventually penetrated their bubble and they broke apart. A line formed, their friends congratulating them and admiring Deb's new ring. Gold and diamond petals surrounded a large yellow diamond mounted on a slender gold band. The sunflower ring was perfect in every way, and a true testament to Michael's love for her.

After the party, Michael led her to the top of the bakery. Since they'd had to renovate anyway, Michael and Nic added a tiny rooftop deck above her apartment, reached by a retractable ladder inside. Just large enough for a double-size chaise lounge, a side table, and a small grill, it was perfect for the two of them.

They sat and shared a glass of champagne. Michael barely sipped; alcohol could bring on a migraine. He draped one arm over her shoulder, snuggling her tight against his side, and played with the fingers of her ring hand with the other. "What kind of wedding do you want? Did you always dream of a huge guest list, with an enormous dress and roses?"

Deb chuckled. "Childish dreams are just that; for children. We're adults, and quite frankly, we have better things to spend money on than some huge production."

"But you deserve have your dreams made a reality, Cupcake Queen. You deserve everything, including someone better than me, but I'm not letting you go." He tightened his arm and kissed her passionately.

Deb broke the kiss. "There's no one better than you. And we both deserve everything." She caressed his cheek, enjoying his scruff against her palm. "But really, I don't need a spectacular wedding for the ages. You, me, our friends, a nice dress and a few flowers. That's all I need."

Michael kissed her palm, then put his hand over hers. "You and me. That's all I need. But let's do the white gown, the tux, and the party, with plenty of pictures and video. We'll need those to embarrass our kids someday."

She laughed. "Yes, that's the reason for a wedding; embarrassing the kids."

"No, it's just a side-benefit." He kissed her again. "The real reason is the same reason I invited everyone tonight. You, the incredibly kind, generous and joyful person who tolerates this grumpy, damaged soldier and makes me a better, happier man, deserve a celebration every day of the week and twice on Tuesdays. But since we work, we'll have to do the next best thing, and have a big blowout, big enough to remember how great it feels until we have time for the next one. And I want to make you happy. Because that's what counts. Your happiness is my happiness, period." He grinned. "But I won't lie. Sooner is better."

Deb snickered. "I think we can do it all. Big party, big dress, quickly. But in the end, none of that matters. You do. My happiness comes from being with you, not a party or a dress. It's only you." Michael pulled her on top of him, and held her tight. Deb kissed him hard, hoping her love was as obvious as his.

They might have been oil and water to start, but in the churn of danger and hardship, they'd come together, rising to meet every challenge, the fires of adversity purifying and building their love into joyous sweetness. Marriage, and children someday, would be the frosting on top, celebrating the love of the cupcake queen and home improvement king forever.

Thanks for reading! Sam and Trevor's book, *Bitter Past*, is next! Second chances are always difficult, and danger heightens every emotion. Releases Mar 19th, 2024!

Want to know how Kim and Nic met? Sign up for my newsletter, Anne's Musings, and get the story:

*Santa Rode a RED HORSE*https://BookHip.com/ZKF CVQV

Also out now, *Saved by the Airman*: **https://books2r ead.com/SavedByTheAirman**

Author's Note

Marcus, Montana isn't a real place, but it's based on Hamilton, Montana, where I live. Find lots of pictures on my Instagram at annemscott_author. Sadly, there isn't a Deb's Bakery, but we have several wonderful bakeries and espresso shops. Her bakery building is very loosely based on the Red Rooster Bakery on 1st St. The old lumberyard has been torn down, but there's still a bulk fuel storage site nearby. There's no Acer Home Improvement, either, but I can recommend an excellent local remodeler if you move here.

Deb and Michael's hunting cabin and escape routes are all based in reality. The drive down the West Fork of the Bitterroot River is beautiful, and there are tons of Forest Service roads you can explore, many with campgrounds and hiking trails. West Fork Road skirts Painted Rocks Lake; I'm told the fishing is great. There are cabins for rent in the area, ranging from rustic to luxurious, but please take "No Trespassing" signs seriously; remain on public lands. Also, watch for deer, elk, and other critters.

If you leave the West Fork and take Nez Perce road, you'll cross Nez Perce Pass and enter Idaho. Then, you're in the Magruder Corridor, a historic, 101-mile, single-lane rather rough road that goes to Elk City, Idaho, crossing the Selway-Bitterroot Wilderness and the Frank Church River of No Return Wilderness. It's primitive but gorgeous! If you go, you'll need a vehicle with good ground clearance (4x4 recommended, no trailers or RVs) drinking water and/or filter, camping supplies, and extra fuel. Under ideal conditions, the road can be traveled in a single day, but if you're going, take a couple of days and enjoy it! No matter what, check with the Forest Service before you go for current conditions. Wildfires and landslides are common.

We drove the Magruder with my brother and his wife in the summer of 2022. Despite a wildfire cutting our adventure slightly short, we had a great time—see pictures on my Instagram.

I hope you enjoyed Deb and Michael's adventures in this little slice of the Last Best Place! We're going a little farther away for the next novel, *Bitter Past*, but those details will be as real as possible, too.

Acknowledgements

First, I want to thank all of you, for reading my books! I truly appreciate the time and money you spend on my stories.

Second, a big Thank You to Cara North for organizing the Home for the Holidays group and including my story in the collection *Santa Wore Combat Boots*.

Third, I'm grateful for The Amazing Sleeping Man. This novel launched on our 30th Anniversary! It doesn't feel like it's been that long and I love you more every day!

Fourth, my sister Lia Huni, fabulous rom-com writer. Thanks for reading all my novels, especially that first terrible one!

Fifth, my sprint group. Thanks to Lia, Marcus Alexander Hart, Sara Ivy Hill, Irene Micheals, Tony Slater, Lou Cadle, and Kate Pickford, along with all their pen name alter-egos! Y'all are the best!

Sixth, my crazy German Shepherd, Zoe, for getting me away from the computer regularly. I hope we can find a way to get you out on daytime walks near the house again.

Seventh, my Team Rubicon friends. Thanks for kicking disaster of all kinds in the teeth!

Eighth, the Ukrainian people and your sunflowers. Your dedication, inventiveness, and determination are an inspiration to all of us. Keep up the good fight!

Finally, I thank God for sending me on this amazing writing adventure. It's an wonderful gift, and I hope You appreciate what I do with it.

Anne M. Scott Biography

Instagram: https://www.instagram.com/annemscott_author/

Threads: @annemscott_author

Twitter: @AnneScottAuthor

Email: romance@amscottwrites.com

Website: https://amscottwrites.com/romance

I love to hear from readers! If you find errors, please let me know at the email address above. I'm on all the normal social media, but somewhat irregularly, so if you ask a question or make a comment, please don't be offended if I don't immediately reply. I'm particularly difficult to contact when I'm on Team Rubicon operations or out backpacking—cellphone towers don't exist in disaster zones or the wilderness!

Also By Anne M. Scott

Strong women and men overcome hardship, survive danger and find love in the beautiful town of Marcus, deep in the Bitterroot Valley of Montana.
Small town, closed-door military veteran romance, with suspense, action and adventure awaits!
Free e-Book, *Bitter Roots*: https://BookHip.com/TQGCATB
Bitter Haven: https://books2read.com/BitterHaven
Bitter Retreat: https://books2read.com/BitterRetreat
Bitter Sweet: https://books2read.com/BitterSweetMarcus
Bitter Past: https://books2read.com/BitterPast

Join the active duty heroes and heroines of the Wild Blue Yonder Hearts! Every story comes with a strong military hero, a determined military heroine, action, adventure, adversity, danger and a sweet happily ever after that won't steam your glasses! Fly away into the Wild Blue Yonder today!

Saved by the Airman: https://books2read.com/SavedBy TheAirman

www.ingramcontent.com/pod-product-compliance
Lightning Source LLC
Chambersburg PA
CBHW021230310726
48971CB00006B/1754